An ordinary girl trying
to follow the rules
never knows what danger
lies right around the corner....

Cold Call

The phone rang. A voice floated back—a thin whisper, barely audible. "Samantha. They're best when they're little."

"Who is this?" Of course I knew who it was. By now I knew.

"More corpses, then little you." The whisper was genderless, but strong, like an icy wind.

"Leave me alone."

"Have you ever touched a corpse's skin? It's cold and stiff. Perfect."

"I said—"

"Soon you'll feel like that. Touch your face."

Suddenly, my whole body felt deeply, painfully cold. . . .

To my mother, Beverly LeBov Sloane,
and in loving memory of Bob Sloane, my dad

ACKNOWLEDGMENTS

First of all, I'd like to thank my agent Deborah Schneider for her enthusiasm and great ideas. And everyone at NAL—particularly Ellen Edwards, the shockingly kind, smart and sane editor of this book, whom I'm so happy to know.

I've also been fortunate to count as friends some truly talented writers who've given me great support and advice: Marlene Adelstein, Abby Thomas, Sharyn Kolberg (who said, "Why not make her a preschool teacher?"), Val Wachs, Richard Hoffman, Kath O'Donnel—not to mention James Conrad and Paul Leone, who've been giving me love, laughs and vodka drinks for the better part of two decades.

Also, the Tuesday Night Babes, Cindy Chastain and Adam Levy, John Burger and all the other dear friends whose stories and boyfriends' names I've ripped off.

I'd like to thank the brave men and women of NYPD's Sixth Precinct. (Which really does have a nice bomb squad sign.)

And most of all, I'd like to thank my husband, Mike Gaylin, for absolutely everything.

PROLOGUE

Your Spiritual Lifeboat

"I'd kill for publicity like yours," said Shell Clarion yesterday morning. Shell has said this many times within the past month, but I've never responded because it annoys me in so many ways.

First of all, there's the tone: I'd *kill* for publicity like yours, as if she were talking about metabolism or pore size.

The truth is, when you're in the papers, everybody stares at you. You can't buy things like condoms or facial depilatory cream. And you can forget all about spitting, or saying "fuck you" to a bike messenger who nearly knocks you unconscious, or doing anything even remotely unphotogenic, because you *will* be noticed and it *will* make Page 6 of the *New York Post* under some self-fulfilling headline like "Is the Pressure Getting to Her?" and then you'll be even more paranoid than you were to begin with.

There's also the unspoken implication that I should be doing something with this publicity—writing a book, for instance. I don't want to write a book. I want to teach prekindergarten and work in the box office of an off-Broadway theater. I've been doing both for years, and neither requires a spokesperson.

Most important, there's the fact that I *did* kill for publicity like mine, and if Shell honestly wants a bunch of cameras shoved in her face when she's buying tampons at Rite Aid, all she needs to do is kill someone too. But she has to understand this first: No amount of publicity can make up for the dreams you have, every night, after you take someone's life.

Of course, I didn't tell this to Shell, because she is an aspiring soap opera actress who *chose* the name of Shell Clarion, and you don't want to discuss existential pain with somebody like that. So instead I said, "I bet if I punched you in the face, we could both make the six o'clock news." Worked pretty good. Wish I'd said it earlier.

My name is Samantha Leiffer. Even before the killing, the last name sounded familiar to people because of my mother, Sydney Stark-Leiffer, self-help author and lover of publicity.

In her latest book, *Your Spiritual Lifeboat*, Sydney talks about the simple ways we can all stay afloat in "the sometimes placid, sometimes roiling sea called living." Meditation or prayer is the life vest—"the puncture-proof floatation device that you wear close to your heart." The planks of the lifeboat, described in the following fourteen chapters, include self-education, exercise, career fulfillment, family, laughter and friendship. The rudder—the thing that gives the boat direction—is love.

Sydney's sold about a trillion of these books, so I hate to disagree with her, but my lifeboat has always been constructed differently than that. Until recently, it consisted of two planks getting tossed around in a choppy ocean, with me lashed to the top. The planks were my two jobs. Love was the school of hungry sharks circling just below the surface. Forget about the life vest; the sharks would swallow it whole.

The odd part is, love was what brought me to New York in the first place. I'd met Nate during my senior year of college when I stage managed *King Lear* and he played Edmund the Bastard. He was so freakishly beautiful, Nate. A shimmering blond museum piece, with brains and talent and an ass you could rest a full martini on, and he claimed to love me. I guess I'm attractive, but not like Nate. Nate literally caused traffic accidents.

I'd often wake up in the middle of the night and stare at his closed eyes—almond shaped, with thick, honey-colored lashes—and wonder, *What is wrong with him?*

Turned out there *was* something wrong with Nate—or, at least, with Nate and me. I found out after I'd followed him to New York and taken the job at the box office and learned, through a series of cryptic answering machine messages and a bouquet of irises on the doormat, that he was screwing his commercial agent, Susan, every day after I left for work, and his theatrical agent, Gregory, on Monday, Wednesday and Friday evenings, when he was supposed to be at his Method class.

Through my mother's most recent ex-husband, a real estate developer, I found a decent-sized, lower Chelsea studio on the twelfth floor of a prewar building, overlooking an airshaft but rent stabilized. Then I called a furniture rental place called Rent 2 Own and ordered a roomful of blond wood and beige cushions. The idea behind that decision was: light, modern, very temporary. Yet I wound up renting the stuff so long I owned it, and found myself stuck with an apartment that looked like a dentist's waiting room.

Still, the place was convenient. Only ten street blocks north of the Space, which is the theater where I work; an additional three avenue blocks east of the Hudson River, where I like to take walks; five street blocks south and two avenue blocks west of Sunny Side Preschool, where I began teaching a year after the breakup, when I decided my lifeboat needed a sturdier, more buoyant plank.

Unconsciously, I'd arranged my life in a tight, safe

circle in which even subways were unnecessary. I had my kids to keep me company from eight 'til noon; my aspiring actor coworkers at the box office to entertain me from two 'til curtain. Then I had a microwavable dinner on my blond wood dinette in front of the Shopping Channel, and bed.

My mother said I wasn't realizing my true potential. "Who moves to New York City to teach nursery school?" she'd ask over the phone from L.A. "Who goes to Stanford to work in a box office?"

I don't know, Mom, I'd want to reply. *Who gets divorced three times in six years and then writes a chapter called "Love Is the Rudder"?*

Mainly, I was happy—the kind of muted happy that you don't notice at the time, but see clearly after it's gone.

There are seven people, including the manager and me, who work in the box office of the Space. That's about six too many. But in a textbook case of putting the cart before the horse, the rich owner believes a busy box office attracts big ticket sales. Or so she says. I think it's a tax scam.

Before I tell this story, I should list the names of my box office coworkers. The kids at Sunny Side have normal, human names like Daniel Klein and Nancy Yu. When I introduce them, you won't go, "What?" and stop paying attention to the story in order to digest the syllables. The Space staff, though—aspiring ac-

tors—have the most blatantly changed names this side
of the porn industry: Besides Shell Clarion, there's En
Henry, Argent Devereaux, Yale St. Germaine and
Hermyn. Hermyn is a woman—a feminist performance artist and the only person I've ever met with
just one name. Each of us has a cubbyhole near the
will-call window, for phone messages, mail and notes
from visitors. On top of each cubbyhole, there's a
piece of masking tape with our initials on it. Hermyn's
just says "H."

Until last month, Hermyn never spoke. Not a word.
She'd taken a three-year vow of silence in order to
shore up vocal power for *Inanimate Womyn*, a one-
person show in which she mutated her voice into a whip,
a brick and a feather.

My other coworkers thrill to the sound of their own
voices. That includes my best friend Yale St. Germaine, but I like the sound of his voice too.

When the rest of them have been sniping and
singing and pontificating so much that it seems they've
stolen all the air out of the room, Yale invites me outside for cigarette breaks. Even though he knows I don't
smoke. Even though everyone knows I don't smoke.
"How about some secondhand carcinogens?" he says.
And I run.

Life would've been so different had I chosen to not
smoke with Yale on that overcast day in February
when I took a walk to the Hudson River instead.

I still wonder what made me stop at that ugly, abandoned construction site in the first place, let alone stay long enough to see what I did. Initially, I assumed it was boredom, or PMS, or possibly the loneliness that used to hit me so often, especially on overcast days in late winter when *everything* looks ugly and abandoned. In interviews, I've attributed it to claustrophobia—an occupational hazard for anybody who works in a box office. But lately, none of that seems right.

I've been thinking it was luck. Whether it was good luck or bad, I'm not sure.

1

Squad Watery

It was Valentine's Day, or, as Yale St. Germaine liked to call it, "the only holiday with a massacre named after it." Valentine's Day depressed Yale because he'd had some gorgeous ones in his life—the kind with roses and candlelight and someone with moist eyes grasping both your hands over a white tablecloth and comparing you to various addictive substances.

I'd never taken Valentine's Day seriously. It was fine for my preschool class, but to my eye it was a kids' holiday, full of sweet but unsubstantial things like paper hearts and candy. And boyfriends.

The only valentine I could depend on was the one from my mother. It was the same postcard her publicist sent out to the media: a black-and-white headshot of her taken circa 1981, the year her first book came out.

In the white space over the photo hovered a pink, cursive inscription: *Open Your* ♥ *and Love Will Sail In.* Despite the two decades that had elapsed since the shot was taken, Sydney looked more or less the same. Like me, with an Adrien Arpel makeover.

Because she still used it as her author photo, it had attained icon status among Stark-Leiffer enthusiasts: the sculpted, dark hair with its warm, professional-looking highlights; the pale eyes, embraced by kohl; the outlined and painted lips compassionately pursed. It was a photo that said, "I know how to accentuate my best features, but right now, I'm thinking about *you.*"

Sydney usually just scrawled her signature on my valentine, but this time she'd added a note. *Have fun, Samantha,* she'd written at the bottom of the card in bright red ink. *Please.*

I was carrying the card in my giant patchwork shoulder bag as I walked to Sunny Side that morning. And I was also carrying more February 14th fun than Sydney Stark-Leiffer could shake her red pen at: twenty cut-out valentine hearts, five extra pads of construction paper, one bag of children's scissors, eight packages of doilies, two jars apiece of red, silver, gold, green and pink glitter (and three extra jars of gold, because the kids loved gold), nine tubes of Elmer's glue and twenty small boxes of crayons.

It wasn't tons of fun, but it felt close to it. Who knew paper products could be so heavy? It couldn't be helped, though. My classroom had been robbed twice. (I still found this hard to wrap my head around. A gang of West Village nursery school marauders.) In the latest heist, they'd made off with all my Chanukah decorations—including the Styrofoam latkes and the giant paper dreidel—so I was relatively certain valentine supplies wouldn't be safe there overnight.

I shifted the heavy bag to the other shoulder, and that's when I felt it. A creeping, cold sensation originating at the base of my spine, winding up through my vertebrae one by one, settling into the sweat on the back of my neck and pressing against it, like puddled ice. For a few seconds, I couldn't breathe.

A man bumped into me as he passed. "Get the fuckin' fuck out of my fuckin' way!" he said. It always amazed me how many times New Yorkers could insert the word *fuckin'* into a sentence, and normally I would've stared at this man, if only to see what someone who said "fuckin' fuck" looked like. But I was too distracted. The awful tingling began to dissipate, though the idea of it lingered.

Dead Man's Fingers. Chills up your spine for no reason. The sign of a bad premonition.

I don't like to think of myself as superstitious, but I am. It comes from my grandmother, who lived with Sydney and me after Dad moved out and chastised us if we wore socks around the house. *(If you wear socks with no shoes, you'll lose all your money!)* Grandma was forever spitting, muttering oaths, knocking wood and tossing salt over her shoulder. My mother thought it was obsessive-compulsive, but I bought right into it.

Ten years after Grandma's death, I still didn't wear socks around my apartment. Occasionally, I whispered *keinahora* to ward off the evil eye.

When you feel Dead Man's Fingers, you're supposed to stop whatever it is you're doing and do the opposite. That way, the premonition might not come true.

For me, doing the opposite would have meant turning around and going home. I imagined myself calling the principal, telling him, "Sorry, Terry. Dead Man's Fingers."

I tried to attribute the sensation to the bitter February cold, to a forgotten bad dream, to Valentine's Day with no valentine. But then it returned, this time in italics: *Dead Man's Fingers.*

I removed my bag again, shifted it to the other shoulder. *Maybe that'll suffice as doing the opposite. Suffice for whom? What am I thinking?*

I pulled my coat closer to my body. It was the same coat that I always wore on cold days—a heavy, black, men's wool coat that I bought at the army/navy store when I first moved to New York—and I found comfort in its enormity. It was about four sizes too big, because there is no such thing as a man (especially an army/navy man) who is my size: five-foot-one, one hundred pounds. For some military reason I'm sure, this coat had a hood, which I never wore because it made me look like a Druid. But one block away from Sunny Side Preschool, with Dead Man's Fingers stuck in my nervous system and the sickening certainty that something horrible was going to happen, I pulled the hood over my head until it obscured the top half of my face.

I need protection, I thought. It seemed to make sense.

My classroom had not been robbed, and I was surprised. Ever since the spine freeze, I'd thought robbery. *Of course. What else could it be? You had a premonition just like this before the Chanukah break-in, didn't you?*

By the time I arrived at my classroom, I'd so convinced myself a theft had occurred, I tried pushing the door open without the key.

But the lock was intact.

I flicked on the fluorescent lights and surveyed the classroom. The tiny, multicolored chairs were spaced evenly around the long red table. The large toy box in the corner was shut. The storybooks were neatly stacked on their low shelves, all seven pieces of colored chalk present and accounted for on the blackboard tray. The three locks on the closet door were secure, and when I unbolted them, I saw that the TV and VCR were untouched, as was the collection of educational tapes piled beneath them on the movable stand. The items I'd placed on the closet shelves: the paint jars, the boxes of thick sidewalk chalk for warm-weather months, the felt numbers and letters, the plastic fruits and vegetables and African musical instruments—not to mention the boom box and crate of CDs (which we'd had to replace after the first break-in)—remained inviolate. My classroom was so undisturbed it was satirical.

"Excuse me."

I recognized the voice of the principal, Terry Mann, even before I looked up and saw his neat little head poking through the open door. Terry had a squeamish way of speaking and winced often, which made it seem like each word had an unpleasant aftertaste. "I wanted to . . . remind you . . . that the . . . police officers . . . are coming today."

"Cops? Why?"

"Police officers." He raised his eyebrows as if the word *cops* was some sort of racial slur. "They're going to speak to the . . . children. It's . . . community outreach."

"Lucky us."

"It's an annual event, Samantha."

"No, it isn't."

"Yes, it is."

"There were no cops here last year. On Valentine's Day, we made valentines. That's it. Believe me, I would have remembered uniformed men with firearms hanging from their belts."

"Yes, well, sometimes we skip a year. The police officers are coming around eleven and will speak to the children about safety."

"Terry, don't you think they might scare the kids? I mean, when I was that age I used to cry whenever I heard a siren. Okay, maybe I watched too many *Fugitive* reruns. But they really are frightening to most young children, with their badges and their boots and their guns and their . . . their hats."

"I'm sorry you had such a negative developmental experience, Samantha. But it is important for children to learn that policemen are their friends. The officers will be here at eleven."

Before he closed the door, he gave me a wan smile. "One of them has a puppet."

I put my head on my desk. Now Terry thought I was anti–safety training as the result of a strong negative influence in my early developmental years brought on by unsupervised violent television viewing, and that wasn't true at all.

I was all for safety training. I had books, videos—even a board game called Walk Home Safe! that I'd bought from one of the nonprofits with my own money. It was a little complex for the kids, but I'd gotten them to play it more than once.

I'd held meetings with the parents, made sure I'd shaken hands with every relative, housekeeper, nanny or honorary uncle who might ever have reason to pick up one of their children from school. Safety training was important to me. More important than Terry could ever know.

But cops? With puppets?

Two years ago, I went to see a reissue of *A Clockwork Orange* at a small theater in NoHo. Halfway through the film, I got up to use the bathroom and when I returned, my purse had been stolen.

Reluctantly, I went to the Fifth Precinct house to file a report. "You left your pocketbook on a movie theater seat?" said the platinum-haired cop at the front desk. "That was stupid."

She went back to her paperwork, as if looking at me wasn't worth her time.

"Can I file a report?"

"You ask me, anyone who does something that stupid deserves to get their pocketbook stolen."

"Well, I didn't."

"Didn't what?"

"Ask you."

After I left the precinct house, I went to the nearest thrift store and bought the most ridiculous-looking shoulder bag I could find. It was a square foot in size and comprised of haphazard brown, orange, antifreeze green and neon-yellow patchwork squares—most of them solid colored, though some sported polka dots, drawn on in black, indelible ink. Embroidered peace sign, happy face and dancing bear patches had been applied in random spots, and a spindly, hot-pink fringe hung off the bottom—embellishments obviously made on the third straight day of an acid trip.

When I'd bought it for one dollar, the clerk had stared at me and said, "Are you *sure*?"

I figured no one would be caught dead swiping this monstrosity. Even so, I vowed never to let it out of my sight. As strange as I looked carrying it everywhere, it beat visiting another police station.

I'd never trusted cops. In my early childhood, they were the sneering giants who'd throw my dad through the door most Sunday mornings, stinking of beer and sometimes bruised. When I was a teenager, they were the assholes who tailed my boyfriend Brian and me all the way across Coldwater Canyon and into the Valley before inexplicably pulling us over, searching the car and asking us questions so rude I can't even repeat them. (My mother didn't mind that I was dating a black guy; these cops, for some reason, did.) And, in New York, they were that bitch from the Fifth Precinct.

I was thinking about how annoying I found Terry and his callow respect for "police officers" when one of my preschoolers, Daniel Klein, showed up. It was only seven-thirty, but Daniel was always early. His father was a stockbroker and dropped him off on his way to work. If I were Daniel, I would've resented all the forced "alone time" with my teacher. But he didn't seem to mind. Daniel was an unusually dignified four-year-old. His parents dressed him in Brooks Brothers casuals and gave him a tiny briefcase to carry and still he looked so comfortable that none of the other kids teased him about it.

"I got a new fish," he said.

"Really, Dan?" I said, opening the shoulder bag, removing some of the paper hearts and placing them along the red table. "A goldfish?"

"No. It's orange, akshully."

"Yeah, they are orange. But they call them goldfish for some reason."

"Who is *they*?"

"The International Society of Fish Namers."

Daniel giggled. He had a surprisingly throaty and infectious laugh for a kid with such a grave face, and it lifted my spirits. I wanted to make him laugh some more, but I couldn't think of anything funny to say (except for a terrible joke about the word *goldfish* being a fishnomer, which wasn't the right material for anyone, let alone a preschooler.)

"Is he your first pet?"

"Yes. Mommy says if I take care of him, I can have a dog when I get bigger."

"What's his name?"

"Squad Watery."

"Squad Watery?"

"Yes. I didn't make it up. He told me his name."

"That's a great name."

"His food looks like little, tiny Corn Flakes, but akshully it does not taste like them."

"Daniel, you shouldn't be eating fish food."

"Someone's at the door."

I turned around, saw the dark outline of a head in the smoky pane of glass. The person rapped on it lightly.

I cracked open the door, and there stood Terry, his face flushed and shiny. I was about to ask what was wrong when I saw the younger, taller man behind him. The man was casually dressed—jeans, black T-shirt, plaid flannel overshirt, leather jacket—and his expression was much calmer than Terry's.

"Samantha, I . . . oh, is Daniel here already?" There was a tremor in Terry's voice—a tinge of anxiety that hadn't been there earlier and seemed to increase as his eyes went from my face to that of the younger man and back again.

As I stepped through the door and closed it behind me, I thought of bad premonitions, holidays with massacres named after them.

"Who are you?" I said to the stranger.

He reached into his leather jacket, inched it aside like a backstage curtain, and I saw the dull glint of steel. *A gun.*

I screamed. The sound bounced off the sides of the enclosed courtyard that held the small playground, echoed back at me and hurt my ears—a horror-movie scream, the scream of someone soon to be murdered.

Our janitor, Anthony Ciriglio, a sweet-but-addled sixties drug casualty, appeared at the far end of the courtyard, his mop raised like a machete. The other teacher, Veronica Bliss, flew out of her classroom and stared at me with her thick jaw hanging open.

"What is the matter with you, Samantha?" Terry said. For the first time since I had known him, I detected anger in his voice.

"What's the matter with *me*?"

The man removed his hand from his jacket and produced a police ID card. "John Krull," he said with the nervous nonchalance that people reserve for the insane. "I'm a detective with the Sixth Precinct. Um . . . I'll be speaking with your kids today at eleven? I thought I'd stop by on my way to work, but uh . . . this is obviously a bad time for you so . . ."

"God, I'm sorry."

"She had a . . . a difficult morning," said Terry.

"You need a Valium, Sam?" said Anthony.

"Are you okay, Detective Krull?" said Veronica, who'd never particularly liked me.

My throat and mouth suddenly felt like they were made of rusted metal. "I . . . I don't need a Valium. It's just . . ." I closed my eyes, swallowed hard. "I saw your gun."

Terry stared at me as if I'd just exploded into a fine powder. "I told you officers would be—"

"You said at eleven. It's not eleven, Terry. It's not even close."

Veronica rolled her eyes and retreated into her classroom.

Anthony said, "How about half a Valium?"

Krull smiled—a nice, uncoplike smile that made me think he might not throw me into the back of his patrol car, turn on the siren and head straight for Ward's Island. "You've got quite a voice."

"I guess I do," I said. "Who knew?"

"It's good to know how to scream. You'd be surprised how many people don't."

For a moment, he seemed miles away. Then he smiled again and it was as if he'd never left. "See you at eleven."

It took me ten minutes to get Daniel to stop crying and another fifteen to coax him out from under my desk.

By the time the rest of the kids arrived, everything was back to normal. Daniel and I were sitting at the long table. We'd removed all the art supplies from my bag, and we were making a valentine for Squad Watcry.

2

Strangers Are Danger

To my relief, Detective John Krull was not the one with the puppet. I'd have hated to think that this actual decent cop was, in reality, a Borscht Belt reject with a talking doll on his lap.

The one with the puppet was named Officer Ricky Genovese Community Relations. (That's how he introduced himself, only with no spaces between the words.) A thin, impeccably groomed, uniformed cop, he sat in front of my class on a collapsible stool that he'd brought himself and opened his stainless-steel ventriloquist's case.

His black hair was short and extremely glossy; it looked as if someone had recently poured ink over the top of his head. Too bad Yale wasn't here; Yale actu-

ally liked guys whose clothes you could bounce quarters off of.

The puppet was a smiling Dalmatian—also meticu-
lously turned out, in a police uniform identical to that
of his master. From the back of the room, I watched
Officer Ricky Genovese Community Relations set the
dapper little dog on the creased thigh of his blue slacks
and thought about how long it must take both of them
to get ready in the morning.

To be honest, Krull was more interesting to look at
than Community Relations or his dog. He had changed
clothes and facial expressions since this morning, and
both looked extremely uncomfortable. He wore an
exhausted-looking blue blazer, rumpled white shirt, a
patternless navy blue tie made out of some sort of
polyester/cellophane blend and gray corduroy pants
that looked as if they'd barely survived the eighties. I
wondered if he always changed into a coat and tie for
work, or just when he talked to kids, which, judging
from the confused look on his face, was not very often.

The kids—who sat in three rows on the floor in front
of Community Relations—were unfazed by the police
uniform and riveted by the dog puppet, which made
me think maybe I didn't know them as well as I'd
thought. As soon as it came out of the stainless-steel
box, they broke into spontaneous applause.

"Hello, everybody!" Community Relations said
cheerfully.

"Hello!" they responded in unison.

"I'm Officer Ricky! The man behind me is Detective John Krull. He works at the police station right near here, and he can answer all your safety questions later!"

Krull waved clumsily.

"I have a safety question!" yelled Kendrick Sullivan, the most skillful four-year-old heckler I'd ever encountered.

"How about you hold off until later, sport?"

"It's a good question!"

"You don't have a safety question, Kendrick, and you know it," I said. "Now let Officer Ricky continue with his presentation."

"Does that doggie go poop?" Kendrick said, sending his nearest fellow audience members into peals of appreciative laughter.

"What's your dog's name?" asked Nancy Yu.

"I have a new fish!" said Daniel.

"I'm Buster the Safety Dog!" the Dalmatian said in a slobbery, animated voice. Officer Ricky was impressive; his lips never moved. He lifted Buster into a standing position, spun the puppet in a pirouette and flopped it back down onto his knee in one fluid motion. "I'm going to show you how to *spot* danger! Get it?"

"Yay!" the class screamed.

"Now, I know a word that rhymes with danger. Do you?"

"Ranger!"

"Danger!"

"Poopoo brain-ger!"

"Kendrick."

"The word is *stranger*! Can anybody tell me what a stranger is?"

"I have a new fish!"

"I'll tell you what a stranger is!" the puppet shouted. "A stranger is anybody you and your parents don't know! If a stranger talks to you, what do you do?"

"Yell loud and run away!" said Nancy.

"That's right, young lady!" said Buster. "If a stranger gives you a candy bar, what do you do?"

"Don't take it and run away and yell loud!" said Serena Martin.

"That's right! If a stranger gives you a Nintendo game, what do you do?"

"Say, 'Thank you!'" Daniel said.

"Wrong-o-roonie! Sorry, young man. Saying thank you is polite, but you're not supposed to be polite to strangers. You know why?"

Silence.

"Because . . . strangers are danger! Say it with me!"

"Strangers are danger!"

"You got that right, Buster," I said, thinking of every fairy tale I knew in which the overly trusting princess was nearly killed by the witch or the troll. And my gaze slowly drifted up, until I was looking at the tiny, evenly spaced soundproofing holes in the ceiling tiles.

"Hello there, princess," he says, *through the open*

window of his dirty red Pinto. No one has ever called me a princess before and so I smile and watch him smile back with his long, thin teeth. He says he has something for me in the car, and I think, Maybe it's a jeweled crown, like on the Imperial Margarine commercials . . .

I shut my eyes tight and forced the memory out of my head, wondering what could have possibly brought it back. I'd obviously thought about strangers before. I'd thought about the ones who broke into my classroom, the one who stole my purse at the movies, the ones whom Yale would meet at clubs or gyms or newsstands, the ones who passed me on the street as I walked home from the box office alone. New York was a city filled with strangers and danger. But I still hadn't thought about the man in the red Pinto. Not for twenty years.

It's good to know how to scream, Krull had said. *You'd be surprised how many people don't.* I caught his eye, and he nodded at me.

Buster the Safety Dog was chanting, "If a stranger calls on the phone, and he asks if you're alone, what do you say?"

"No!" the class shouted.

"If a stranger says, 'Come with me! I've got something for you to see!' what do you say?"

"No!"

"I can't heeeeeear you!"

"No!"

"Now, let's all say it together, as loud as we can . . ."

"No! No! No!"

After the presentation, the kids mobbed Officer Ricky as if he were a rock star. I walked up to Krull and said, "Looks like he was a hit."

"I think he used to play Atlantic City."

"Listen," I said. "I just wanted to tell you again how sorry I am about this morning."

"It was actually pretty funny."

"Funny?"

"I mean, the principal, Mr. Mann, told me when we were walking to your room that he 'suspected you have some authority issues.' Something like that . . . Basically, he was saying you don't like cops."

"That isn't true."

"It's no big deal. *I* don't like a lot of cops. But I was getting ready to turn on the charm and change your mind, you know? Because this is the first time I've done community outreach and I wanted to make sure everybody was happy. But I get to your room, and before I can even say 'hello' you scream at me."

I started to laugh.

"I'm thinking, 'Man, I must really look like a cop.'"

"You didn't," I said. "That was the problem."

"Really."

"Well, if you were wearing then what you are now I'd have definitely known you were a cop."

Krull looked down at his clothes.

"That came out wrong."

"This tie has been in my family for years."

"I'm sorry, I—"

"Kidding."

"Detective Krull," I said, "can I just apologize now for anything I may say or scream in the future?"

Out of the corner of my eye, I saw Nancy holding out her valentine and asking for Buster the Safety Dog's autograph. Officer Ricky clamped a pen between Buster's wooden paws, and, holding them together, skillfully "helped" the dog to sign.

"There you go, princess," he said, handing it back to her. My stomach seized up.

"You okay?" Krull said. "You look a little pale."

"Yeah, I'm fine. I just . . . remembered something."

I didn't feel like going home between jobs, so I had a long lunch at the University Diner consisting of an egg-salad sandwich, five cups of coffee and the *Village Voice*, which I tried to read cover to cover.

Actually, I was just staring at the print, trying to figure out why I'd gotten Dead Man's Fingers. My classroom hadn't been robbed, none of the kids had hurt themselves, even the cops had been personable.

Maybe the Fingers were a premonition of something that hadn't happened yet—a hostile customer at the box office, for instance. Or maybe I'd get mugged on the walk home. I looked at my sandwich. Maybe this egg salad would turn out to be bad. *"Keinahora,"* I whispered.

I opened my shoulder bag, took out Sydney's valentine, and reread her hand-written message: *Have fun, Samantha. Please.*

The red ink was deep; she'd practically pushed the pen through the card.

Something happened at the box office. It wasn't horrible, but it was so completely out of sync with the reality I'd come to know, I found new justification for believing in Dead Man's Fingers—even if I was forced to rethink their meaning. What happened was this: Hermyn told a joke.

I had known the woman for three years and even before the vow of silence, she didn't have much to say. But things change, which Hermyn proved when she breezed into the box office half an hour late, threw off her heavy camouflage jacket and black watch cap, ran both hands through her spiky brown hair and said—in a voice loud enough and cheerful enough to rival Officer Ricky's— "What's purple and goes slam, slam, slam, slam?"

When no one responded, she said, "A four-door grape!"

Hermyn's laughter was hearty to the point of operatic—laughter saved up over a three-year period and released from the coddled lungs of a performance artist in the cramped subscription room of an old theater box office.

Everyone in the room was silenced—even Yale, who had bet Argent Devereaux and me five dollars apiece that he could make it all the way through "I Am the Very Model of a Modern Major General" without breathing. Yale loved Gilbert and Sullivan almost as much as he loved the sound of his own singing voice, but with Hermyn's laughter lacing the air like a gas leak, he stopped dead in the middle of "animal and vegetable and mineral" and asked, "What's wrong?"

Hermyn stopped laughing and smiled at us. Her left front tooth was adorned with a tiny, gold butterfly. "I'm happy," she said. "I'm in love."

"Tell me it isn't true. I can't believe it. Can you believe it? I mean, look at her! I can't believe it, can you?" Shell Clarion, who spoke quickly to begin with, tended to talk even faster when she got emotional. Now she sounded like an auctioneer on Ritalin.

I was in the small stone courtyard outside the box office, not smoking between her and Yale. Shell was talking only to me. She'd been referring to Hermyn, of course, and the fact that she saw me as a fellow jealous hag bothered me a lot.

I said, "This kid in my class—Daniel? He got a new fish."

"Really?" Yale said. "Tropical or freshwater?"

"Hello," said Shell, enveloping my face in smoke. "I'm *talking* here!"

"It's a goldfish," I said.

"I had a goldfish as a child, but it got eaten by my sister's cat . . ."

"Sammy, I'm serious. Look at her. Turn around, and look in that fuckin' window and fuckin' look at her. She probably hasn't even gotten laid in her entire life and here she is engaged? It's im-fuckin'-possible."

"It isn't impossible, Shell," I said. "It's happened. Hermyn has a fiancé named Sal."

"I thought she was gay. Didn't you think she was gay?"

"I never gave it much thought."

"You are so naive!"

"No, I just don't particularly care."

"Maybe Sal is a woman," Yale offered. "My gal Sal . . ."

I started to laugh.

"I wasn't speaking to you." Shell plucked a speck of tobacco off of her tongue and flicked it into the air. "I am speaking to Sammy, who understands the problem."

"What *is* the problem?" Yale said. "Hermyn is engaged, which we all should be terribly upset about because . . ."

"Because it should be one of us."

"Speak for yourself," I said.

"Oh, for God's sake." She whirled around and glared through the big subscription room window. "That weird-ass butch bitch is engaged to a mother-

fucking dentist from fucking Scarsdale, and you're as
pissed off about it as I am. Only difference is I'm honest enough to admit it."

She crushed the cigarette butt under the sole of a
black patent-leather boot and stormed back into the
box office without saying another word to either one of
us. I looked at Yale. "I don't want to be engaged to a
dentist from Scarsdale."

"How about a urologist from Short Hills?"

I took a drag off Yale's cigarette, coughed. Together
we turned and peered through the window. We
watched Hermyn hug Argent, watched our septuage-
narian boss Roland slap the bride-to-be on the back,
watched Shell grab Hermyn's hand, stare at the large
diamond on her finger, drop it like an unwanted flyer
and stalk off into the ticketing office.

"She's all id, isn't she?" said Yale.

"Yep."

"Well, we'd better get back in there before Roland
gets pissed."

"Hey, Yale?"

"Yeah?"

"It isn't like Shell said. And I'd only tell you this.
But I think I *am* a little jealous. Not about the engage-
ment. Just . . . I don't know. The way she seems to feel,
I guess."

Yale put out his cigarette and patted me on the back.
"Me too, hon," he said. "Happy Valentine's Day."

                *   *   *

Despite Shell's new theory, Hermyn had not bought the diamond ring for herself. She was engaged to a (male) dentist named Sal Merstein, whom she had met six months earlier. An avid performance art fan, Sal drove into the city like he always did on Saturday nights and went to his favorite bar/space, Industropia, just to see what was going on.

As it turned out, more was going on at Industropia than the NEA-supporting DDS could ever have imagined—and according to Hermyn, he had a very active imagination. Dr. Merstein caught a midnight performance of *Inanimate Womyn* and fell instantly and irrevocably in love. He explained his way into her dressing room and proposed to her that night. Hermyn, who wasn't speaking at the time, shook her head and mouthed the words "Are you nuts?"

Hermyn remained skeptical; Sal remained persistent. And adorable. And incredibly funny—at least to a woman who liked jokes about gasoline-powered fruit. Half a year later, at dawn on Valentine's Day, he'd affixed the butterfly to Hermyn's tooth and reiterated his proposal. And that's when she'd said, "Yes."

"He's got to be crazy. Maybe he's kinky. I hear that a lot about dentists. Too much nitrous oxide." Three hours later and Clarion was still at it. She was whispering in my ear, so as not to be overheard by Roland as we sorted prepurchased tickets ("will call," as we say in the trade) at the small, speakered window where customers would later pick them up. I was pondering physics. With a perfectly executed jerk to the right, I figured I could knock out both of Shell's front teeth, caps and all. Sal could fix them. Maybe throw in a root canal.

Hermyn was answering phones in the subscription office. I could hear her voice, friendly and musical, saying "Thank you so much for calling the Space."

Shell wondered aloud how much money Sal "socks away" every year after taxes and began quoting huge dollar amounts, her whisper disappearing and her vocal pitch rising alarmingly.

"Unless that's the price for your silence, we're not interested!" Yale's voice resounded from the subscription room.

Shell shrieked, "Eat me!"

"All right. That's enough!" said Roland.

"I'd rather eat arsenic," Yale said.

"I heard that, you twat!"

"I said that's enough!"

I looked at Shell.

"What."

At times like this, I found myself wishing I were back at Sunny Side with the grown-ups. I grabbed my shoulder bag and coat, walked out of the ticketing office, into the subscription room. "I'm done with the tickets. I'm going to take a little walk before the window opens."

Roland nodded as he checked off spaces on the seating chart and stopped briefly to turn down his hearing aid. I looked at Yale on my way out. "Breath of Clarion-free air?" he asked.

I nodded.

"Well, lucky you."

Hermyn, sitting at the desk across from Yale's, was smiling with her eyes closed. I wondered what she was thinking about, and felt a stab of envy as I walked out the door.

3

Worked Up

I was born in Venice Beach and raised in Santa Monica. And, while there were a lot of things about southern California that I didn't like—the lazy way that people talked, earthquake drills, strip malls, pastels, stage three smog alerts, Eagles reunions—I always loved the ocean. The thick, salt-laced scent and the continuous whoosh of the waves always worked like a tranquilizer on me.

The Hudson River wasn't the Pacific Ocean, but the Pacific Ocean wasn't walking distance from the Space, so I was willing to compromise.

On stressful days, even blisteringly cold ones, I would walk to the piers, close my eyes and listen to the water lapping at the wooden supports. The result was an instant, almost Pavlovian sense of well-being. I'd feel the way I did as a kid, when Sydney and I would stand on the beach and watch the sun set over the dark, rolling waves.

I couldn't get to the river fast enough that day. My hands balled into fists, I clutched my bag as though it were a poorly designed life preserver and slammed my feet into the sidewalk.

Before I expected it, I saw the thick gate that shrouded the few remaining piers, the intermittent signs that read *Area Peligrosa. Area Unsafe.*

When Yale had first moved to New York as a seventeen-year-old, gay men used to sunbathe on the Peligrosa Piers, as he called them. *You'd know it was spring when those tiny basket shorts cropped up on the Peligrosa Piers. They were more reliable than crocuses . . . Prettier, too.* During the sticky, fragrant summer nights, the men would return, making *Area Unsafe* a well-known double entendre.

Not anymore. Some of the piers had been dismantled to make room for the big gym complex with its bowling alleys and family restaurants. Others, like these, crumbled into the river like old corpses. Only the signs remained, with some of the fence corners cut and folded back, historical evidence. *Unsafe.* I shivered a little. So many ghosts. So much bad luck.

I'd been walking along the river for about fifteen minutes before I saw the construction site. There was an *Area Peligrosa* sign on the fence in front of it. And, even though the fence corner had been cut and folded back, I couldn't imagine anyone wanting to crawl under it.

Three tall stacks of concrete blocks bounded the area, the farthest edge of the farthest pile touching the end of a rusty, sad-looking trailer. Faded red letters stretched across the trailer, reading *Shank's Dredging and Construction,* and a broken *RK AND RIDE* sign was propped up against it, even though there was nowhere to park and nowhere to ride.

Perhaps it was the sign that drew me in. *Who would ever park a car in this place? Who would ever ride away from it, knowing they had to return?*

Or it could have been the construction company's name. Shank's, as in butchered body parts.

I knew these should have been reasons to leave—warning signs, literally—but they had the opposite effect on me. *No one's here. No one will be here. No one ever, except you.*

I crawled under the folded-back fence corner.

On the other side, I stood up and took a few steps toward the trailer.

I couldn't quite hear the water—I was still several car lengths away from the river, and the trailer seemed to block out sounds. To the left of the trailer was a huge rusty bin that was nearly overflowing with broken chunks of cement. I wondered when they'd been dumped there, and by whom.

I crept closer, saw some dead, brown weeds shooting through the concrete, then a few deviant, crumbling cement blocks and, finally, the oily green water of the Hudson. Placed neatly next to the bin like a spectator's seat was a smooth, rectangular block of cement with a blue chalk scrawl of *1/3/00* across the top. More than thirteen months old. *No one will be here . . .*

I sat down on the block. An icy gust flew off the river and bit at my face, but with the hood of my coat still up, I didn't mind. *No one ever, except you.*

My father left home when I was five years old, and I haven't seen him since. He's more a voice than a face to me—a loud laugh in the hallway; a hoarse, angry whisper in my parents' bedroom; a tinny mumble on the other end of the phone, asking Sydney for help. Picturing him is difficult, but if I clear my mind and close my eyes really tight, I can sometimes see his profile.

It's a purely mental exercise—not emotional at all—because I really don't feel one way or the other about him. Fact is, if Dad hadn't left, Sydney would never have written her first book (*PMS: Post Marital Survival*) and become instantaneously famous among self-help enthusiasts. She'd still be a social worker. He'd still be spending most of her salary on twelve-packs of Mickey's BigMouth. So it's probably best he got out when he did.

That said, I used to be crazy about him. One of my happiest memories was the time he'd taken me on the Ferris wheel at the Santa Monica Pier. When our cage turned upside down, I'd laughed instead of screaming like the other kids. And he'd patted me on the arm and said, "That's my brave girl."

Funny how I could remember the Ferris wheel ride as if it had just happened, but I couldn't remember the day he took off. Especially since, according to Sydney, I'd been the first one to notice the note he'd left on the kitchen table.

Listening to the sound of the river, I closed my eyes and tried to picture Dad. The hair was easy. It was long and dark and shiny; he usually wore it in a ponytail. But the features were blurry, and the eye color was a complete mystery. I knew they were brown, but were they amber colored like Nate's, or were they darker? My own eyes are pale green, like Sydney's, so they were of no help.

I'm losing Dad, I thought. It depressed me more than it should have.

I pressed my palms into the freezing cement block. The water sound was nice. I'd concentrate on that, block out everything else. Nate had once taught me how to meditate. It wasn't the type of rules-driven meditation that you learn at weekend retreats in upstate New York mountain towns. It was just an *inner chant* that his acting teacher had come up with in order to relax the class before scene work. *Breathe in, breathe out*, it went. *Think of anything. Think of nothing.* It sometimes helped if you said the words aloud, so that's what I did, over and over and over . . .

"Relax, princess," says the man in the Pinto. "Stop moving." But I can't. There's no crown in the car. Not in the front, not in the back. The vinyl seat is hot, sticky on my bare legs.

"Where is my crown?" I say.

"Where is my crown?" he repeats, his voice a squeaky imitation of mine. "Princess needs a crown . . ."

His hand clamps the back of my neck. It's big and rough and feels like it's made of sandpaper. He starts to laugh, and his laugh is big and rough too. "Princess needs a crown," he says, still laughing. "That's funny, princess."

Stop, I want to say. But I can't. My mouth opens and closes. He squeezes tighter. Pinches my skin between the stubby tips of his fingers. He jerks my head back, then down, like you'd do with a big doll.

I'm looking at the floor beneath the dashboard. "No crown for prin-cess," he sings.

On the floor I see a coiled rope. Next to it I see a roll of thick gray tape. They remind me of two snakes—a mother and her baby.

"I have something else, though. Something else princess can wear . . ."

I try to scream, but still nothing comes out. I am a doll. Can't move. Going to get broken.

"You can wear this on your neck." He holds something up to my eyes. It's silver mostly, but he's holding it so close that I have to blink to see what it is.

It's a long, sharp knife with a black leather handle.

*I'm wondering why I can't cry, can't yell, can't move
when his hand isn't over my mouth and he's only holding my neck. I'm thinking maybe he's magic. Maybe
I'm under a spell. He whispers, "Little bitch."*

*His breath smells of beer, which reminds me of Dad.
I wish he was Dad, because Dad wouldn't say that,
wouldn't hate me like this.* Dad wouldn't, *I think, as he
presses the cool side of the blade to my throat, then
shoves my head down farther . . .*

I opened my eyes, breathing fast and shallow. *Some
meditation exercise.*

I understood now why I'd blocked the memory for
so long. It had nothing to do with the knife or the rope.
It was the dry calm of the voice in my ear. And it was
how I couldn't move.

Here's how I escaped: A pigeon wiped out on the
Pinto's windshield. The stranger loosened his grip and
dropped the knife and said, "What the fuck?"

Saved by a kamikaze pigeon. Finally, I'd managed to
open the car door and run home.

*No, I don't open the door. I stare at the flattened feath-
ers. At the bright smear of blood. I don't move. I can't.*

*"What the fuck?" He leans across me, opens the
door, pushes me out. My knees hit the concrete. "My
car, my fucking car, fucking bird."*

*"Fucking bird," I whisper as I run and run and run.
"Fucking bird, fucking bird . . ."*

*   *   *

With the memory echoing in my brain, I didn't quite notice the sound at first. But then it became clearer, more defined. It was a scraping. The scraping of a heavy object across a floor. After a few seconds, I realized it was coming from the trailer.

Rats, I decided. But rats didn't scrape, they scurried. Besides, this sound was much too heavy for rats, even big rats. The scraping got louder and culminated in a thud on the concrete between the bin and the trailer. *It's not rats.* Instinctively, I jumped to my feet, tightened my grip on my bag and backed up. Soon, I'd made my way behind the bin and had almost reached the fence. I stopped for a moment. From where I was standing, I couldn't see the whole space between the bin and the trailer. But there was no more sound. *Maybe I imagined it.*

I used to imagine things a lot when I was a kid— monsters under the bed, snakes in the kitchen cupboard, Dad's car outside our apartment. Grandma said I was special and intuitive; Sydney said I was making things up to get attention.

When I tried to tell them that a pigeon had saved me from a strange man who thought I was a princess and tried to kill me, even Grandma wasn't buying it. "If you didn't want to go to your Brownie meeting," she said, "all you had to do was say so."

Sydney added, "You're too big a girl to be making up stories." After a while, I began thinking that Sydney and Grandma were right; I really had imagined the whole incident. *What if I had?*

No. I was saved from a murderer by a damn pigeon, and I am not hearing things. It was probably a homeless guy. A homeless guy dragging something around. And now I am going to leave him alone. I got up and walked back toward the fence.

But why didn't I see the homeless guy earlier? I looked through the trailer's windows. It was empty.

I turned around again, made myself stare at the big space between the bin and the trailer.

Two people stood there, a man and a woman. He was facing the water with his back to me, his dark hair cropped so close it looked like a shadow. He was a tall man in a long black trench coat; she was smaller with blond hair, wearing a red dress. She wasn't wearing a coat, even though it was freezing. Her dress had short sleeves.

She must be cold in those sleeves, I thought. They were bending over, pushing against something that I couldn't see.

I could hear it scraping the concrete, though. And when they straightened up, I saw it: a pale blue ice chest. Small, to be making such a scrape. *Prettier color than the water . . . a clean, shiny blue.*

Both of them bent over again, and pushed it hard. I heard a dull splash, and as they stepped back, I saw the white lid sinking into the Hudson. *Not so clean now. Not so shiny . . . Why am I watching this?*

For a long time, they both stood there, staring at what they'd just done. The woman's bare arms and back seemed to shake violently, though the rest of her body remained perfectly still.

"Crying," I said. The woman didn't move, but the man spun around fast and stared at me.

The bottom half of his face was covered by a thick black scarf, but I wouldn't have noticed it had it been visible. He had a smooth forehead, black eyebrows. But the eyes . . . *Where did you come from where did you?*

The irises were, literally, mirrors. The fading sunlight refracted off of them, made points of light on my black coat. For a second, they seemed to transform into two laser beams.

"Oh, Jesus," I whispered. "I am insane."

Heart pumping, fingernails digging into my palms, I held my breath and ducked under the fence. On the other side, I walked fast, but I refused to run. I crossed Tenth Avenue, headed east on Fourteenth. *It's okay. Too much emotion in one day. Weird things happening. Dead Man's Fingers. Cops in the classroom. Safety lectures, bad memories. Hermyn told a joke. You're worked up. You're not crazy. Not insane. Just worked up. But where did they, where did he . . .*

Maybe Shell had slipped something into the box office coffeepot. Maybe the egg salad had been bad.

I passed a group of laughing teenage girls. One of them, the one with the pierced lip, looked like a vampirette from a cheap seventies movie; another had a snake tattooed on her forehead, but they all looked real. None of them had mirror eyes.

Whatever it is, it's wearing off.

I had noticed something else, though, something harder to dismiss. I took a deep breath and tried to forget about it. *Breathe in, breathe out.* I opened the box office door. *Think of anything, think of nothing.*

Still, it stuck in my mind. More than once during the walk, I'd heard footsteps—and breath—moving closer and closer to my back. But each time I turned around and looked, no one was there.

En Henry was brushing his teeth one morning after twenty-four hours on ecstasy when he saw Christopher Marlowe's ghost levitating behind him in the mirror. "Write movies," the ghost intoned. So En, who was then called Stephen, lopped off the first five letters of his name (for numerological reasons), swore off both acting and ecstasy and vowed to write what he called the "Great American Screenplay."

Far as I knew, he had yet to complete a scene, but he was working towards it. In the past year, En had taken up yoga, bought a computer and joined several online dating services catering to writers.

When I returned from my break ten minutes late and closed the door behind me, the first thing I saw was En Henry's headless body propped upside down against the wall beside the filing cabinet that held the subscription order forms.

"Oh, God, no."

En's quavering voice said, *"Namaste,"* and I realized that I was looking at neither the aftermath of a brutal murder nor some kind of waking dream. It was only a yoga position.

En's head was thrown back, his chest resting lightly on the floor. He appeared to be balancing on his forearms.

"What the hell is that supposed to be?"

"It's the scorpion, man," he said through his stretched throat. "Speaking of which, did one happen to crawl up your ass and die?"

"Sorry, En. I'm just tired." I removed my coat and hung it on one of the hooks near the door. I shouldn't have been shocked. Ever since his bathroom epiphany, En worked only evenings and warmed up for "human-on-human contact" by holding a yoga pose in the subscription room for several minutes.

Roland was on the ticket office computer checking for orders on our brand new Web site, thespace.com. He did this every night after the window opened, in the desperate hope of filling half the theater. "Sorry I'm late," I called out to his back. He didn't even turn around.

"Hearing aid's down," whispered Argent, who was sitting at a desk and thumbing through a book of sheet music, a fat pink highlighter in her hand.

"Why are you whispering?" I asked.

"I don't want to bend En's aura."

Yale sat cross-legged on the floor, his back up against Argent's desk, reading the latest *Post*. He winked at me. "Don't worry," he said. "It's almost over."

"What's almost over?"

"Valentine's Day."

"Oh, right." I knelt down on the floor next to him.
"Did you drink any of that coffee that Shell made?"

"Yeah. Why?"

"Did it make you feel . . . I don't know . . . funny?"

"No. Why? You sick?"

I thought about telling him what I'd seen, rehearsed it
in my head. *Well, to tell the truth, I was at this construction site, and I thought I saw this couple materialize out
of nowhere and push a very nice ice chest into the river.
The guy turned around, and his eyes almost burned a
hole in my coat. That ever happen to you before?*

No, I decided. The best thing to do was forget about
it and calm down. And if I saw anything like it again,
I'd get the name of a good, cheap therapist. I was
pretty sure En was seeing one.

"Just a little queasy," I said. "Probably the egg salad."

"You really should try eating a vegetable every once
in a while."

"Yes, Mother." I tried to think of real, nonthreaten-
ing things, like En's yoga poses, Daniel's fish,
Hermyn's joke about the four-door grape. Yale had
gone back to reading Liz Smith's column, and I sat
down next to him and stared over his shoulder until the
words ran together.

Argent flipped on a table lamp as twilight soaked in
through the windows. It was after five, and tickethold-
ers and purchasers would soon start to arrive. Then, at

seven, the play would begin and there'd be nothing left to do but field complaints.

The play, *No Tears for Addie,* was a musical version of *As I Lay Dying* and a total disaster. Audience members had been storming out of the theater, usually during Addie's big number ("This Dang Mortal Coil"), and demanding their money back. There wasn't much we could say. No one in the box office could stand it either, except for Shell, who desperately wanted the part of Dewey Dell.

Until today, I hated listening to complaints, but now I couldn't wait for them. I wanted angry subscribers storming the window. I wanted them in my face, looking for a fight, irritating me back to reality. I wanted to look into their unfamiliar but human eyes through the streaked glass and say, without fear, "No refunds."

Instead, I found myself gazing out the subscription room window, trying to make out the details of shadows at the reaches of the courtyard, wishing I'd never have to open the door and leave the box office again.

"Shell and Hermyn off tonight?" I asked Argent.

"Mmmm hmmm," she whispered. "Hey, that's great about Hermyn's engagement, huh?"

"It sure is." I closed my eyes, listened to the soothing squeak of Argent's highlighter and En's deep, nasal breathing and tried to relax. But the only thing I could really hear was my own pounding pulse, which seemed to drown out every other sound in the room. I hoped it wouldn't bend En's aura.

4

Sailor Knots

"You look terrible."

I usually didn't take Veronica Bliss seriously when she said this to me. My fellow preschool teacher expressed concern over my looks so often that it was practically a greeting. But as she stared at me through her thick, plastic-framed glasses, a newspaper mashed into her pillowy chest like a saved baby, I knew she was telling the truth.

"I had a rough weekend."

I saw envy creep into her studious gray eyes, and I wanted to laugh and cry at the same time.

I'd barely slept since Friday. And since *Addie*'s dismal attendance meant I wasn't scheduled to work at the box office, I'd left my apartment only once, to go to the corner deli and buy enough bread, peanut butter, Diet Coke and M&M's to subsist on until Monday.

I could hardly sleep for fear of nightmares. I couldn't go out for fear of what I might see. I couldn't speak to anyone because if somebody said, "What's wrong?" I didn't think I'd be able to answer.

So I'd stayed in, letting my machine pick up the phone, eating peanut butter sandwiches in front of the TV, alternating between the shopping channel and the porn channel so consistently that, when I closed my eyes, I saw dicks wearing collectible doll dresses and nipples pierced with cubic zirconia rings.

But I couldn't help remembering what I'd seen at the river. It made me want to get up and pace the room in compulsive circles. Not a good idea, because of my downstairs neighbor, Elmira Bean.

A sixtyish woman with a penchant for Day-Glo negligees and matching mules, Elmira had moved in around six months earlier. As soon as boot season started, she took to pounding on her ceiling with a broom handle, or possibly a battering ram, whenever I left or returned from work. I'd thought maybe it was some kind of greeting—until she'd shown up at my door threatening to call the police if I didn't remove my boots immediately.

I doubted I'd get arrested for wearing shoes in my own apartment, but I always tried to comply anyway. The woman scared me a little.

*   *   *

At eleven o'clock on Sunday evening, I'd called Sydney.

She answered the phone like a doorbell ("Ye-hes!"), which told me she was in a bad mood. The angrier my mother was, the more singsongy her phone voice became.

"What's wrong?"

"Oh, Samantha," she sighed. "It's Vito."

I sighed right back. Vito Paradise was her hairstylist, with whom she was involved in a consuming, vaguely masochistic relationship that had outlasted three of her four marriages. They fought and reconciled and fought again, but the topic—Sydney's hair—never changed. "What did he do this time?"

"It's not what he *did* do, it's what he *didn't* do. He *did* my roots today, but he *didn't* put the deep conditioner in. Vito said I didn't need the deep conditioner. Vito said my hair had graduated beyond infusion treatments. Well, now it looks like I've got a goddamn wad of cotton candy stuck to my head and I'm on *AM Los Angeles* first thing tomorrow morning and the passive-aggressive bastard won't return my calls."

"I'm sure it doesn't look that bad."

"You should see me, Samantha. I swear to God you could insulate a house with it. He's violated me. The overpriced son of a bitch has violated—"

"Mom, I need to talk to you."

Click. "That's my call waiting. Hold on a sec. It might be *him*."

When she returned to the line, announcing, "Well, I think Vito and I may have reached an understanding . . ." I said, "Does seeing people who may not exist make you insane?"

"What?"

"I saw a man with . . . mirrored eyes."

"You mean mirrored sunglasses."

"No. I mean mirrored eyes. They refracted sunlight, just like a mirror."

"Okay . . ."

"And he and a woman, they were . . . putting something in the Hudson River."

"Samantha, what were you doing at the Hudson River?"

"I was at a construction site, trying to relax."

There was a long pause—so long that I'd thought our connection might have died. "Hello?"

"You're on drugs."

"I am not on drugs."

"Don't tell me that. I am an expert in human behavior and I know what 'trying to relax' means, and let me tell you I am deeply disappointed in you."

"Mother . . ."

"What kind of drugs are you on? Special K? Ice? Methamphetamines?"

During the next half hour, I somehow managed to convince Sydney not to fly out to New York and stage an intervention. By the time we hung up, my voice was hoarse and my head was pounding. But for the first time that weekend, I wasn't afraid of what was going on inside it.

I left my apartment and walked six blocks in the freezing cold to the nearest place to get a drink—a nautical-themed gay bar called Great White. There, I'd downed three scotch/rocks and watched abnormally gorgeous men interacting with each other amidst the billowing fishing nets, dotted with sequined shells and starfish, that had been suspended like fake ghosts from the high ceilings. No one seemed to notice me, which was nice. No one seemed to have mirror eyes, which was nicer.

Half a scotch more, and I gave the abnormally gorgeous bartender a huge tip, walked home in the dark and passed out on top of my pull-out couch with my coat still on.

This morning, I'd awakened with throbbing eyes, tapioca-colored skin and a tongue that felt like it was wearing a sock.

I knew it could only get worse. A nursery school classroom is no place to be when you have a hangover. And dependably, the bright red table, taxicab-yellow chairs, electric blue bookshelves and whitest of white walls made me squint as soon as I opened the door and flicked on the fluorescent lights.

I'd collapsed into my desk chair, leaned back and closed my eyes gingerly, craving a cold compress and praying that Daniel wouldn't show up any earlier than he normally did.

That's when Veronica had barged in, screaming, "Do you have any extra chalk?"

"Take all the chalk you want, Veronica," I said now, as she continued to eye me enviously. *How could anyone be jealous of a hangover?* "Just leave me one piece. And some aspirin if you have any, please."

"I don't have any aspirin!" she said. "Try water. You should be drinking eight glasses a day, anyway, for your skin. My mother's been doing that for years, and she looks a *lot* better than you do." She smiled. Her teeth matched my walls.

Veronica had always resented me; I couldn't figure out why. There wasn't anything about my life that was remotely resentable—except, possibly, for my hours. I taught an eight a.m. to noon class for kids whose parents could pick them up in the middle of the day, while she went straight through to five o'clock. Her class was a good deal bigger than mine was, but she had two assistants to help her out, plus she made twice as much as I did and Terry seemed to trust her more.

So recently, I'd begun to suspect a different reason for the resentment. Observing her over the past two years, I'd noticed certain things about Veronica—how she blushed when any man addressed her directly; how she'd never once mentioned a boyfriend, or an ex-boyfriend, or even a date, but talked about the lives of her parents (with whom she lived) with an attention to detail that bordered on obsessive; how (according to one of her assistants) she'd nearly swallowed her own tongue when a girl in her class asked her what a penis was. At thirty-five, Veronica Bliss was still a virgin. I was pretty sure she resented most of us who weren't, but, since my classroom was right next to hers, I was the most convenient target.

"Wasn't that actor you used to date named Nate Gundersen?" she asked.

My stomach flopped over like an empty hot water bottle. "You have an excellent memory."

"Well, my memory was jogged a little bit this morning." Veronica's smile grew to chilling proportions as she opened the *New York Post* she'd been clutching and placed it on the desk in front of me. "No wonder you were so upset when he dumped you. He's *dreamy*."

Just in case I didn't notice the forty-eight-point type or the breathtakingly shirtless photo of Nate, Veronica had outlined the article—which graced the front page of the entertainment section—in red Magic Marker. "Nate Gundersen," the headline read. "TV's Newest, Hottest Heartthrob."

Veronica said, "You can keep the paper if you like."

I grabbed the bathroom key out of my desk and ran down the hall. Fortunately, I made it into the girls' room before I threw up.

The hangover wasn't Yale's fault. Neither was the strange image that continued to haunt my brain; nor the sadistic virgin with whom I worked; nor the news—courtesy of the sadistic virgin and her overzealous Magic Marker—that Nate hadn't become suicidal or penniless or even fat since I'd left him, but quite the opposite. He'd become a soap star—*Live and Let Live*'s Lucas, a.k.a. TV's Newest, Hottest Heartthrob in forty-eight-point type.

The one thing I could pin on Yale, however, was the agonizing string of syllables I was now forced to wrap my acid-tasting tongue around: "I have a Gumbie Cat in mind, her name is Jennyanydots/The curtain-cord she likes to wind and tie it into sailor knots."

I'll tell you what I'd like to tie into sailor knots . . .

Five months earlier, Yale—whose then-boyfriend was understudying the part of Rum Tum Tugger—had snagged free matinee tickets for me and my class to one of the last performances of *Cats*. I was never much of a musical theater fan to begin with, and I found the concept of grown men and women frisking around a stage in whiskers and spandex disturbing. But I'd figured the kids would love the show, and my instincts had proven correct. During recess, several of them regularly reenacted scenes, leaping around the jungle gym like crazed, miniature theater majors. Ever since I'd told them that *Cats* was based on a book, they requested *Old Possum's Book of Practical Cats* at least three times a week for story hour. (The book was also courtesy of Yale, who'd been only too happy to donate it to my class after Rum Tum gave him the heave-ho.)

Terry thought it was marvelous that the kids enjoyed

T. S. Eliot. So did I, most of the time. But on this par-
ticular day, with my hollow stomach sucking up
against my spine and my mind tied into tighter sailor
knots than any Gumbie Cat could ever hope to create,
"The Wasteland" would've been far more appropriate
reading material.

"She sits upon the windowsill. Or anything that's
smooth or flat/She sits and sits and sits and . . ."

"Ms. Leiffer, read slower!" shouted Kendrick, who
was not heckling but making a legitimate request. I
was rushing through the poem, in the hopes of speed-
ing up story hour and the day and my life. If I had to
say *Gumbie Cat* one more time I thought I might
scream. And, as Daniel knew all too well, that wasn't
a sound any child should hear.

"Louder please!" said Nancy.

"I want a cat," said Daniel.

"I am a cat," said Serena, licking her palm. "See?"

"No, you're not," Nancy protested.

"Am so. A Gumbie Cat."

"Gumbie Cats smell."

"Okay, listen up! You guys settle down or else I
close the book."

"Sorry, Ms. Leiffer," Serena said.

"That's . . . all right. I'm just a little tired today,
kids." *I am a hungover, dried-up, gay-bar-frequenting
preschool teacher. And Nate is a heartthrob.*

I cleared my throat, forced a smile. "She sits and sits
and sits and sits and . . ."

Since I'd more or less memorized this poem, I kept reciting it—as slowly as I could—as my eyes meandered from the book to my watch and back again.

On the facing page, over the title of "Growltiger's Last Stand," was a handwritten word. It hadn't been there on Valentine's Day. I knew this because I'd read "Growltiger's Last Stand" on Valentine's Day after the cops had left and, faint as the word was, I would have noticed it.

"And that's what makes a Gumbie Cat," I said.

As I paused between stanzas, I squinted to make out the four ghostly letters—letters written by an adult, with a pencil that had barely touched the page.

I must've stretched out the pause a little too long because Daniel said, "What's the matter?" In an attempt to appear calm, I opened my mouth to say, "Nothing," but my breath caught in my throat and no sound came out.

The word on the page was *hide*.

"Peekaboo, teach!"

Yale's voice, achingly cheerful. The kids had finally left for the day and I'd been cleaning the room up slowly, avoiding the *Book of Practical Cats*, which sat, sprawled open, at the center of my desk. I looked up and saw Yale standing in the classroom with a poorly concealed grin and cheeks that were flushed for reasons other than the cold weather. "I'm in love and I'm taking you out to lunch!"

Oh, Christ almighty. "I still have some stuff to do around here . . ."

"I'll wait."

I collected a few unused scraps of modeling clay and rolled them into a ball.

"Need help?" Yale asked.

"No."

"So . . . why don't I tell you who I'm in love with."

I tightened the lids on the jars of water-soluble paint and lined them up on their long, plastic tray as he launched into a monologue about his significant-other-of-one-night-so-far. The guy was a waiter named Peter Steele, but beyond that information, it was just a bunch of words to me, irrelevant as the brand names on the sides of the jars.

". . . took him home from an after-hours bar, Sam. I haven't taken anyone home from an after-hours bar since they arrested Jeffrey Dahmer . . ."

I placed the paint tray on top of the VCR, wheeled the entertainment system into the closet.

"But, God, he was flawless . . ."

I shoved the ball of modeling clay into its container, closed the lid, stuck it on a closet shelf.

". . . Drop-dead, soul-swallowing gorgeous as a fucking Venetian opera. Don't look at me like that. You would've done the exact same thing."

I closed the closet door. Bolted the three locks. *Click, click, click.*

"Cat got your tongue?"

I looked at him. "You have no idea what a poor choice of words that is," I said, and showed him the T. S. Eliot book.

Yale squinted at the word. "Who wrote that?"

I shrugged my shoulders.

"Okay . . . Let's retrace your steps. Exactly where have you and the book been lately?"

After reading "Growltiger's Last Stand" at story hour on Valentine's Day, I'd marked the page and stuck it into my shoulder bag. I often did this with *Old Possum's Book of Practical Cats* as it was so frequently in demand and—replaceable though it was—a potentially catastrophic disappointment for my class if stolen.

Since I hadn't removed it from the bag until today's story hour, the book had been everywhere I'd been: the University Diner, where I'd had lunch, the box office, the abandoned construction site, the Happy Face deli, where I'd bought the food that had sustained me through the weekend, Great White and, finally, back to Sunny Side again.

I told him about all of it—except the abandoned construction site.

After I was through, Yale strode up to my desk and leaned against it like a TV attorney interrogating a witness. "What about Miss Jean Brodie?"

"Veronica? Not her style. Too subtle."

"That principal of yours is a little odd."

"Terry would never go into a woman's purse, and

he'd never deface a book, even with a pencil. Besides,
I think he's sort of scared of me."

"Why?"

"Because I screamed at a cop."

"Excuse me?"

"Terry didn't write *hide* in my book."

Yale paced a full circle around my desk, then re-
versed direction.

"Yale, you're bringing back my hangover. Why
don't you just forget—"

"I've got it."

"Oh, really."

He rested both elbows on the edge of my desk and
smiled. "The message wasn't directed at you."

"Then who was it directed at, Nancy Drew?"

"Your bag, of course." Yale explained: Since no one
in the box office disliked me enough to write *hide* in
my book, and since I wasn't in the deli long enough for
someone to remove it from my bag, write in it and put
it back without my knowledge, the culprit was obviously "some nasty queen at Great White." And not just
any nasty queen. A nasty queen with *a passionate aes-
thetic sensibility.*

"That's just so obviously it," he said.

"Someone is writing threatening notes to my *bag*?"

"You take that piece of hippie hell into Great White
and *someone* is going to tell you to hide it. Probably
thought he was doing you a favor."

"But—"

"You were bombed, right?"

"Well, yeah I guess."

"Bombed enough to turn your back on the bag for a few minutes?"

"Maybe."

"And was there anything else in aforementioned bag, besides aforementioned dog-eared page of aforementioned book that someone with a need to express himself regarding aforementioned desecration of natural fiber could've written on?"

"I don't think so."

He smacked his hand against the desk. "I rest my case."

I looked at Yale, tried to smile. I hadn't told him about the man at the river. And, as I remembered the head with its pencily shadow of hair, turning to reveal those impossible eyes—eyes that could refract light and burn holes through flesh, eyes without pupils— another thought came to me: *Maybe I'm the one who wrote the word.* "We should go," I said.

"First, tell me about the cop you screamed at."

I sighed. "He was here for community outreach, but he didn't have on a uniform and he showed up early. I saw his gun and—"

"Oh, Sam."

"He was nice about it. Let's get out of here. I've had enough of these fucking primary colors."

Yale clasped my shoulder and gave me a look that was much too concerned for my liking. I half expected him to put a hand on my forehead and check my temperature. "You need to relax." *Relax, princess.* "You drink too much coffee." *Stop moving.*

"I happen to enjoy coffee!"

"Sorry. Just trying to help."

"I . . . know you are."

Yale searched my eyes with his own. It wasn't the first time I noticed how sweet and pure a blue they were—like a baby's blanket, a few cottony white flecks sprinkled around the pupils. Yale was three years older than me and smoked and drank and stayed up all night on a regular basis, but he still had the eyes of a child—bright and uncorrupted, no lines in the delicate skin around them. He said, "There's something else bothering you, isn't there?" and I heard myself reply, "If I told you that I think I might be going crazy, would you take me seriously?"

"Sam."

"Um . . . Okay then . . ." My mouth was dry, and I was beginning to sweat. I felt like an actor at an audition, only my monologue was unmemorized, unrehearsed. I returned my eyes to Yale's, let them rest there a while, and realized how lucky his scene partners were. They probably never had stage fright. "I know this is going to sound weird," I began, "but have you ever heard of Dead Man's Fingers?"

When I was through with the story, Yale stared at me, his expression unreadable. *Please don't accuse me of being on drugs*, I started to say. He cleared his throat. "So?"

"So . . . what?"

"So . . . what do you think was in the ice chest?"

"You mean you don't think I hallucinated it?"

"Of course not."

"But . . . the eyes . . ."

"Sam, I moved to New York eight years ago. Since then, I've seen a woman with no nose knitting a scarf on the nine train, a man—actually the head, arms and chest of a man—propelling himself down Fifth Avenue on a hand-made gurney, a guy with three balls, Shell Clarion . . . I'll buy you saw a man with mirror eyes."

"But he disappeared—more than once."

"Did you see him fade into thin air?"

"No, but . . ."

"Maybe you were just so afraid, you thought you heard him following you, even though he wasn't. Did you ever consider that?"

Actually, I hadn't considered that.

"You're too damn superstitious is the problem here," said Yale. "I mean, Dead Man's Fingers. Puh-lease." I felt a palpable relief, starting at the base of my neck and spreading throughout the rest of my body like clear, warm water—until another thought cut off the flow.

"So, if the couple was real," I said, "what if something horrible was in the ice chest? I mean, it wasn't big enough to hold a dead body. But what about . . . body parts?"

"I highly doubt it. A young couple? Dressed up like that? In broad daylight? On Valentine's Day? They could've been getting rid of any number of things—trash, battery acid, old clothes, maybe evidence of an affair, maybe even the ice chest itself. It could've had fish or cheese in it for too long. You can't get rotten cheese smell out of anything, ever."

"Old clothes?"

"Well, why not? Besides, don't you think a man with eyes like that would try to hide them if he were disposing of body parts in broad daylight? I mean, sunglasses are not hard to come by."

"What about the note in my book?"

"A design queen with too much time on his hands, and nothing to write on but a children's book. You really should hide that purse, though. It's a point well taken, if you ask me . . ."

"Oh, wait a minute. There is something else he could have written on." I fished around in my bag. "So. A guy with three balls."

"I was hoping you wouldn't catch that."

"I'm assuming it's not Peter Steele."

"No, wiseass," he said. "It was someone I met years ago, at the Spike."

"I don't recall you ever mentioning a gentleman friend with three testicles."

"Oh, hmmm . . . I suppose it just didn't come up. 'Hello, Sam, and how was your evening? Watched a documentary on PBS? That's nice. I fucked a guy with an extra marble in his pouch.'"

"I would've told you."

Yale rolled his eyes. "He was a student at Hunter. Adorable. Not as handsome as Peter, though. Of course no one's as handsome as Peter. Michelangelo's David is not as handsome as Peter. I can't wait for you to meet him, I'm taking you to his restaurant for lunch, and I swear you are just going to die when you see him, and not just because he's the most beautiful man you will ever see in your life. There's something else about him—something about his voice . . . and the way he uses his eyes. You know what I mean?"

Yale waited for a response, but I didn't have one to offer. I was too busy staring at a different set of eyes—Sydney's eyes on the valentine headshot. Someone had drawn X's over them, pressing down hard with a pencil.

5

Magic Mirrors

Since it was reasonably close to Sunny Side, we decided to walk to Ruby Redd's Brewing Company, the touristy West Village restaurant where Peter Steele worked. Yale wanted us both to have at least an hour to stare at the Most Beautiful Man You Will Ever See in Your Life before we were due in at the Space, so we were running a little late on his clock. My friend moved fast to begin with, and since the eleven inches he had on me was almost all leg, I was jogging to keep up.

I hadn't shown Yale the defaced valentine. I figured he'd probably make up more excuses about crazy bar queens and I wasn't ready to hear them, wasn't ready to talk about it at all.

"So what exactly *does* Peter look like?"

Yale responded with dependable creativity. And as he described the waiter's "lethal" abs, "ergonomic" bone structure and lips "that would be considered a delicacy in most countries," I did my best to picture him. But, hard as I tried, my mind replaced each of Yale's images with these: mirrored eyes staring at the back of my head, a man's hand clutching a pencil.

It was a good thing I was no longer hungover, because the interior of Ruby Redd's Brewing Company was nearly more overpowering than my classroom.

"There's so much red," I said, staring at all of it. Red-and-white checkered tablecloths, tiny bunches of red carnations at the center of every table in red glass vases, brass ceiling lamps with red Tiffany-style shades, red vinyl booths facing red wooden chairs. "I mean, okay, Ruby Redd's. We get the point. It's like *The Shining* in here."

The waiters wore red-and-white checkered bow ties that matched the tablecloths and red butchers' aprons that matched nearly everything else. All of them looked cute enough to be on a TV commercial, though none was exactly ready for the *Galleria dell'Accademia*.

I watched my friend's face as he scanned the room for Peter Steele, but his expression remained neutral, his baby blue eyes darkened. "Do you think he was lying about working here?" he asked.

"Who would lie about being a waiter at Ruby Redd's Brewing Company?"

Yale and I sat on two crimson counter stools, and a young waiter with spiky burgundy hair and a red name tag that said "Tredwell" approached us.

"Hi, Tredwell," Yale said as he accepted two long, rectangular menus encased in cherry velveteen. "Did you color your hair to match the restaurant or vice versa?"

"Huh?"

"Never mind. We're looking for Peter Steele?"

"You guys are friends of Peter's?" Tredwell said.

Yale exhaled audibly. "He does work here."

"Yeah. His shift doesn't start 'til later, though."

We decided to stay anyway. I hadn't eaten a thing since before I'd puked, and I realized I was starving. I ordered my typical posthangover meal: a cheddar omelet with a side of bacon, buttered rye toast and black coffee.

Yale gave me a disdainful look and pointedly asked for grilled vegetables and green tea.

"Oh, I never shared my other lovely news," I said, after the waiter walked away. "You remember Nate, don't you?" I whipped the *Post* out of my bag and placed the entertainment section in front of Yale as Tredwell returned with our steaming red mugs.

Yale stared at the article. "You have *got* to be kidding."

"Stupid, huh?"

Yale jerked his tea bag up and down, up and down. "Well . . . it's not as if he's on Broadway."

"No. He's making more money than that."

"How'd you two kids like some cream with your coffee and tea?" asked Tredwell.

"He cheated on you with a man and a woman!" Yale was inadvertently using his stage voice, and I could feel customers turning to stare at us, or, rather, at me.

"Could you possibly keep it down?"

"Nathan Gundersen bisexually cheated on you and he gets to make more money than the emcee in *Cabaret*? What the fuck kind of karma is that?"

"Tell me about it."

"Well," he said. "There is more to life than just making money as some flash-in-the-pan, so-called 'hunk' on an inconsequential daytime soap opera."

"You guys know Nate Gundersen?" Tredwell said.

Yale ignored him. "The minute that ass drops—and let me tell you it *will* drop—not a soul in the universe will return his calls. Male, female, canine, bovine . . . No one. Because beneath that . . . that gaudy exterior, he has no substance. No . . . intelligence."

"He graduated from Stanford summa cum laude."

"Oh, for shit's sake!"

Tredwell was still standing over us, a tiny red pitcher balanced on his palm.

"We would not like any cream!" said Yale.

I said, "You sound angrier than me."

"I know. It's just . . . God. I hate Nate for what he did to you. He doesn't deserve anything."

"We're in agreement there."

"And, not to sound selfish, but it isn't fair to me either."

I looked at him.

"Hey, I work hard, and I strive to be a good person, and I've never cheated on anyone, let alone *bisexually* cheated on them, and that prick can do any play that he wants while I'm lucky to get a chorus part at a dinner theater on Long Island. He's clearly stolen *my* hard-earned good fortune."

I couldn't help but smile a little.

"And . . . and then you tell me he's summa cum laude? I mean, he has money and fame and fans and . . . and that ass, and now I can't even take comfort in his possible stupidity? What am I supposed to do about that?"

My smile grew broader. Yale had a talent for making himself the injured party in any given situation—particularly the ones that were actually damaging to me. It was oddly soothing, the way he asked me to help him with my problems. "You have a very nice ass," I said.

Yale gave my hand a squeeze. "Get this away from me." He folded up the *Post* and stuffed it back in my bag.

Meanwhile, the waiter was lingering like bad breath.

I said, "I swear to God we don't need anything else."

Tredwell put down the cursed pitcher of cream, knocking over a saltshaker in the process. I pinched up some salt, tossed it over my left shoulder and glared at him.

Tredwell stared unblinkingly over our heads, and then slowly, his lips parted. "Whoa," he said softly, and proceeded to knock over my coffee.

Tredwell brought new meaning to the words *economy of movement*. With hot coffee streaming over the edge of the counter and onto the decidedly nonwaterproof shoulder bag that sat in my lap, he waited several seconds before slowly reaching behind him, grabbing a stack of paper napkins and placing them in front of me without so much as offering to help. As Yale used some of the napkins to dam off the coffee, I tried to sop up my purse. "We could use a few more napkins here, buddy," Yale said, but Tredwell just stood there like a lamp.

A deep, inflectionless voice behind us said, "Turn around, Bright Eyes."

Yale gasped. "Peter . . . don't you look . . . striking today."

"Can I have some seltzer water?" I said, but Tredwell remained paralyzed. I didn't care how good-looking Peter Steele was, this little creep wasn't getting a tip.

I looped the shoulder strap over the counter stool so the bag was facing out at the room behind me. "I guess I'll just have to *air this out* then."

Peter's voice was saying, "Well, come on. What do you think?"

"They're definitely interesting," Yale said.

"They're one of a kind. At least that's what the guy at the contact lens place told me. I can't decide whether they're hot or scary."

"I'd say they're a little of both."

"Know what they're called? Magic Mirrors."

I spun around on the counter stool and looked at his face. "Shit."

"Who's she?"

I cleared my throat. "I'm Yale's friend Samantha."

"Golly," he said. "Taking the gals to meet me already."

"Sam's my best friend."

"Not to be rude, but what an ugly bag. Not you—your purse."

"I told you, Sam."

"Magic Mirrors," I said.

"Cute name, huh?"

"Cute."

Yale said, "I hate to break it to you, Peter, but I don't think those contacts are one of a— Sam! You *kicked* me!"

"Sorry. It was an accident."

"I need something," Peter said. He reached out and took Yale's hand in his, then slowly brought it up to his mouth. Watching my face, he ran his full lips along the length of its underside, from the base of the palm to the tip of the middle finger. "That's better," he said.

Yale opened his mouth and closed it again, his cheeks coloring.

"I have to go to the bathroom." I grabbed the damp shoulder bag and headed for the rear of the restaurant on stiff, uncooperative legs.

All the while, I felt Peter's mirrored eyes staring at the back of my head.

"Okay," I said to my reflection. "Okay, okay, okay."

I wasn't sure how long I'd been in this giant cor-puscle of a bathroom, with its red toilet, sink and light bulbs; nor how long I'd been repeating the word, but it was starting to sound foreign. "Okayokayokay . . ."

I looked deep into my own pupils, maroon under the tarty lights, and thought about Peter's eyes, how they didn't have pupils. I thought about how, when he'd turned towards me, all I could see in them were tiny, distorted segments of my own face. When he'd mouthed Yale's hand, I'd seen doubles of my top lip.

They were the same eyes as the Hudson River man's, and Peter had said his contacts were one of a kind. "Okayokay . . ."

Peter had close-cropped, dark hair, a broad, smooth forehead, black eyebrows. "Okay."

What an ugly bag, he'd said, bits of orange and brown embroidery in his eyes. The bag had been everywhere with me—the construction site, the box office, Great White. Was he letting me know he'd seen it before? Was he letting me know that he'd seen it— and me—before he tracked down and seduced my best friend? Was he letting me know that he could go any-

where, be anywhere at any time, that there was
nowhere for me to go, nowhere for me to *hide*?

Yale would think I was insane if he were to hear me
muttering into the mirror of the world's reddest bathroom, considering the possibility that his gorgeous
new boyfriend was a murderer and stalker who had
spent Valentine's Day dumping a picnic cooler full of
body parts into the Hudson.

He would think I was insane, and I wouldn't blame
him. Peter was probably not the same man I'd seen at
the river. And even if he was . . . *body parts*? More
likely there was something harmless in the ice chest.
Something along the lines of trash, battery acid, old
clothes . . .

Why couldn't I shake off this suspicion? Why was I
afraid to leave the bathroom? Why couldn't I imagine
myself saying, "Hey, Peter. Didn't I see you and a
woman down by the piers?" if there wasn't anything
wrong with Peter and a woman being down by the piers?

I splashed cold water in my face. "Okay," I said
again. The muscles at the base of my skull clenched
up, my headache was starting to return. I had to eat
something. Somebody knocked on the door. I clutched
the edge of the sink and took a deep, trembling breath.
Finally, I unlocked the door and headed back for the
counter.

"That's the men's room, you know," a male voice
called after me.

*   *   *

"Are you all right?" Yale asked when I returned.

"Yeah, why?"

"We thought you fell in," said Peter.

"I was . . . in the men's room."

"Well, that explains it." Peter winked a mirrored eye at me. I could see part of my cheek in it, a wisp of my hair.

Peter had taken my seat at the counter, and Yale stared at him as if he were watching *Les Mis* for the first time. "Sam, Peter. Peter, Sam . . ."

"You look familiar," said Peter. "Have we met before?"

I watched Tredwell put my lunch in front of the empty seat on the other side of Peter and said, "I don't think so." My eyes darted back to his. Now they were filled with the faint black and gray pattern on my V-necked sweater.

Yale was right. His face was beautiful. It looked as if someone had spent long, loving hours sculpting every smooth inch of it, and his skin was glowingly tan despite the time of year. He had the ripe, bloated mouth of a *Cosmopolitan* model. I imagined it covered by a black scarf.

"You're staring at me," Peter said—not unkindly, more like he was used to it. "Do I have something in my teeth?" In his eyes, I could see where the pale skin of my neck met my black T-shirt collar.

"I really hate those lenses."

"Sam!" said Yale. "You have to forgive her, Peter. She saw someone else with contacts like that and . . ."

"Shut up, Yale."

"You couldn't," Peter said. "They're one of a kind."

"Then maybe it was you I saw."

"Maybe it was," he said through pearlescent teeth. "Maybe that's why you look so . . . fa-mil-iar."

"Maybe."

"Sam, why don't you sit down?" Yale said. "You're making me nervous."

I obliged, more out of hunger than anything else, and shoved a piece of toast in my mouth.

Peter said, "I saw you throw salt over your shoulder before. I know a lot about old superstitions. You know what you were doing when you did that?"

I dug into the lukewarm omelet. "Not really."

"You were trying to blind the devil!" He started to laugh.

"What's so funny about that?"

"Come on. A grown, educated woman in New York City throwing salt in the devil's eyes? I mean, it is kind of . . . stupid when you think about it."

Yale chuckled. "That *is* funny. Well, let me tell you, Sam is *soooo* superstitious. My God, it's practically a psychosis. I mean, if you're in a hurry to get somewhere, and the closest distance between two points happens to be under a ladder, then you can just forget about it. She will literally go *blocks* out of her way to avoid stepping under that ladder. I've seen it happen. She's *crazy*."

Peter stopped laughing.

I stared at Yale.

"I don't mean crazy. I mean . . . fun."

I shoved more omelet in my mouth. At least my headache was starting to go away. "So," I finally said to Peter. "You do anything else besides wait tables and pick up complete strangers at after-hours bars?"

Peter turned his body towards me, and I felt my heart speed up. I avoided his eyes, watched his mouth. "I breathe," the mouth said. "I eat. I smoke. I fuck." Abruptly, he leaned in so close I could feel his warm, odorless breath on my skin. "I bet *you* don't . . . smoke. I bet you haven't *smoked* for *years.*"

"Oh, for God's sake. How can you keep your vegetables down, Yale?"

His face flushed. "What do you mean?"

"Oh, nothing. I just thought you might be feeling as nauseous as I do." I pulled a handful of bills out of my ugly bag and tossed them onto the counter.

Peter turned back to Yale. "You've got great friends."

"Whatever, good-bye." As I reached for my bag, I noticed a tattoo on the back of Peter's neck. It was a dark red pentagram, just about the size of a quarter. The small shape was thickly drawn and amateurish—almost as if it had been put there with a branding iron—and it made me feel as if someone were squeezing all the air out of the room. "You better come too, Yale. We're going to be late for work," I said, my voice shaking. "I'll meet you outside."

"Wait a minute, Sam!" Yale said, but I kept walking until I reached the front door and stepped outside and onto the freezing gray sidewalk.

When Yale left the restaurant a few minutes later, he already had a lit cigarette in his hand. "What the fuck is wrong with you?" he said, exhaling blue-tinged smoke.

"What's wrong with *me*? What's wrong with *you*? Is your brain that firmly embedded in your pants? He's an asshole, Yale. A hostile, misogynous asshole. I can't believe you wanted me to meet him."

"Number one, he is not a misogynist—he just has a slightly off sense of humor, which you might have even appreciated if you weren't so hell-bent on hating him. Number two, you were the hostile one in there. I mean, Jesus. *You do anything else besides wait tables and pick up complete strangers?* What kind of a question is that?"

"Yale . . . I think he might be the same man I saw at the river."

"Oh, spare me. Did you feel Dead Man's Fingers again?"

I glared at him.

"You get chills up your spine, you see a couple dumping trash, and your mind just spins out of control. Think about it. Just do me a favor and think logically—"

"Did you see the way he glared at me when he told me I look familiar?"

Yale blinked. "You know what you need? You need a good night's sleep, you need a few healthy meals—"

"Peter himself said the contacts were one of a kind."

"He bought them this morning."

"What?"

"After you left, I asked."

"And you believed him?"

"You think little Tredwell would've been that shocked if he'd worn them during his weekend shifts? Peter's contact lens salesman lied to him, the couple was not disposing of body parts, and you are not psychic. Now, if you don't mind, I am going to walk to work by myself and smoke an entire pack of cigarettes."

Yale buttoned up his cashmere coat. It was deliciously soft and chocolate brown and to wrap it around your shoulders was to feel unconditionally loved. His parents had given it to him for Christmas. I'd been at his apartment when he'd opened the UPS box. "And you don't have to worry about Peter, because you scared him off. He says *no one's* worth the company I keep."

I stood there for several seconds, watching Yale's brown cashmere back disappear up Sixth Avenue. I hadn't mentioned the tattoo; not that it would've made any difference.

My throat felt raw and knotted, and pressure was building up behind my eyes. I knew I wouldn't start crying on the corner of Sixth and West Fourth in broad daylight with thick groups of pedestrians rushing past me towards the subway, but I wanted to.

I looked at my watch. It was two ten already, with at least ten more minutes to get to the theater, even if I ran. There was a pay phone on the corner, so I fished around in my bag for a quarter and called work.

"Thank you so much for calling the Space."

At first, I didn't recognize the voice, but then it hit me. "Hi, Hermyn. Roland's got you answering phones now, huh?"

"Oh, hi, Samantha. I thought you were my mother."

I wasn't sure how to respond to that. "Can you tell Roland that Yale and I are running late? We both had to run a few errands."

"Okay. He was wondering where you guys were, so he'll be glad you called . . ." Hermyn's voice tilted up at the end of the sentence, like she wanted to talk. I was freezing, and although I felt sorry for her, sitting on her hard little chair near the door with Shell Clarion staring bullets through her back, I was in no mood to discuss her wedding plans. "Bye," I said, and hung up before she could respond.

Two minutes later, I was navigating my way through a slow-walking family of eight on West Tenth. "Excuse you!" shouted the grandmother when I brushed by her mink. I stopped and examined her. Like the rest of her family, she had pink cheeks, a huge head and a thick, sturdy body. They were, I decided, on vacation from a safe, friendly state, embraced by land on all sides. "Fuck you," I said, because I didn't feel like saying "sorry" to some landlocked old mink-wearing bitch right now.

I increased my pace, focused on the clear, flat stretch of sidewalk ahead of me. Maybe Yale was right. Maybe I was a paranoid, relationship-ruining nightmare.

My bag tugged at my shoulder, and I realized it was because the *Post* was still in there. I pulled it out and looked at Nate, eyeing the camera in all his shirtless, gleaming celebrity, framed by Veronica's studiously drawn outline. Much as I hated the photo and the headline and the article, Veronica's outline irritated me most of all. She had actually used a ruler.

Without thinking, I ripped the page in half. It felt better than I'd expected. I tore it into quarters, then eighths, then random little bits. The tension in my chest began to lift; I almost wanted to laugh. There was a trash can nearby, so I decimated the entire tabloid and tossed it up and in, like confetti. It felt so good I considered buying another *Post*, just so I could do it again. Then I felt two hands on my shoulders and my heart jumped into my mouth.

"What the—" I spun around. It took me a few seconds to recognize the pinkish face, the burgundy hair. *"Tredwell?"*

"Sorry, dude," the young waiter said. "I didn't mean to scare you."

"Did I forget something?" I grasped my bag.

"No . . . You walk fast." He smiled broadly and panted. "Ummmm . . . Where'd your friend go?"

"Yale? He's . . . smoking. Did he not pay his share of the bill?"

"No, no, no, no . . . It's not that. I . . . I wanted to talk to you," Tredwell finally caught his breath and smiled again. "Whew!" He jammed his hands into the pockets of his red butcher's apron. He wasn't wearing a coat. "Whoosh! Cold! Hooo boy!"

The conversation was starting to annoy me, and I was about to tell this AWOL waiter as much, but when I looked into his eyes, I detected an emotion that didn't match the grin, the slouch, the ridiculous exclamations. It was fear, and it shut me right up.

When his fake smile dropped away, Tredwell looked about ten years older and suddenly intelligent. "I need to talk to you about Peter," he said.

6

Verbal Judo

Tredwell was on the verge of hypothermia, so we ducked into the nearest bar—a windowless crater called Cheap Trix that had no business being open during the day. Since it was empty, the bartender noticed us immediately. "Nice apron," he shouted over needlessly loud techno music as he eyed the shivering Tredwell. "You know you can't just come in here for the heater. You have to order something." I thought, *What the hell? I need it,* and asked for a draft beer while Tredwell ran to the bathroom, explaining, "I'll be right back. I just g-g-gotta put hot water on my hands."

By the time Tredwell returned, I'd finished around three quarters of the beer and was considering ordering another. "What took you so long?" I said, but when he launched into a speech about thinking the door was locked, even though it wasn't, it was just sticky, you know how old doors get sticky sometimes and you think they're locked even though they're not, I'd already heard too much. "Tell me about Peter."

Tredwell took a swallow of my beer before replying, "Peter Steele is evil."

I held my breath and waited for him to say more, but he didn't. He just looked at me until frustration seeped out of my skin.

"Are you going to maybe elaborate on that? Because you can't just say somebody's evil. It's not like saying he's got brown hair or that he's a Methodist or something. You say somebody's evil, you have to give examples."

"All right . . . Ummm. He gives off bad energy? I know you felt it; otherwise you wouldn't have run to the bathroom like you did. And, shit, man, those contacts. You can't tell me you didn't notice those freaky, freaky contacts. Whoa. I can't believe he *bought* those . . ."

"I noticed the contacts, Tredwell. And I felt the *energy.*" I polished off the beer and leveled my eyes at him. "What I'm trying to figure out right now is why you chased me three blocks in the freezing cold with no coat on, just to tell me stuff I already know."

"To tell you stuff you already know," he repeated— or replied, I wasn't sure. My headache was back again, and I felt a dull pain at the core of my stomach. If there were two things I didn't need, they were a beer on top of a cheese omelet and the company of this kid.

"Thanks for the warning," I said. "I have to go now."

I started to put my coat back on, but he grabbed my arm. Tredwell's grip was surprisingly strong. "There's more," he said. "It's just a little difficult to express."

"I'll give you thirty seconds."

"I'm not totally gay."

"Okay . . ."

"But I used to . . . I used to *be* with Peter. And . . . and he made me . . . do things I didn't want to do." Tredwell eased me back onto the barstool.

"What kind of things?"

"Name it," he said. "Drugs I'd never done before. K. Crystal meth. Lots and lots of amyl." He watched my face warily, like he expected it to detonate.

"I'm pretty sure Yale is beyond drug peer pressure."

"The amyl was for the sex. Because it kills the pain—"

"All right, now you're giving me too much information."

"No, wait. This is important . . . Peter got me to . . . experience real pain." He glanced at the bartender, then leaned in close. "Peter hurt me," he whispered. "I let him."

Tredwell stared at me so intently that I had to look away. "I didn't want to, but I did. It was like I . . . couldn't move."

There was a sudden, strange intimacy between us— between me and this twenty-year-old, one-named guy who had spilled coffee on me less than half an hour earlier—and it made me feel raw and embarrassed. "He hurt you," I said, more to myself than to him.

Tredwell rubbed his eyelids with his palms. "He'd look at you, look inside you more like . . . and you'd be forced into doing whatever he said. Bondage. S and M . . ."

I put a hand on his arm, frail as a bird's wing under the long, white sleeve.

"I have scars."

"It's okay," I said, like you would to a frightened child. "It's okay, honey."

Tredwell drew a shallow, trembling breath and placed his hand over mine. His palm was cold and sweaty.

"What, honey? You can tell me."

Suddenly, he squeezed my hand so hard it hurt. When he looked up at me, I noticed his eyes were wet. "Peter convinced me to worship Satan."

I couldn't believe I was going to actually say the words *Satan worship* to anyone, much less a cop, but I was.

What I'd seen at the river had been Peter and a woman involved in a Satanic rite. I was now sure of it. I remembered the scraping sound I'd heard, the ice chest's heaviness. It had been small, but large enough to hold a severed body part, or a collection of them. I remembered the woman's exposed arms, shaking uncontrollably. Shaking like Tredwell's hand.

Back at Cheap Trix, I'd stared at Tredwell, who, like the woman, wore clothes that surrendered his body to the cold. I'd looked at his red apron and recalled the woman's red dress. I'd listened to him tell me about Black Masses and inverted crosses and red robes and red candles "signifying virgin blood" and thought of all that red light in Ruby's, how comfortable Peter had seemed there. I'd remembered the bloodred pentagram branded into Peter's neck, and how he'd laughed at me for trying to blind the devil, and the question had floated out of my mouth so effortlessly, like a ghost: *Did you and Peter ever sacrifice anything?*

And Tredwell had said nothing, just looked away.

"Sorry to freak you out. I just wanted to warn your friend," he told me after we left the bar. "I was Peter's slave, and I'm not anymore, so he's looking for a new one."

I envisioned the woman again, trembling in her uncomfortable dress. "What makes you think he doesn't already have one?"

"Huh?"

"Don't worry, I'll take care of it."

Tredwell smiled. "I think you will." He gave me a kiss on the cheek, which didn't feel strange at all. And I watched him run back to work in the freezing cold, weaving around clusters of pedestrians with the grace of a new angel.

*   *   *

The bartender at Cheap Trix had given me directions to the Sixth Precinct, and it was surprisingly close. Half a block past Ruby Redd's Brewing Company, in the other direction.

When I passed the restaurant on my way to the precinct house, I pulled my hood over my head, a poor attempt to disguise myself lest Peter catch sight of me through the large window—particularly poor, since I'd been wearing the hood at the river.

A woman in a long camel coat was leaving Ruby's as I went by, and when she asked me if I had a light, I did my best to pretend I was invisible, even though there was no one else she could have been addressing. "Hey, Patchwork Bag!" the woman shrieked. "I'm talking to you!"

Thanks a lot, sister. I stopped and glared at her. Her hair was so smooth and gold that it looked as if it had been cast, rather than styled. She wore huge Jackie Onassis–style glasses and perfect red lipstick and looked familiar in a famous way. Local anchorwoman or soap opera actress, I decided. I wondered if she knew Nate. "I don't have a light."

"Sorry. I just don't like it when people ignore me."

When I turned around, I could still feel her eyes on my back.

Across the street, four doors down, I saw a building too ugly to be anything but a precinct house. As I approached it, I saw that indeed it was—a squat, beige seventies-style fortress wedged between walk-ups with a huge blue-and-white police shield painted on the front. There was an unfurled scroll emblazoned with the words *Greenwich Village* at the top of the shield, an outline of the Washington Square Park Arch at the center and the words *6th Precinct* in smaller, more modest letters at the bottom. It struck me as sweet and collegiate—not cop-like at all, which soothed my nerves a little.

I crossed the street and pushed open the heavy glass door. The interior was quite a match for the facade, with its draining fluorescent lights and walls the color of old teeth. I tried to ignore the queasiness that came over me when I saw two huge cops drag a skinny boy across the bustling front room. The boy's cheeks were striped with runny mascara. "I'm sorry. I'm sorry. I'm sorry," he kept saying. The cops pushed him into what must have been the booking room as four other uni-forms rushed past them and out the front door, oblivi-ous. I noticed the guns in their holsters and it hit me that the boy and I were possibly the only two people in the building who weren't packing.

Think of the shield outside. Think of that adorable shield with the Washington Square Park Arch painted on it and walk up to that front desk this minute.

The desk was manned by a tall cop with cornrowed hair who looked like African royalty, even in her uni-form, and strong enough to beat the crap out of me without breaking a sweat.

"Hi." I cleared my throat. "I'm here to see Detective Krull?"

"Your name?"

"I'm Samantha Leiffer." Even as I said it, I doubted he would remember. "I'm a prekindergarten teacher? He met me on Friday, when he came to speak at my school, which is called Sunny Side . . ."

"Samantha Leiffer to see you," she said into her phone.

"Prekindergarten teacher," I said, but the desk sergeant had already hung up.

"He'll be right down."

"He will?"

I thought about sitting down on one of the plastic chairs near the front desk but as it turned out, I didn't have time. A door across from us opened and there he stood, like a game show prize.

Detective John Krull wore a brown, synthetic suit that he'd probably owned since high school graduation, without benefit of a tailor. The jacket winced against his powerful shoulders and the sleeves ended about two inches too soon, displaying the cuffs of yet another tired white shirt, adorned by yet another cheap, patternless tie—this time mud colored. "Hey," he said. "Nice surprise."

"You remember me."

"Isn't every day I look at someone and make them scream."

The desk sergeant raised her eyebrows.

"Listen, I need to talk to you about something I . . . uh . . . witnessed."

"You're reporting a crime?"

"Um . . . sort of . . ."

His smile faded. "Come on upstairs to the squad room."

I followed him back through the door, up a staircase that reeked from decades of cigarette smoke and down a hallway that housed several offices—one of which bore a red, B52-shaped sign that said *Bomb Squad*, in Prussian-style letters. Like the police shield out front, I found the sign out of place and charming. Very Greenwich Village, not at all Sixth Precinct. "Cute sign," I said. Krull didn't hear me, and I was glad. What a ridiculous thing to do, complimenting a bomb squad sign.

The detective squad room was beyond compliments—one hundred percent government issue—and it resuscitated my anxiety. Torturous bright lights and narrow windows, fascistically lined-up Formica desks and about a dozen badly dressed men of varying ages—all of them, no doubt, packing. Despite the huge coat, most of the detectives stopped their conversations and gawked at me like I was nude. I felt dizzy from testosterone, like I'd inadvertently walked into a high-school football team's locker room or a men's prison. They must not see many females with a pulse in here, I thought.

Krull guided me to one of the few detectives who wasn't gawking—a heavy guy in his fifties with a face like a rare steak. "Nope," he said into his phone. "You heard me . . . No . . . What part of the word *no* don't you . . . Oh, really? He said that? Well, he can go *fuck* himself with *the proverbial ham sandwich*, but that's off the record. Peas." He hung up without saying good-bye, then turned his attention to us. *Peas?*

Krull said, "I'd like you to meet one of my partners, Art Boyle. Art, this is Samantha Leiffer."

"Johnny's told me a lot about you."

"He's lying," Krull said. "He has no absolutely no idea who you are."

Boyle chuckled and shook my hand. His grip was tourniquet strength.

"*One* of your partners? I thought you guys worked in teams."

"We work three to a unit in this precinct," Boyle said. "Our other partner is in the hospital."

"I'm sorry."

"Nothing to be sorry about. She's having a baby."

"Oh, well, that's great."

"Definitely. Amanda is damn lucky. Baby born on the Aquarius/Pisces cusp like that, Mercury fresh out of retrograde. Could be president of the United States, that kid, especially if he winds up with earth rising."

"Art's wife is into astrology." Krull winked at me. "It's rubbed off a little, hasn't it, Art?"

Boyle stared into his coffee cup. "You'd be surprised at how accurate some of it is . . ."

As Krull led me into one of the adjacent interrogation rooms (which he referred to as an "interview room"), I whispered, "Why would Art say peas to someone?"

"What?"

"Didn't you hear him say *peas* to whomever he was talking to on the phone? Right before he hung up."

Krull grinned. "Not peas. Peace. He always says that to reporters. Thinks it pisses them off."

Whatever Krull or the NYPD chose to call it, this room was no place for an interview. Granted, there was a tape recorder plugged into a wall. But the only furniture in the cramped space was a metal table and four hard chairs that had interrogation written all over them. The room had no windows, unless you counted the small piece of one-way glass on the wall that faced the squad room. It made me nervous, but I supposed that was the purpose. "Promise you won't think I'm insane," I said to Krull, once we were situated across from each other at the interrogation table.

"That's a tough promise to make." He tried smiling at me again, but I just looked at him.

"I'm kidding."

Besides the tape recorder, the only thing on the table was a small tin ashtray that made me wish I smoked. For several seconds, I stared at it as if it were a crystal ball that could tell me whether my suspicions about Peter were correct. But Tredwell had already been my crystal ball, hadn't he? How lucky that he'd caught up with me, that I'd listened to him long enough to know that he was more than just an idiot with a bad dye job.

I pictured a tiny version of Tredwell in the center of the ashtray, on his knees with his hands clasped, begging me to speak. Tentatively, I began. I told Krull about the blond woman, whose face I never saw, and the ice chest, and then I told him about the man with the mirrored eyes. I ventured a glance up at the detective, half expecting him to accuse me, as Sydney had, of being on designer hallucinogens. But his expression remained neutral, even kind.

I opened up my bag, showed him the word *hide* in my book, showed him my mother's eyes, X-ed out on the Valentine's Day postcard she'd sent. I watched him as he carefully examined both items, running his fingertips over the pencil marks.

It grew easier and easier to talk.

When I got to the part about meeting Peter, Krull interrupted me. "So there are now two guys with this type of contact lens."

"No, it's the same one."

"It is?"

I took a deep breath, replayed my conversations with Peter and Tredwell. It was oddly cathartic, hearing my own voice say it all. Even phrases like *S and M* and *Satan worship* helped solidify the events in my mind and make them less frightening, like describing a nightmare out loud.

After I finished, Krull said, "Okay. Now I want you

to tell me something, but I want you to think hard before you say it."

"Yes?"

"What do you think the crime was?" He sounded like I did when I spoke to my class. *Where do you think Elmo is hiding? Can you make a letter* B*?*

Anger trickled into my veins. I felt my back stiffen. "What do you *mean*, what do I think the crime was?" I said. "Weren't you listening to me at all? This guy . . . he's a *freak* and he obviously sacrificed something—*someone*—and disposed of the body parts in the river, and he . . . he followed me, and . . . and defaced things in my purse, and then he seduced my best friend—probably to send me some kind of sick message . . . He's a *Satan worshiper*, for godsakes."

"I know it's easy to infer things from what you saw—"

"Infer things!"

"Listen to me for a second."

"I am not inferring—"

"Hold up . . . please. Wrong choice of words. Okay? My fault." His voice was measured, skilled. I remembered a magazine article I'd once read about a technique used by cops to soothe and manipulate overemotional witnesses. It was called verbal judo. They even offered courses in it at the police academy.

He's using a talking technique on me, I thought. I wanted to slap Krull across the face. *I'll show you verbal judo, you fucking cop . . .*

"Samantha?"

I glared at him.

"I'm going to give you two scenarios and you tell me, from an objective point of view, which makes the most sense. Okay?"

"Fine."

"Scenario one: Just like you said, you stumbled on a bisexual devil worshiper making human sacrifices at the Hudson River with his female slave accomplice, and he subsequently stalks you and seduces your friend—to send you a message."

"I know it sounds weird, but that's what hap—"

"Scenario two: You see two people at the river: a woman, and a man with a pair of weird-assed contacts. They've taken a few bucks under the table to illegally dispose of medical waste in ice chests, which—unlike human sacrifice—is a common thing to do. Since you're a witness to what is, in fact, a criminal act, he gives you a nasty look, maybe even starts to follow you. But then he gives up and forgets about it. Later, some asshole at—what was it, Great White?—doesn't like seeing a woman in a gay bar so he takes out his pencil and writes a little note in your book, X-es out the eyes of your mom, who by the way, looks a lot like you. Later, your friend meets a different guy with the same contacts. Maybe the guy is into sadism, I don't know. That's not unusual in this precinct, and it isn't a crime between consenting adults."

"I know that."

"Now, I don't doubt you saw some people dropping an ice chest in the river. But until that ice chest is recovered and we can look inside it, the only crime you've got to report is littering. Okay?"

I stared silently at Krull, and he stared right back at me. The fact that I'd mistaken him for anything other than a typical shithead policeman could only mean I was disgustingly superficial, capable of allowing my entire perspective on life and law enforcement to be swayed by . . . what? A smile? A few kind words?

"I am not an *idiot*! I'm not shocked by sado-masochism. I know when someone is—is littering. I know what I saw and I know what to *make of* what I saw . . . and . . . *you* . . . you are making a big mistake, Detective."

I wasn't sure when I'd jumped to my feet, but I was standing now. Krull looked up at me. "I never said you were an idiot. You are an intelligent person. When you've calmed down a little, do me a favor and think about what I've said. I'm pretty sure you'll realize it makes sense. Because you *are*. You're very intelligent." That was it. The sickly sweet icing on the verbal judo cake.

"You must be a black belt," I said.

"What?"

"Nothing. I'll find my own way out." I more or less jogged out of the squad room. Someone shouted, "Nice work, Krull!" as the door slammed behind me.

It took me several minutes to locate the staircase, but at least I didn't ask anyone for directions.

7

Two Hours Late

No Tears for Addie was the biggest flop to abuse the Space's stage since *My Baby's a Hat!* the Oliver Sacks–inspired musical comedy that nearly shut the place down just after it opened in 1989. That was a good thing for me, because if it had inconvenienced any customers, the fact that I'd shown up for work two hours late would've been grounds for dismissal.

As it stood, Roland did the next best thing, which was dragging Yale upstairs to back him up at his weekly meeting with the theater's owner and stationing me at the buyers' window between Shell Clarion and Hermyn—a punishment if there ever was one.

I hadn't been able to say anything to Yale, which was all right because I didn't know what I would have said to him given the chance. When I'd first come in, all he did was shake his head at me like I was a bad idea. Why wouldn't anyone believe me?

The only crime you've got to report is littering. I could practically hear Krull say it again as I separated and alphabetized the evening's few will-call tickets, and the back of my neck heated up. I wished I'd slapped him when I'd had the opportunity.

"What the fuck is going on with you?" asked Shell Clarion. Apparently, she'd been talking to me for quite some time.

"Man trouble." It wasn't a lie. First Nate's picture, then Peter Steele, then Yale, then Krull. If men didn't exist, my day would've been trouble free.

"Men suck," Shell said, glaring at Hermyn.

"Why are you looking at me, Shell? I'm not a man."

"Could've fooled me."

"Pardon?"

"Can you picture *it* in a wedding dress?" she stage-whispered. "Talk about a drag show."

I did my best to ignore her. "Where's Argent?"

"She's auditioning," Hermyn said, "for *Cats*."

I recalled the hand-written word in my book and shuddered. The fact that *Cats* now terrified me made me even angrier at Krull. *Hide* in my book was not about littering. The way my mother's picture had been violated with a pencil was not about littering. And it certainly wasn't about being a woman in Great White.

Krull was right about one thing. My mother's picture looked a lot like me. At the time it was taken, she'd been just five years older than I was now. Give me a little kohl liner and a frost-and-tip, we'd be identical. Especially the eyes. The X-ed-out eyes. My throat clenched up.

I said, "I thought *Cats* closed."

"Not Broadway," Hermyn said. "The production is in New Hope, Pennsylvania."

"Large Arge in a unitard? Don't make me puke."

Shut up, Shell, I thought, like a mantra. *Shut up Shell. Shut up Shell. Shut up Shell* . . . "New Hope. That's a commute."

"It is, but I bet she gets the part," Hermyn added. "Argent really does have a beautiful voice. I'm thinking of asking her to sing at my wedding."

"I suppose that's one way to get somebody to come. Where are you renting your tux, by the way . . . Her-*man*?"

That was it. My last nerve of the day, and Clarion had snapped it in two. I turned and glared at her, sitting on the metal stool in her black velveteen leggings and her black patent leather boots and her tight black turtleneck with pink, fuzzy valentine hearts all over it, commenting on Hermyn's looks, Hermyn's clothes. Shell, with that beige bleach job and that junior smoker's voice, like a rubber band twanging, and nothing, absolutely nothing on her mind that didn't spill out of her mouth. Shell, with her soap operatic jealousy and her shallow opinions and her hatred of Hermyn and Yale and Argent and En—of everyone except me. *How insulting.*

I said, "You are a bitter, bitter cow."

"What did you say?"

"The world does not revolve around you and whether or not you're getting laid, which you're obviously *not* or else you wouldn't be so obsessed with Hermyn's wedding. A performance artist who hasn't said a fucking word to you or to anyone for the past three years, and you hate her because she's found a little bit of happiness with a dentist you've never even met? Is your life so pathetic and petty and small that a woman you've never spoken to marrying a man you've never met is enough to rock the core of your existence? You stupid bitch, look at it out there! You have no idea how lucky you are just to be safe!"

Shell Clarion stared at me, her pink lips forming a tiny *o,* the color draining slowly from her face. I'd never spoken to her like that, mainly because I felt sorry for her. I knew she couldn't do anything about her awful sense of humor or the uncontrollable urge she had to talk behind people's backs in front of their faces. I also knew she had no friends. I'd held my tongue with Shell because she sometimes reminded me of one of my preschoolers—she was that helpless in the world.

I looked down at her legs, dangling like a child's over the edge of the stool, her feet at least two inches shy of the floor, even in those heels. I wanted to say *I'm sorry Shell*, but I couldn't make myself do it.

She narrowed her eyes at me, swallowed so hard I

could see her throat moving under her turtleneck. "I *am* getting laid," she said.

After Shell stormed out the door for a cigarette break, Hermyn said, "Well, *I* wouldn't fuck her," and I started giggling, somewhat hysterically. Hermyn began laughing too, and minutes later when En showed up, lay down on his back and thrust his ass into high-noon position, his sneakers kissing the floor behind his head, it was nearly all we could take.

"Grow up. It's yoga," he said, which only made us laugh more, until tears streamed down our cheeks and our intermittent screams pierced the air and it felt as if we'd never be able to stop.

One hour later, Hermyn was on the phone with her mother, and she was the only one talking.

I was remembering how Tredwell had closed his eyes as he described the feel of candle wax on his bare skin. How he'd seemed, for a moment, to savor the memory.

The candles represent hellfire. Hell burns with the fire of lust. That's what Peter would say. The fire of lust. Satan's sustenance. Only he'd say it backwards. Natas. In Satanism, you say names backwards. He'd call me Llewdert when we fucked . . .

Red candles?

Red for blood. Virgin blood. Like the robes. We were naked under the robes, did I tell you?

Did you and Peter ever sacrifice anything?

"No," Hermyn said into the phone. "No, no thank you, no no, nope, no, ma'am, no way, abso-tootin'-lutely not." Her voice was calm, but the denials became more and more emphatic until finally, she erupted. "I said no, Mother! I'm the one who's getting married and I do not want to do the hora. Mother . . . I . . . I don't care what Aunt Gussie thinks . . . I refuse to be lifted over people's heads in a chair . . . I just refuse, I don't have to give a reas— Okay, okay. It's degrading and traditionalist and . . . and . . . scary. I'm afraid I'll fall."

I glanced at Shell, who hadn't said a word to me or to anyone since returning from her break. You'd think she was drowningly absorbed in the month-old *National Enquirer* that she'd plucked out of Argent's cubbyhole, only she hadn't turned the page once. I tried smiling at her, just for the hell of it. She diverted her eyes long enough to glower at me, then pointedly raised the tabloid so that her entire face was hidden behind the cover, which read "Whitney Goes Wild!"

En was sitting at the computer at the far end of the ticketing room, ostensibly checking seat reservations on the Space's Web site but actually responding to posts on a site called www.ScreenwriteRomance.com. Earlier, I'd sneaked up behind him and peered over his shoulder. "When I'm not playing semipro football, I'm penning a brutal Faulkner adapt," he'd typed, before sensing my presence and throwing both hands in front of the screen.

En didn't look like any football player I'd ever seen. He was five-six, 120 pounds soaking wet and probably didn't need to shave more than once a week. At age thirty-two, he still couldn't buy a pack of cigarettes without getting carded. Did he ever meet these women in person?

"Hey," I said. "You'd better get off that site before Roland gets back from his meeting. He is not in a pretty mood today."

"And whose fault is that, Two Hours Late?" Shell said.

I sighed heavily. "Look, Shell. I'm sorry I said you weren't getting laid."

"I'm not speaking to you. And like I said, I am."

"Anybody I know?" said En.

"Shut up!"

"Good-bye, Mother. I've had enough of this . . . I'm not talk—I—All right . . . all right . . . ALL RIGHT! I'LL DO THE HORA!" Hermyn slammed the receiver back on its cradle and let her head drop into her hands.

I patted her on the back. "My mother's a pain in the ass, too."

"Why'd I have to start talking again?"

I thought about my conversations with Peter, Yale, Krull, Shell. "I might take a vow of silence. But only with certain people."

"You guys should check your mail," En said as he got up from the computer. "I actually had two ticket or- ders."

I sat down in En's still-warm chair and logged on. The only person who ever e-mailed me at thespace.com was Sydney, who regularly sent me excerpts from her own books that she thought "spoke directly" to whatever she perceived to be going on in my mind. I'd repeatedly explained to her that 1) I already owned all of her books and 2) My e-mail address was for ticket-related issues only (not entirely true, but whatever). Neither point deterred her. I received motherly, self-help-guru e-mail at least twice a week. And, after the previous night's phone conversation, I knew I was in for a lengthy document. "At least your mother just wants you to do a folk dance at your wedding," I said to Hermyn. "Mine thinks I'm a drug addict."

"Why?"

"Because I like to take walks by the river."

"That doesn't make any sense."

"Welcome to the Wonderful World of Sydney." I saw two new letters in my mailbox, and sure enough, the first was from my mom. I recognized the subject line as a chapter title from *Your Spiritual Lifeboat*: "Healthy Habits Are the Oars." I didn't bother opening it.

The second one bore an unfamiliar return address: ER425160 at one of the major Internet providers, and the subject line was blank. When I opened it up, I saw just one word on the screen: *Your*. It was probably a mistake—some disgruntled *Addie* patron, angry at me over the theater's "no refund" policy, someone who had started to write *Your rules are unfair*, or *Your poli-*

cies leave much to be desired or *Your job is history* and had hit the send button too early. All of us got angry e-mails, especially since *Addie* had opened.

There were, however, two unusual things about this note. The first was that I hadn't had a run-in with a customer in over a week and a half—and that person, a Southern woman who had actually accused Roland and me of pocketing her money to finance "that disgusting May-December thing y'all have going on," had already sent us a nasty letter, by regular mail, from West Virginia. The second was that the word *your* was centered on the screen.

"Happy days, kids!" said Roland. He was smiling, a rare sight, particularly lately.

Shell said, "Did you fire St. Germaine?"

"No, my dear. He's gone home. We're canceling *Addie*. And you've all got a week off, paid."

I sensed movement in the courtyard, and when I looked out the window I saw several cast members leaving the theater in their street clothes.

"Yes!" said En. Hermyn let out a huge whoop. Shell said, "You're shitting me."

"I'm going to miss you guys." After I said it, I realized I wasn't being sarcastic.

"How about helping me close up?" said Roland.

"Sure." I wondered why Yale had left so quickly. Probably to avoid me, but at least it wasn't to meet Peter. *He says no one's worth the company I keep.*

"Miranda! Miranda!" Shell said into the ticket window microphone. She'd been peering out the window over my shoulder, and her voice was like broken glass in my ears. "Miraaaanda!"

Miranda, an actress who naturally possessed the blond, patrician looks Shell strove for, played Dewey Dell in *Addie* and had made the mistake of introducing herself to the box office staff at the start of the show's run.

Having seen *All About Eve* several times too many, Shell thought that the quickest route to stealing the part for herself was to glom onto Miranda like some sort of deranged fan, shrieking her name whenever she passed the box office, which had been happening less and less. I watched the young actress, her shiny, butterscotch hair backlit by a streetlight, shielding her face with a black glove as she pretended to search for something near the heel of her boot.

"Why don't you give it a rest?" I said. "The show is over, so you're not going to get the part."

Shell was already out the door.

"I can't believe she wanted to play *that* part in *that* show at *this* theater," En said as he buttoned up his coat. "Imagine aiming that low and still not getting what you're after."

I emptied the thin envelopes, made a small pile of unclaimed will-call tickets, and placed them in the drawer. "Do you want me to enter these into the computer?" I asked Roland.

"Nah, I'll do it later. Just make a sign for the door, if

you would, and I'll see ya next week." He paused for a moment. "Don't be late."

"I'm sorry, Roland. It won't happen again."

"I know it won't. It wasn't like you."

"Nothing is like me lately."

"Sammy!" Shell seemed to have decided to speak to me again.

"Just a second. I'm making a sign."

"Guess what Miranda's doing now that *Addie*'s closed! She's up for a big part on *Live and Let Live*! Opposite Nate Gundersen! Didn't you used to date him?"

I capped the pen and rubbed my temples. The headache was back, with newfound superpowers. I turned towards the doorway where Shell held Miranda captive. "Yeah, I used to . . ."

Miranda wore pupilless, mirrored contacts.

"Shit."

"Is he nice?" Miranda said. "I'm totally nervous about this audition. It's my first major TV part, you know? Especially opposite a big star like him. I've done under-fives, but that's it."

"Where did you get those lenses?"

"Aren't they fabulous?" Shell said. "Everybody's getting them. They're called Magic Mirrors."

"*Everybody's* getting them?"

"Well, they're totally going to be hot in about a week," Miranda said. "The makeup artist on *Addie*? She's got 'em too, and so does my friend William who works at *Allure*. I even saw this clerk at that toy and hobby store on 28th who was wearing them. Scared my poor niece half to death. 'He's probably a club kid, honey,' I told her. As if a five-year-old would know what a club kid is. Anyway, I'm sure a month from now they'll be so over it'll be embarrassing."

I had a sudden urge to take my throbbing head and bang it against the wall.

After Shell and Miranda left, Hermyn tapped me on the shoulder. "Are you okay? You look pale."

"I'm fine. I just realized I may have been wrong about something."

"You want to talk about it? I've got a date with Sal, but not 'til later."

I forced a smile. "Get out of here. Go have fun."

"Call me if you change your mind." she said, disappearing out the door and into the night. It was only a little after six, but already dark outside. I'd always hated that about East Coast winters. Like someone shutting the lights off in a windowless room and lying to you that the day is over. That didn't happen in L.A. Or maybe it did, but I hadn't noticed.

I glanced at Roland, busy at the computer, then looked down at the note I'd just written: NO TEARS FOR ADDIE *HAS BEEN CANCELLED. NO REFUNDS OR EXCHANGES.*

I uncapped the red pen and added the word *SORRY.* It made me feel a little better.

8

Another Round

When I got back to my apartment, I saw that the red message light on my answering machine wasn't blinking. Big surprise. I hadn't had a date in six months, my mother preferred e-mail and my best friend hated me. Who did I think was going to call?

I headed for the couch, but a furious, floor-rattling banging made me freeze. *Jesus Christ, Elmira.*

I wondered what she was using down there. It felt like a mop with a brick attached. She was probably ruining her ceiling. "All right! All right!" I collapsed to the floor, slipping off my boots and then my socks.

I lay flat on my back and listened to the banging subside. The wooden floor felt grainy where it connected with the back of my head, the palms of my hands and my bare heels, but I didn't want to move. I tended to lie on the floor whenever I got depressed. I figured it had to stem from a need for punishment, especially given how dusty my floor was. I rolled my head to the side, looked at the billowy gray poufs under my couch and felt tremendously sorry for myself. *Is this what it's going to be? Just me and my dust bunnies for all eternity?*

I closed my eyes, thought about Peter Steele, whose contact lenses were obviously not one of a kind. I could hear Yale's voice in my head saying, *What the fuck is wrong with you?* I was beginning to wonder the same thing myself.

What's the worst thing Peter ever did to you?

That's hard to say . . . There were so many things.

Did he cut you?

Yeah . . . And then he'd taste my blood. Like Dracula, man. He's way into blood.

Did he bite you?

Sometimes.

Did he brand you?

Brand me?

Where did he get that tattoo?

What tattoo?

The one on the back of his neck. The pentagram.

I gave him that. He made me.

Whether or not he called it Satan worship, all Tredwell had told me about was sex—theatrical sex that was maybe distasteful, but not criminal. The only one to mention sacrifice had been me . . .

*You get chills up your spine, you see a couple dump-
ing trash and your mind just spins out of control.*

"My fault." I opened my eyes and went for the
phone. "My fucking fault."

I tried Yale's cell phone first, but it was turned off so
I called him at home.

Yale's machine picked up. His best stage voice, with
Patti LuPone belting "Don't Cry for Me Argentina" in
the background. *Hello, you've reached Yale St. Germaine. Don't keep your distance—please leave a message.* I'd heard it hundreds of times; now it made me
feel nostalgic.

"I'm sorry. I'm sorry. I'm sorry," I said. "I jumped
to conclusions. If jumping to conclusions were an
Olympic event, I'd win a gold medal and set a distance
record." I took a deep breath, then added, "If you forgive me, I'll buy you a drink. Three drinks . . ."

About thirty seconds after I hung up, the phone
rang. I picked it up fast. "Do you forgive me?"

"I was just about to ask you the same thing." It
wasn't Yale's voice. It was huskier, with a faint Jersey
accent that was vaguely familiar.

"Who is this?"

"It's John . . . Detective Krull."

I wasn't sure why I agreed to meet Krull. It was
probably more curiosity than anything else—he'd
been so insistent about getting together and I had no
idea why. But there was also the way his words so

closely mirrored the message I'd left for Yale. "I feel like I jumped to conclusions in the interview room, and I'm sorry . . ." I took it as some kind of sign.

He'd said he supposed I didn't want to go back to the precinct house, and I'd told him, "You got that right," and he'd said, "Can you meet me for drinks, then? Please?" *Please* was the clincher.

So here I was, doing something I never would've imagined myself doing an hour earlier: having a scotch on the rocks in a cop bar with Detective John Krull.

We were sitting across from each other at a small table in a fake English pub called the Blind Lion that was about a block west of the precinct house. Krull had changed out of his coat and tie and into natural fibers—a black pullover sweater and beat-up jeans. He looked much more comfortable physically—his neck, I noticed, was better made for loose sweaters than dress shirts and ties. Nonetheless, he seemed oddly nervous, and his eyes cut into mine with an intensity that seemed inappropriate given the conversation. "So what do you think of our New York winters?" he asked me for the third time.

"I still don't mind them." I took a sip of my scotch. It felt surprisingly warm and comforting as it blazed down my throat, erasing the last remnants of headache. I was tempted to drain the entire glass right there, in front of this antsy, muscular cop with his untouched bottle of light beer. I hoped I wasn't becoming an alcoholic.

"Those kids in your class are great. You must like kids."

"Yeah, I do. They're funny, and they're honest too, which is refreshing considering my other job, which is with a bunch of wannabe actors who, ummm . . . tend to exaggerate sometimes."

"I spoke to your boss at the theater. He seemed like a nice guy."

"Roland's not an actor. He's seventy-three, and he used to have a real job in advertising or something and he actually likes selling tickets."

"I hope you don't mind my asking him for your number."

"No, I don't, except *why* did you want my number?" I took another sip.

"I don't know," he said. "I like you?"

I wasn't buying that at all. "Did my screaming in your face do it," I asked, "or was it the charming way I exploded at you this afternoon?"

"Maybe I'm a masochist."

"Which isn't a crime between consenting adults."

Krull smiled, but only briefly, and only with his mouth. His eyes remained fixed on me in that deeply unsettling way. "I just wanted to talk," he said finally. "I was thinking about our conversation today. I was wrong to act like I did."

"No, you weren't," I said. "Sometimes I see things and I overdramatize them. I guess I expect life to be a lot more frightening than it actually is . . ." My voice trailed off. His black eyes clouded in the dim light, and I knew something had crossed his mind that I couldn't begin to understand. It made me nervous, like I had inadvertently said something offensive but didn't know how to apologize.

Two uniforms passed our table. One said, "Hi, Detective," and Krull nodded without removing his eyes from mine.

"What's wrong?" I said. "Have I done something illegal?"

Finally, he took a swallow of his beer. "Do you remember what the ice chest looked like?"

"The ice chest."

"Yeah. I'm wondering if you could sort of . . . think about it and try to remember what size it was, what color, anything . . . distinguishing you might have seen on it."

"You don't have to humor me, Detective Krull."

"It's John, and I'm not humoring you."

I closed my eyes, if only to avoid his stare. "It was small."

"How small? Show me with your hands."

I drew both hands out and down in approximation of the shape, until I'd made a more or less accurate, invisible rectangle on the table.

"Okay. The color?"

"It was blue."

"Dark blue or light?"

"Like a pale, metallic blue, maybe with white trim. But I'm not positive about that. About the trim."

"How many handles?"

"There was one on either side. He was holding one, and she had the other."

"What brand was it?"

"I don't know Det . . . John. I really only looked at it for a few seconds. I was sort of distracted by the man."

"Of course."

I opened my eyes to find him still looking through me. "What's this about?"

He took one of my hands in both of his. A gesture for widows, I thought, and my pulse sped up. With my free hand, I raised my glass of scotch and downed the rest of it before repeating the question.

"An ice chest was found near the piers a couple of hours after you left the station. It's going to be in the papers tomorrow, so I wanted to tell you first . . . It fits your description—you won't see that in the press. We don't like to give too many details. It makes it easier to weed out the fake information that comes in."

"I . . . I take it there wasn't medical waste in it."

He took my other hand, and I didn't want to hear the answer. I wanted to run out of the bar and into the street, or, better yet, to wake up. "Samantha," he said. "There was a child inside."

I started to say something, but no sound came out. *A child. A small child, because the ice chest was small . . . Large enough to hold a severed body part, or a collection of them. An arm, I imagined, a pair of hands. Even a head. But an adult's head. Not a child, not a child bent and shoved into that small, rigid box.*

"I'm not an expert," Krull said. "But it looked to me like there were some markings of a ritual murder."

The woman in her red dress. Red signifies blood. Virgin blood. The woman's shaking arms. She's crying. But why? Her child? Her baby? "What . . . kind of markings?"

"I'd rather not tell you right now. It wouldn't be great for the investigation, and also I don't think you want to hear about it. Can I get you another scotch?"

"I do want to hear about it. I'm the one who told you about these people in the first place. And besides, what makes you think you know what I do and don't want to hear about?"

"Because you like kids, and I can tell you're sensitive, and you're only going to get upset."

"John. I. Am. Upset."

He called the waitress over, ordered another round, though his beer was still close to full. When she left, he looked at me and said, "There was something done to the child's eyes."

Through Art Boyle's press contact, Krull had managed to secure a printout of the article that was to run in the *Post* the following day. After I finished my second scotch and had calmed down enough to put a sentence together, he pulled it out of his briefcase and showed it to me. The tentative headline was "Child's Watery Grave."

At four o'clock in the afternoon, two construction workers had found the strangled body of a three-year-old girl in a "small, picnic-sized" ice chest that had been wedged under one of the piers north of the Village by the stiff current. One of the workers, who spoke under the condition of anonymity, said, "When we opened it, my buddy cried."

According to the *Post*, the girl's identity had yet to be determined. "Because of the sensitivity of this matter, we are not releasing any further information," Detective Arthur Boyle told the newspaper. "However, anyone with any knowledge of the crime is encouraged to contact the Sixth Precinct detective squad. There will be a $10,000 reward for information leading to a conviction."

The phrase *ritual murder* was not mentioned in the article but *serial killer* was. The *Post*—not Boyle—had hinted that the way the girl had been killed was similar to another unsolved child murder—that of a six-year-old boy whose body had been found in a Tenth Street Dumpster two years earlier. When the reporter had asked Boyle about it, he'd refused comment. I looked up from the article, pointed to the section. Krull slowly nodded.

"The boy's eyes?" I asked.

"Yeah. And other similarities as well."

I lifted my empty glass slowly, like I was under deep, black water. "I want another drink."

"I think we should get some food too. Have you eaten?"

"I'm not hungry."

"I know, but you're too small to hold all that scotch without a buffer. How about some nachos?"

"You think it's Peter?"

"We're looking into all possibilities." He called the waitress over again, ordered nachos, fries and wings.

I asked for another round and watched her leave before I said, "The contacts aren't one of a kind."

He nodded. "We've already collected more than a hundred Magic Mirrors receipts from optical stores. But I figured we would. Nothing's one of a kind in New York . . . except maybe you."

I raised my eyebrows at Krull. He smiled, this time with his eyes too. "Well, you scream like nobody else . . . No, I take that back. There was an actress I saw in a Roger Corman movie once . . ."

"Very funny." I tried to smile, but couldn't. *Children's eyes, widening in horror . . . Eyes . . . Mirrored Eyes . . . X-ed-out eyes.* "The valentine from my mother . . ."

"Yeah, I'll need that. The book too."

I reached into my bag, handed him the card just as the waitress set down our drinks and food. I gave him the *Book of Practical Cats*, wondering how I was going to distract the kids into not asking for it at story time tomorrow.

I didn't want to think about Peter. I didn't want to think that I could've sat down next to a child murderer and eaten lunch, didn't want to think Yale could've slept with one. I picked up my drink, emptied half of it down my throat. "Hey, try to eat something," Krull said. "Your blood/scotch ratio is starting to disturb me."

"I'm not an alcoholic." I leaned forward and tried to focus on his face, but Krull's eyes blurred into one and back again, as if to illustrate his point. Reluctantly, I picked up a wing. "You have beautiful eyelashes." I couldn't believe I had just said that.

"Alcoholics can handle their booze better than you," he said. "Now, take a bite."

I did. It wasn't bad.

"Good. How about one more?"

"You know what my grandmother used to do when I wouldn't eat my vegetables? 'One bite for your grandpa up in heaven,' she'd say. 'One more bite for your great uncle Charlie who was cursed with the cancer. One for your poor cousin Lucille who got run over by a bus.' For a long time, I couldn't look at vegetables without thinking of dead relatives."

"I promise I won't make you eat vegetables."

I dug into the nachos. "I appreciate that, Detective."

"John."

"Right . . . How come you care so much about whether or not I eat something?"

"Because I'd rather not get puked on."

"And . . . because you like me." I couldn't believe I had just said that either. This last round had been a bad idea, I decided, but still I felt myself leaning closer to him, attempting to look seductively into his eyes. My gaze settled on his nose instead. "You said you did, and I think I believe you now. Don't you like me, John?" I licked my lips. "You're not married, are you?"

Krull squinted at me as if I were a foreign language he was trying, unsuccessfully, to decipher.

Why was I doing this? Why did I want this cop to come home with me so badly that I was willing to make a complete ass out of myself? It wasn't his broad shoulders. It wasn't his kind smile or his powerful neck or his big hands or the sense that there might be an actual soul somewhere in that hard detective's body. It wasn't even the scotch. It was, I realized, fear. It was the fear of remembering everything Krull had told me and everything I'd read in the article, sober and alone in my dark apartment, where I knew the silence would hum in my ears, where I knew my mind would create images of dead children with X's branded into their eyes. "I'm sorry," I said. "I've obviously had too much to drink."

Krull slowly raised his beer to his lips and took a swallow. "I'm not married," he said with a slight smile, and I felt my cheeks color. "Look. I know you drank too much because you're scared and I don't blame you. All I can tell you is we're going to get this asshole. The ice chest and the body are with the Crime Scene Unit. You wouldn't believe the kind of evidence murderers leave on their victims, and CSU can do so much with one hair, one tiny piece of fiber. Plus, there's Art and me. Amanda too. When she heard about this, it was all we could do to get her to stay in the hospital."

I finished the rest of my scotch. "That makes me feel better," I said, rather unconvincingly. "And thanks for being so understanding."

Krull said, "By the way, I really do like you." Before I could reply, his cell phone rang. "Yeah?" he said. "Interesting. Wonder why he did that. Okay. Okay. Bye."

"That was Art," Krull said. "He was supposed to question Peter Steele tonight at ten o'clock at the restaurant where he works. Steele stood him up."

9

Ariel's Grave

Detective John Krull was lying next to me on my pull-out bed. We were both naked and I could feel the warmth coming off his body, but I wasn't sure how we'd gotten there or where our clothes had gone. Must be the scotch, I thought, must be the scotch . . . .

Krull was stroking my chin with the back of his index finger. His black eyes glowed, as if they held lit matches.

"You want them?" he asked, his lips curling into a grin. His finger traced the outline of my mouth. "You want them?"

Want what?

"You want them?" Like a caress. But what did he mean? I couldn't answer. Not until I knew. His face began to change. "You want them?" His voice now sounded different—flat, inflectionless.

"You want them." I realized it had been him all along as I looked into Peter Steele's mirrored irises. "YOU WANT THEM!" shouted the bloated mouth. The hand went to my neck, tightened around it as the other shot in front of my face, a clenched fist opening. "WANT THEM!" Opening to reveal two bloody eyeballs.

"NO!" I screamed, wrenching my eyes open, waking up on my pullout couch, heart pounding, pouring sweat, naked and disoriented but alone. All alone. "Holy fucking shit."

I patted around in the dark next to the bed and found an empty trash can on the floor, next to a full glass of water, which I gulped down greedily. Nobody had put a trash can next to my bed since college. "What the hell?" I said, but then I remembered Krull's voice. *I'm putting this here just in case.*

I rubbed my eyes. Slowly, they began to adjust to the darkness. I spotted the digital clock on my VCR. Five o'clock a.m. What had happened to me? An unpleasant stiffness settled into my muscles, intensifying as the rest of the evening replayed itself, like scenes from a movie on which I deeply regretted spending money.

Me, reaching across the table, grabbing Krull's bottle of beer and draining it.

Krull taking out his wallet, saying, "My treat." Saying, "We should get you home."

"*How about you get me into bed?*"

"*Hey, are you okay? Let me help you up.*"

My face smashed into Krull's chest in the cold night air. "*I think I drank too much.*"

"*I know you drank too much.*"

"*Can you please walk me into my apartment and make sure there aren't any murderers in there?*"

"*Sure.*"

Krull turning on the lights in my apartment, pulling out the bed.

Me, toppling forward, the pillow slamming into my face.

"*Samantha? You should at least take off your sweater and shoes.*"

"*I can't move.*"

"*Can you breathe?*"

"*I don't think so.*"

My shoes coming off, then my sweater. "*Try and roll over. That's good. Can you get under the covers?*"

"*Get under the covers with me.*"

"*I don't think that's a good idea.*" *Footsteps, retreating into the kitchen, water running.*

Me under the covers, pulling off my jeans, my shirt, my bra, my panties.

Krull's footsteps returning from the kitchen. "*I'm putting this here just in case. And water, which you'll want later.*"

"*I'm totally naked under here.*"

"*I'll talk to you tomorrow.*"

"I'm not wearing panties anymore."

"Good night, Samantha."

The soft click of the light switch. The thump of the door closing.

I moved my hands up and down the cool sheets, felt my balled-up jeans next to my hip, my shirt draped over the upper edge of the bed. I sensed cloth wrapped around my left ankle and identified it as my underwear. *Oh no, no, no . . .*

At least I wasn't afraid. I was too embarrassed to be afraid. I should've enjoyed the feeling.

The girl in the ice chest was wearing purple jeans and a *Little Mermaid* T-shirt. A sad bit of irony for a three-year-old whose final destination was under water. Until they had an official identity for her, the *Post* would refer to her by the mermaid's name, Ariel. None of this information was in Boyle's advance copy of the article, but it was in the version I saw on page three of the newspaper, which I bought the following morning at the Happy Face Deli. The headline had been changed to "Watery Grave for 'Little Mermaid.'"

Purple jeans. One day, about a month earlier, Serena had shown up at school dressed entirely in the color— bright purple tights and turtleneck, lavender jumper, deep grape sweater, three or four violet ribbons tied haphazardly in her short, curly hair. "My mommy let me pick my clothes today," she'd announced, at which

Nancy had started to cry. "That's not fair. I wanna be purple."

Purple was a color made for little girls, and I was sure Ariel had loved it too. Loved it right up until she could no longer see it. I folded up the paper, stuffed it into my bag, pulled my coat closer around me.

It was only a few minutes after 6:00 a.m. and barely light outside. The sidewalk was empty, and what few cars were on the road buzzed by with a luxurious speed. I knew I was very early for work, but I'd already been up an hour and I couldn't stay in my apartment anymore. Making my bed and folding it back up had been close to torturous when I remembered, again and again, what I had said and done in it the night before. *I'm not wearing panties anymore. Jesus.*

During the moments when I was able to put my own humiliation out of my mind, other thoughts replaced it. Thoughts of devil worship, ritual murder, dead children with damaged eyes. Peter Steele.

In the shower, all I could think of was the pale blue ice chest, sinking into cold, dirty water.

So I'd dressed and left early. If I was lucky, maybe I could find an all-night bookstore and replace the *Book of Practical Cats*. Otherwise, I'd just get breakfast at a diner. There was a good one called Brugerman's a block and a half away from Sunny Side. Big menu. Excellent ham and eggs. I'd been there a bunch of times with Yale because it wasn't far from his apartment. Maybe, after breakfast, I'd stop by.

The more I walked, the less the all-night bookstore appealed and the more my empty stomach took precedence. Thanks to four glasses of water and a couple Advil, my hangover wasn't as debilitating as the one from the previous day. But a big, fatty breakfast—eaten nowhere near Ruby Redd's Brewing Company—was becoming increasingly necessary.

I finally got to Brugerman's, sat at the counter, ordered coffee, ham steak, fried eggs over easy and buttered rye toast. I took the *Post* out of my bag, but I avoided page three and went straight for Liz Smith. Liz never said anything frightening.

My breakfast arrived, quick and hot and better than anything I'd ever eaten in my life. Liz was waxing on about some gorgeous Spanish pop star, the waitress said, "Can I get you anything else, honey?" and for a few minutes, it seemed like everything was going to be all right.

Then I heard a man's voice behind me, so close it made my shoulders shoot up.

"Where the hell have you been?" It was Yale, and he looked awful.

"What do you mean?"

"I tried calling you all night. Your phone was off the hook. Then I go to your apartment and buzz you, and no one answers."

I stared at Yale's face. His skin was dead white, his eyes puffy and red rimmed. Tufts of his blond hair stuck out at eccentric angles, dotted with odd, white flecks. "I was at a bar," I said. "What happened to you?"

"I've been out all night," he said. "Feel free to say I told you so."

"What do you mean?"

Yale sighed. "I had a date with Peter last night."

"But you said I scared him off."

"Yeah, well, what was I supposed to tell you?"

"Oh, Christ, Yale—"

"Peter and I were supposed to meet at Temple Bar at ten o'clock. So I go there, and I wait for two fucking hours and he never shows up. Don't waste your breath because everything you're going to say to me I've already said to myself about five hundred thousand times."

"At ten o'clock last night—"

"I figure, whatever, he's a huge flake. So I go back to my apartment, and it seems the lock has been picked."

"No."

"Yes. And after I walk in, I discover that every breakable thing I own has been smashed to bits—my dishware, my glass-topped coffee table, my Tiffany-style lamps, my comedy/tragedy masks. That asinine porcelain dog I won on *Wheel of Fortune* during my trip to Hollywood five years ago. Oh, no, he did not discriminate at all."

"You think it was Peter?"

"Who else would it be? He knows where I live, and

he knew I wouldn't be there. And besides, he left his stupid checkered waiter's bow tie on the kitchen floor. It must've fallen off while he was decimating my china."

"Did you call the police?"

"I was too humiliated."

"You should've—"

"I went to your place and you weren't there and I wanted to be with *people*, that's all, and I certainly didn't feel like going to another bar . . . So I saw the second half of *Rocky Horror*."

"That's still playing?"

"At certain theaters, yes. *Rocky Horror*, Sam. I hated that movie in high school, and it's just . . . gotten . . . worse."

I reached over, plucked a white fleck out of his hair. "Rice."

"I've got rice in my hair from *Rocky Horror*. God help me, I've hit rock bottom."

"Yale—"

"After the movie was over, I . . . I needed to talk to someone. And . . . I wanted to feel safe, so I went to David's."

"David?"

"Rum Tum Tugger."

"Oh, no."

"And he's got a new boyfriend."

"Oh no."

"Who lives with him. I show up at his apartment at

three in the fucking morning with *rice in my hair*, and his personal trainer boyfriend answers the door in a jock strap. Life does not get worse than that. I've been wandering from diner to diner ever since."

"Yale. It's my fault."

"No, it isn't. You were a little rude to him at the restaurant. Big deal. That's no reason to trash all of my—"

"I think he trashed your stuff because I called the police on him. I think he saw me going into the station to report him. It's practically across the street from Ruby Redd's Brewing Company, and this incredibly loud soap opera actress called attention to me."

"You called the police on him?"

I turned to page three of the *Post*, showed him the article.

"That's horrible, but of course it's a coincidence, Sam. You don't honestly think Peter would—"

"It's not, and I do. Honestly." I told him the whole story, from my conversation with Tredwell to my visit to the Sixth Precinct to the discovery of the ice chest, and how Krull had said my description had matched the one found by the construction workers. I told him about Peter's proclivity for devil worship and sadomasochism and the ritualistic nature of the girl's death. How something had been done to her eyes—just like something had been done to Sydney's eyes in the valentine photo. I told him how Peter had skipped out on Detective Boyle, who was also scheduled to meet him at ten o'clock the previous evening.

Yale just stared at me, his skin growing even paler. When I was finished, he asked if he could have a sip of my water, and when he took the glass, I noticed his hand was trembling. He drank all of it before he was able to speak. "I had sex with a murderer."

I put my arm around his shoulders. "You didn't know."

"A . . . a sick fuck who k-kills little kids."

"You didn't know, Yale. You had no idea."

"But that doesn't change the *fact*."

He put his head down on the counter, and I patted his back. I wished I could change the fact. I wished I could change everything, or at least make it go away for a while. "You want to know what I did last night? I asked Krull to walk me home, and when he was getting me a glass of water, I took off all my clothes and begged him to get into bed with me."

"No, you didn't," Yale said into his hands.

"Oh, yes I did."

When he looked up at me, I saw that his eyes were moist. "You stripped in front of an NYPD detective? The same one you screamed at?"

"Yep, and you know what else? He turned me down."

"We're quite a pair, aren't we?"

"You want some of my ham and eggs?"

He cleared his throat. "Sure. Screw nutrition."

I asked the waitress for another fork and knife, and we both ate off my plate in silence.

After we were done with breakfast, Yale asked if he could wash up at Sunny Side because he still didn't feel like facing his apartment. I said, "Why don't you just sit in on my class and we can spend the day together?" He took me up on the offer, though neither of us said much on the walk there.

As I opened the main door to the school, I turned to him. "Hey," I said. "Can I ask you a personal question?"

"Of course."

"When you and Peter were . . . together, did he, I mean . . . Did any of those things that Tredwell said sound familiar?"

"No," he replied. "If anything, I thought he was a little too vanilla for me."

"That's odd."

"Isn't it? Maybe I'm not what's he's looking for in a slave. Maybe I'm too . . . threatening."

"You are pretty butch."

"You think?"

"Definitely."

Yale beamed at me, but just for a moment. His expression darkened again, and I could almost see the thoughts entering his head. "I want to kill him."

"Me too," I said. "No more of that talk, though. You're entering a nursery school."

We walked through the courtyard. Anthony, who was sweeping up outside Veronica's classroom, waved to us. "You Sam's boyfriend?" he called out. "You are one lucky guy."

Is anyone more clueless than Anthony?

Before Yale or I could respond, Veronica poked her head out of her door. No matter what hour of the morning I showed up, she was always there first. I figured her parents wanted her out of the house as early as possible, and who could blame them? "That's not her boyfriend," she said, peering at Yale through her thick glasses. "Obviously."

Yale put his arm around my waist with such confidence it startled me. "How do you know Sam hasn't *changed* me?" He winked at her, and she slammed the door.

"Well, there's something that's going to keep her up for the next couple of nights," I said.

"Good. I won't be the only one who's too disturbed to sleep."

I opened the door to my classroom, unlocked my desk drawer and tossed Yale the boys' room key. "Go wash up," I told him. "I don't want you scaring my kids."

Just as I was unlocking the closet, I heard light footsteps coming into the room. I turned and saw Daniel Klein wearing a red-and-white striped Oxford shirt, navy sweater and overcoat, chinos, red duck shoes and his usual serious expression. He looked like a miniature president on retreat at Camp David and I thought, *Maybe I'm seeing into the future.* "Hey, Dan! How's your fish?"

"His butt's where his tummy should be and little brown strings come out of it. That's his poo."

Correct, Mr. President. "You want to help me set up for today?"

"Okay."

I took several pads of white drawing paper out of the closet, as well as a bag of Magic Markers and three large boxes of crayons, which I handed to Daniel. "You can put these on the table, Dan. Put one box at either end, and one in the middle. Okay?"

"What are we making?"

I had no idea. Usually, I thought about what I'd do with the kids while I was taking care of busywork at the Space or when I was getting ready for bed or at least during the walk to school, but lately, my class had been the last thing on my mind. I felt extremely guilty. "Ummm. I thought we'd . . . draw our favorite animals today and try and spell their names. You can draw your fish."

"His name is Squad Watery," Daniel said.

"That's right. How could I forget?" *Squad Watery . . . contact the Sixth Precinct detective squad . . . Watery Grave . . .* "You can draw him if you like, and my friend Yale will be here to help out."

"Is he the man Daddy and I saw out there?"

"You've met Yale before, sweetie."

"The man outside with the sunglasses?"

"Ummm . . . What?"

The door opened, Yale entered, his face scrubbed, his hair damp and combed, flanked by Nancy, Serena and Kendrick. "Class is here, Teacher!" he announced, tossing me the bathroom key.

"See, Dan? Yale. Remember?"

"He's not the same man."

"Crayons!" yelled Serena, as several more of my kids arrived. "I wanna draw my name in gold with stars around it!"

"I'll help you," said Yale. "Serena is a lovely name."

"What about Nancy? Nancy!"

"Beautiful as well. Do you know what letter it begins with?"

"N!"

"Fabulous."

"I'm gonna draw my butt!"

"Not acceptable, Kendrick."

The school day went fast, with Yale doing most of the talking. The kids drew their favorite animals—mostly cats, of course, plus several renderings of Buster the Safety Dog, a shark, three Lion Kings, Squad Watery and Kendrick's butt (which I managed to turn into an unusually fat bird for his mother's sake). When the kids begged me to read from the *Book of Practical Cats*, Yale saved the day by treating them to a booming, acapella rendition of "Memory," for which he received a standing ovation and several hugs.

Before too long, their parents started to show up, complimenting pictures, helping with coats and mittens, taking their small hands and escorting them out the door. It was amazing how quickly the sound level dropped, even with just a few of them gone.

Daniel's mom had yet to arrive. I spotted the boy across the room, folding up his picture and putting it into his little briefcase. "Hey, Dan," I said as I approached. "Did you and your dad really see a man outside, wearing sunglasses?"

"Yeah."

"That's kind of funny, since it's so cloudy out, huh?"

"That's what Daddy said."

"What else did the man look like?"

"Ummm. I don't remember."

"Did he have very, very short hair, about the same color as mine?"

"Yeah."

"How tall was he?"

"Like Yale."

"Okay. Did he have a tan?"

Daniel touched his face. "Yeah, sort of."

"What was his mouth like?"

"Big."

"Did he say anything to you?"

"Ummmm . . . He said, 'Hi, Daniel.'"

"He called you by your name?"

"Yeah. He said, 'Hi, Daniel. You want to play with me later?' "

"Daniel, I don't want you ever playing with that man. Or with anyone you don't know. Do you understand me?"

"I told him, 'No!' I yelled it at him, like Buster said to do."

"Good for you."

"And then he . . . he reached out and he . . . squeezed my nose. Really hard. It hurt."

"Oh, no. Oh, Daniel. What did your daddy do?"

"My daddy hit him in the head with a sword."

I stared at him.

"And then he . . . he flew away."

"He flew away."

"On a broom. And he turned my daddy into a mouse."

"Are we telling stories again?" It was Daniel's mother, Erika Klein. I didn't know how long she'd been standing there. "You have to forgive him, Samantha," she said, adjusting dainty, wire-framed glasses. "He's at this phase where he just makes up stories all the time. I think you're turning into quite the young novelist, eh, Daniel?"

He smiled shyly. "Yes . . ."

"Now, what do we call making up stories and acting as if they're true?"

"Lying."

"And is lying a good thing?"

"No . . . I'm sorry, Ms. Leiffer."

"That's okay, Dan. Why don't you show your mom Squad Watery." As he took out the picture, I recalled how much my own mother's voice had sounded like Erika Klein's.

"You lied to me, and you lied to your grandmother."

"But, Mom . . ."

"There was no man in a Pinto with a princess crown for you, and you know it."

"But . . ."

"There was no pigeon that saved your life."

"Yes, there was."

"You were lying to get attention. Admit it."

"He tried to kill me . . ."

"Are you a little baby, Samantha?"

"No."

"Then stop making up stories. Admit you were lying. That's the first step to growing up."

"But—"

"Samantha Elizabeth Leiffer!"

"I'm sorry I lied, Mom."

"That's a good girl."

As Daniel's mother started to lead him out, I put a hand on her arm. "Please make sure and always listen to Daniel. Sometimes the strangest-sounding stories turn out to be true."

Erika blinked at me. "I'll keep that in mind."

*   *   *

After all the kids were gone, I straightened up my desk while Yale cleared the art detritus from the rest of the room.

"Do you always keep the bathroom key on the chalk tray?" he asked.

"What? No. It goes in the desk."

Yale tossed me the key and looked closely at my face. "Given the current situation, this may seem like a stupid question," he said. "But what's on your mind?"

"Daniel Klein, actually. He said something weird." I pulled out the top drawer, put the key back in and started to close it. But stopped when I saw the bottom of a ripped-out magazine ad. I hadn't put it there.

"What did he say?" Yale said.

"He . . . said . . ." With the short fingernails on my thumb and index finger, I slowly pulled the ad out of the drawer and stared at it, my pulse getting faster, my breath more shallow. Blood pounded in my ears, and I was only dimly aware of Yale's voice.

"Sam? What is that?"

It was an ad for a doll—Schoolteacher Barbie. Her hair in a glossy bun, Barbie wore a pink cardigan and jeans and stood in front of a miniature chalkboard, her name dancing across it in familiar, cursive letters. Several student dolls sat before her, little backs to the camera, raising chubby plastic hands. Barbie appeared to be deciding on whom to call, but it was difficult to tell, because the top half of her face was hidden by a thick smear of dried, reddish brown liquid.

It had been applied to her eyes with a finger, and had dripped down the side of the page before drying.

Yale and I sat at either end of my dinette table, with the magazine ad at the center like a ticking bomb.

I knew I should have called the Sixth Precinct from school and had a cop take the ad. As Yale had pointed out, I could have spoken to anyone there; it didn't have to be Krull. Still, I couldn't bring myself to do it—not there, not then.

So I'd put my gloves on, gingerly placed the ad between two pieces of the white drawing paper we'd used in class that day and carried it home like a relic.

Yale and I had taken a cab to my apartment because it seemed like the safest place to be. The more we were out on the streets, the more likely Peter was to track us down, to follow us, to watch us through windows. My apartment overlooked an airshaft. Only neighbors could watch us here.

My phone was still off the hook, and I wanted it to stay that way. He'd gotten into my classroom, into my locked desk drawer, into my best friend's bed. It was only a matter of time before he got into my phone, before he learned my number, my address. I wasn't listed, but what difference did that make? Peter Steele would find his way in.

Yale said, "We need to call the police."

"Can't we wait?" I said. "Can't we just sit on the

couch and watch TV and eat peanut butter sandwiches and wait until it . . . it blows over?"

"As tempting as that is, all my things have been destroyed and, okay, my valuables aren't all that valuable and I have some insurance, but this is the thing, Sam. He's going to kill you if we don't do something."

I forced a grin. "You sound so certain."

Without a word, he pointed to the smear across Barbie's eyes. It was blood, I knew, and too thick to have come from a pricked finger.

"All right," I said. "But can you do me a favor and put the phone back on the hook and bring it over to me? I . . . I don't feel like moving right now . . . I'm sorry."

He patted my hand. "Abject fear means never having to say you're sorry."

Yale was only able to make it a few steps before the floor started slamming and shaking beneath him. "What is happening . . ." he said, arms straight out and knees bent, as if he'd suddenly been dropped at the center of a tightrope.

I smiled at him. "That's just my crazy downstairs neighbor, Yale. She moved in about six months ago."

"This hasn't happened before, and I've certainly been here in the past six—"

"You were probably wearing sneakers or something. Elmira has a thing about boots."

"Sweet Jesus, what a horrible, horrible . . ." Yale unlaced his thick, brown hiking boots and stepped out of them. I winced at his socks on the bare floors, but didn't say anything. Yale hated it when I brought up superstitions.

Elmira eventually stopped banging, but he still backed away from his shoes as if they were venomous snakes.

When he reached the phone and placed it on the hook, it rang immediately. Yale jumped back. "Your apartment is trying to give me a heart attack!"

"Please, can you pick it up?"

Yale took a massive breath and steadied himself, shaking the tension out of his hands, cracking both sides of his neck, gently slapping himself in the face. It was the same series of motions he went through before beginning an audition monologue.

"Hurry up."

"All right, already . . . Hello? . . . Yes, she is. May I say who's . . . Certainly. Okay . . ."

He placed his hand over the mouthpiece and raised an eyebrow at me. "Detective Krull."

"You're kidding."

Yale walked across the room and handed me the cordless.

"Hello?"

"Samantha . . ." He said my name like a drawn-out sigh. "I was worried about you."

"You were?"

"Your phone's been off the hook. I've been trying to call you . . ."

"I think I must've forgotten to hit the button after I hung up with you last night . . ." I felt my face heating up. Yale was gesturing dramatically at the magazine ad, making it even harder for me to concentrate. I spun around in my chair, put my back to him. "Look, Detective . . . I'm really sorry about last night."

Yale said, "Oh, Jesus Christ, would you please tell him about this fucking thing!"

"Shut up."

"Why?" Krull said.

"Not you. I was talking to my friend."

"No . . . Why are you sorry?"

"Uhhhhh . . . Because I . . . Because I . . ."

"You didn't hit me, or steal my wallet, or say terrible things about my mother."

"Oh, come on, Detective . . ."

"John."

"John, you know what I did."

Yale said, "We interrupt this episode of *Live and Let Live* to bring you important information about a *murderer*!"

I held up my index finger, mouthed the word "Wait."

Krull's voice was quiet, a little tense around the edges. "What you did . . . was you made me a very nice offer. Of course you were about two minutes away from comatose."

"I didn't scare you?"

"Are you insane?"

I covered my face with my hands.

"And if you're sorry about getting so drunk, don't apologize to me. Apologize to your digestive system."

"God, John. When I woke up this morning, I just felt so . . ."

Yale grabbed the phone out of my hands. "Maybe you and Sam could continue your conversation in person. She received some sort of note in her desk at school today with blood on it . . . Yes, blood . . . I'm almost positive that's what it is. She found it there after the children left. And Peter Steele vandalized my apartment last night . . . Right . . . Yeah, that's me. Her friend Yale who slept with the psychopath."

I listened to Yale giving Krull my exact address and then his address, as well as his super's name and apartment number so that police could begin dusting his place for fingerprints. I felt a powerful warmth welling up in my chest and spreading. *He's going to take care of this.*

"Oh, and Detective," Yale said, just before he hung up, "I wouldn't wear boots over here if I were you."

Krull showed up fast and made directly for the dinette table.

On Yale's recommendation, he slipped off his shoes and I noticed they were surprisingly tasteful—soft and black and Italian looking. They contrasted sharply with the rest of his outfit: the same brown suit he'd worn the previous day, a faded oxford shirt of beige and brown plaid and the kind of colorless, rectangular knit tie my seventh grade math teacher used to wear. "Nice shoes," I said.

Krull didn't reply. He opened his briefcase, removed a large, plastic evidence bag and a pair of tweezers, and carefully slipped the magazine ad in. For several moments, he stared at Barbie's bloody face through the clear plastic.

I said, "Thanks for coming by."

Still no answer.

"Are you mad at me?"

Slowly, he shifted his gaze from the doll's face to mine. He didn't say anything; he didn't need to.

"What changed between the phone and here?"

Krull shoved the bag into his briefcase, snapped it shut. When he finally spoke, his voice was excruciatingly tight and measured. "Why didn't you call me from school?"

"I . . . I felt like I'd be safer at home."

"Instead of calling me, you went outside and onto the street, where you could've easily been attacked. And you risked contaminating the evidence to take it *home*? Because you felt *safer* there?"

"I'm . . ."

"Let me ask you something. If I hadn't called you, would you have—"

"We were just about to call the police," Yale cut in. "That's why I put the phone on the hook."

Krull stared at me hard. "Not the police," he said. "Me. Would you have called *me*?"

I stared right back at him. He was starting to make me mad. I didn't need that—anger on top of embarrassment and confusion and fear and all these other unpleasant emotions. *What happened to the verbal judo? The least you could do is patronize me.* "I don't know. Probably not. I think I would have called Art."

Krull said nothing. His eyes were like sharpened pieces of jet.

Yale said, "I should've taken that damn bow tie with me. Peter left his bow tie. That's evidence, isn't it?"

Krull did not respond.

My jaw tightened, but I refused to remove my eyes from his. "I feel more comfortable around Art," I said through my teeth. "I think Art would be more understanding."

Finally, he looked away. I felt a hollow satisfaction, having won this ridiculous staring contest. He unsnapped his briefcase again, removed a cellular phone—a long, fold-up model from the nineties—then a business card and a pen. "This phone was issued to Amanda," he said as he wrote on the back of the card. "It's an NYPD phone, and everyone knows she's on maternity leave so you don't have to worry about getting her calls."

He handed it to me along with a charger, then gave me the card. "This is my card, but I've written Art's direct line and cell number on the back. If anything happens . . . or if you . . . feel scared, call me. Or him. Suit yourself."

He took a notepad out of his briefcase and turned his attention to Yale, asking him a series of questions and putting together a timeline related to the break-in the previous night. "You know what the phrase 'under the umbrella of suspicion' means?" he said to Yale after he closed the pad.

Yale replied, "Only insofar as it relates to John and Patsy Ramsey."

Krull smiled. "It more or less means that Peter is a possible suspect—but not a probable one," he said. "Even if he did wreck your place, it's not necessarily connected with the child murders. We don't have any solid proof he's even a devil worshiper."

I walked out of the room, into the kitchen area.

Krull went on. "I guess what I'm saying is I know this is difficult for you. But try not to think too much about it now. The important thing to remember is you haven't done anything wrong."

From where I was standing, I could see Yale's face, his eyes glistening slightly. "Thanks, Detective," he said.

Knows exactly what to say to everyone but me.

"I'm going to your place to see how the crime scene guys are doing. When you get a chance, stop by the Sixth Precinct on West Twelfth Street, okay? We'll need your fingerprints so we can exclude them."

"My first fingerprinting."

I said, "Good-bye, Detective," and Krull finally looked at me. His eyes were no longer sharp and hard, just sad.

After Krull left, Yale exhaled dramatically. "Well, it certainly feels good to have the authorities involved."

I glared at him.

"Sorry, but I don't give a rat's ass who's winning the Tournament of Mind Games."

"I made *one mistake*. He doesn't have to—"

"I don't understand you, Sam. You're terrified of spilled salt and chills up your spine, but Bloodbath Barbie isn't all that big a deal?"

"I . . . don't feel like talking about it."

"That's fine. Just one reality check: human sacrifice."

"Krull said there's no proof Peter is a devil worshiper."

"He was only trying to make me feel better, and you know it. I have to say he's pretty sensitive for a straight man. A straight cop, no less."

I looked at him. "How do you know he's straight?"

"Oh, please." Yale started to put his coat on.

"I'm serious. He works out of the West Village precinct, he turned me down when I threw myself at him—and I'm sorry, I was *drunk and nude*. He's not married. He obviously spends a lot of time at the gym . . ."

He shook his head at me. "Samantha, dear," he said, as

if he were teaching a child to read, "no self-respecting gay man would be caught dead dressed like that."

"Oh . . . right."

"Not to mention he's hot for you."

I stared at Yale.

Yale finished buttoning up his coat, then grabbed his boots and headed for the door. "God, you're dense sometimes. Must be all that L.A. smog you inhaled as a child."

"What do you mean?"

"Figure it out for yourself, Stanford girl," he said. "I have locks to change, fingerprints to give, an investigation to aid."

"Be careful."

"You be careful. Lock your door." Yale closed the door, and I bolted it. Through the peephole, I watched him put on his boots before heading down the hall to the elevator.

I settled back at the dinette table, picked up Krull's card, turned it over and over between my fingers. I looked at the thick black ink on the back of it, at Art Boyle's name printed in calm, capital letters. *Call me. Or him. Suit yourself.*

"Oh yeah. He is so hot for me."

I folded up Amanda's cell phone, shoved it in my pocket and wandered into the kitchen. I desperately wanted a beer, but decided to make myself coffee instead.

The cupboard with the filters in it was sticky, so I

had to pry it open with my big, wood-handled kitchen knife. I always needed to do this, yet I never could stop myself from putting the filters back in that cupboard when I was through with them. Perhaps subconsciously, I enjoyed the extra work I had to go through every morning to get to them. Or maybe it was because I hardly used the knife for anything else and I liked the feel of the thick pine hilt in my hand. It was probably sexual.

I jammed the long thin blade through the crack, then worked it back and forth until the door drifted open. I was setting the knife back down on the counter when the phone rang.

It was so loud and close that for a second, I thought it was the cell. But then I realized it was the cordless; the receiver was still on the dinette.

I hurried out of the kitchen and picked it up fast. "Hello?"

But there was no answer, just breathing.

"Hello."

Still no reply. My back tensed up. The call had come just after Yale had left the building. *He knows I'm alone. He's watching.* I wanted to hang up, but for some reason I couldn't. It was as if the receiver was part of my hand. I listened to the breathing, the deep inhale and exhale, slow and controlled and strangely hypnotic. So calm. He had all the time in the world.

From the hollow sound of it, I could tell he was breathing through his mouth. I pictured Peter's full, reddish lips, taking the air in, pushing it out. *I breathe. I eat. I smoke. I fuck.*

I pictured his long, tapered finger, coated in fresh blood. *I kill.*

"It's you, isn't it?" I heard myself say.

And then came the response, out of the slow breathing with no voice behind it. "Eyes."

The caller hung up, but I stood frozen against the table, holding the dead receiver to my ear for a long time.

10

Black Box

Strange how it added up so fast as I stood at the dinette, the images clicking in and out of my mind perfunctorily, like slides on a screen. *Click.* The word scrawled in my book: *hide. Click.* The e-mail I'd received at the Space: *your. Click.* The disembodied whisper at the other end of the phone: *eyes.*

Click. Sydney's eyes on the valentine. *Click.* The bleeding eyes of Schoolteacher Barbie. *Click.* Hide your eyes. *Click.* Hide your eyes.

I found myself thinking of eyes I'd never seen—Peter's real eyes behind the mirrored contacts; the eyes of the murdered boy who'd been found two years ago in a Dumpster on Tenth Street; Ariel's eyes. *Something was done to the child's eyes*, Krull had said, not telling me what was done to them. Not wanting to tell me.

I thought of Daniel's imaginary man, the Man with the Sunglasses. And I believed he was real. I believed he was Peter, wearing dark glasses to shield mirrored eyes from anyone who might live to remember them. Were those eyes watching Daniel? Is that why he'd made up a fairy tale about the strange man? Because he'd felt those eyes on him, because he'd seen that hollow smile?

I heard Peter's voice in my head so clearly, as if he were standing over my shoulder. *You were trying to blind the devil!* I could hear his laughter too, and suddenly, I wished he *was* standing over my shoulder—so I could pick up the plastic receiver and force all my strength and anger into it, so I could sock him in the eyes until they bled.

"Ruby Redd's Brewing Company!" said a chirpy female voice.

"Hi. I was looking for a waiter by the name of Peter Steele. Is he there?"

"No, but his shift starts any min— Yep, I see him coming through the door right now. If you want to wait a few seconds, I can get him for—"

"That's not necessary."

"Should I tell him who called?"

"No need, I'm on my way. Bye."

Well, I am on my way. I folded up the cell phone and shoved it back in my pocket. *I'm on my way to getting his sick ass fried.*

What I needed was solid evidence against Peter, and I knew where to find it: in the Space's computer. Whether or not his fingerprints were on the magazine ad or in Yale's apartment (and I was sure he'd been smart enough to wear gloves), the word *your* was sent to me from a personal e-mail address. If it wasn't Peter's, then it belonged to someone who could make the connection. Since Peter was starting his shift at Ruby's, I could go to the theater and print it out without being followed.

I slipped on my coat and boots, and I wasn't scared or unsure or even apprehensive. I was proud, to tell the truth, as I felt around in my shoulder bag and quickly found the sharp, familiar comfort of my work keys. I was proud to be doing something, rather than sitting around my apartment eating peanut butter sandwiches and waiting for it all to blow over.

Words echoed in my head, and then I said them out loud; shouted the sentence so I could listen to it bounce triumphantly off the walls. "I am going to fry your sick ass, Peter Steele!"

I had no doubt I'd succeed as I ran for the door, ignoring the furious banging beneath my floor except to think, *If only Elmira knew. If only she knew.*

I'd been in the box office after nightfall before. These late winter days, when nightfall was at around 4:30 p.m., it seemed I was barely there in daylight. And I'd been in the box office alone, to close up for the evening. But I'd never *entered* it after nightfall, alone.

It was my second day job after all. I was accustomed to bright office lights when I showed up, to booming actors' voices that had already been filling the two rooms for hours. So it was odd, unlocking the box office door in the dark, cold night and seeing more darkness inside. The subscription room was stuffy and dry from radiator heat and so quiet you could actually hear the silence. Since the only big window faced the courtyard rather than the street, even occasional traffic sounds were muffled. "Somebody honk a horn for godsakes," I said to no one. My voice sounded high and squishy in the darkness.

I turned on the lights, saw the identical desks, the beige carpet, the blank white walls and lifeless Teletron machines. It really was a dull, corporate place, I realized, without its cast of characters.

I walked into the tiny ticketing room, booted up the computer and logged on. My two e-mails were still waiting—one from my mother, the other from ER425160. What could that screen name mean? I thought as I printed it out. There were too many numbers for it to be a birthdate or a street address and what did ER mean? Emergency Room? The TV show?

I closed my eyes, repeated the name: "ER425160." Did the letters relate to the numbers, or did they stand on their own? I thought about numerology, how En had lopped off the first five letters of his name to en-

sure his success as a writer, and wondered if Peter
had cut the first three of his for his screen name. I
doubted it. For one thing, En was not a devil worshiper. For another, the ER on the address was in
caps, which made me think, initials. But there had to
be something with those letters. I debated calling
Ruby's again and asking for Tredwell, because he
could probably clear it up. And I was on the verge of
doing just that when I remembered what Tredwell
had already told me . . .

*In Satanism, you say names backwards. He'd call
me Llewdert when we fucked . . .*

And you called him Retep, didn't you? I thought.
And if you called him by his full name, you called him
Eleets Retep. Eleets Retep . . . ER . . . *And four and
two are six, and five and one are six and six and
zero . . . 666. The number of the beast. ER666.*

God, you're predictable.

I turned off the computer, folded up the printout and
slipped it into my bag. *Eleets Retep 666. Give me a
break.*

Before leaving, I walked to the area near the will-
call ticket window and checked out the staff cubby-
holes. Shell's held three spare tubes of lipstick and the
National Enquirer she'd pilfered from Argent. In Argent's, there was a copy of *Casting Call* and a note
from a visiting friend with huge, girlish handwriting.
En's held the *Yoga Journal*. Hermyn's, a red envelope
with *For My Butterfly* printed neatly on the front.

Yale's cubbyhole seemed empty and so did mine, at first. Then I noticed a shadow at the very back and peered in. *Balled-up newspaper?* "Which one of you assholes put your trash in my cubbyhole?" I said, a little uneasily.

I looked into the dark space again, then stuck my arm in and reached back until I felt soft newsprint against my fingertips. *Just trash. Bet Shell did it.* But as I started to grasp it, I grew aware of a weight inside—mostly round but irregular, about the size of a tennis ball. "Oh . . ."

Slowly I pulled it out. A lumpy, globular thing, encased in Want Ads, resting in my palm. My fingers touched the oily paper, removed it as gently as a bride's veil. And without breathing, I stared at what had been wrapped inside.

It was the plastic head of a doll, a pale little girl. Its wavy hair had been colored, cut and styled exactly like mine. And its eyes had been cut out.

A small sound escaped from my throat and I jumped back, the doll's head flying out of my hand and hitting the wall on the other side of the room. And then, like a sudden, hard slap, I heard Peter Steele's voice.

"You bitch," he said, and when I turned around my gaze shot from his mirrored lenses to his checkered waiter's bow tie to his black leather trench coat to his gloved right hand, grasping something short and thick and dark. A gun. *It's happening again, it's the man in the Pinto all over again, again with a weapon in his hand, a weapon meant for me, again calling me bitch, only this time I have to move. I have to move please. Let me move . . .*

There were a few feet of space between his shoulder and the ticket room door, and I threw myself into it with such force that I knocked him off his feet. I heard a yelp and a thud behind me as I flew at the side door to the subscription room, pushed it open and fell into the still courtyard.

"Get back here!"

I headed for the street, which was maddeningly empty. A cab whizzed by, "Off Duty" sign blazing, and then there was nothing again.

I heard the box office door opening, and without thinking, I bolted for the theater, unlocked the heavy door, slammed it shut behind me, heart pounding up through my throat. When I reached the center of the aisle, I collapsed on the floor. *Tough shit, Peter. You don't have a key.*

There is no lobby in the Space. It's what they call a black box—a simple 150 seater with movable rows of chairs, facing a decent-sized, square stage and a rudimentary catwalk for hanging lights. *Addie*'s set, such at it was, had yet to be struck. It consisted of a bunch of dirt; a cheesy diorama painted with horses, rain clouds and shacks; a plain wooden coffin; and a small upright piano, shoved against the far wall.

The theater was absolutely dark. For at least a

minute, there was no difference between closing my eyes and opening them. But slowly, they adjusted. I began to discern shapes, like the neat rows of chairs, the few ladders that had been placed along the walls, the shadow of the coffin at the center of the stage.

I'd seen the show once. Once was all I could manage. I remembered the opening scene, in which eight shirtless pallbearers in baggy overalls rushed onstage, dropped the coffin and ran off without speaking a word. I remembered a bony character actress popping out of it like a Gothic jack-in-the-box, her face coated in thick white makeup, a black shroud draped stolelike around her shoulders. She'd shrieked, "Hey, fellas! The dead have feelings too!" And then the pianist had started to play.

You have a cell phone. Call the police. What's the number? 911, you idiot.

I pulled the phone out of my pocket, looked for the *on* button or the *power* button or whatever it was I was supposed to look for, in complete darkness. *Come on, you little piece of . . .*

Finally, I tapped a button and the face glowed green. I felt like kissing it in gratitude.

"Kkkkkk," went the door.

The phone dropped out of my hand, clattered to the floor. *I thought you locked automatically, you fucking fuck of a fucking door.*

I ran for the stage, though I knew there was no backstage area, no wings to wait in. They put black scrims up for some productions, but not this one. Actors entered and exited through the stage doors. I tried one of them. It was locked. Of course it was locked. What was this, some kind of door conspiracy?

The theater door slammed shut. I heard his shoes scuffing the cold floor, the metal legs of a chair he'd made contact with whining and toppling.

I had maybe seventy-five, eighty seconds before his eyes adjusted to the light. At least I'd seen the show.

I backed up until I felt Addie's coffin against my leg, and slipped inside. There was no squeak as I closed the lid, no sound at all save the whisper of plywood cutting through air.

I held my breath for several seconds. Let it out as slowly as air seeping through a pinprick and wished I could deflate all the way, until I was flat, two-dimensional.

The coffin lid was just inches away from my face and body. If I stuck out my tongue, I could probably touch it. *Breathe in, breathe out . . .*

I tried to see starry skies, tried to hear ocean waves, tried to find a place in my mind, far away and safe. *Think of anything. Think of nothing.*

But all I could think of, all I could see, was that grinning doll's head—black, round holes where its eyes once were. *He cut its hair to look like mine.*

I heard a crash, and knew Peter had knocked into something large. Maybe a group of chairs. Maybe a crate of props.

"Aaaah," he said.

The footsteps continued down the aisle, then stopped. Was he looking under a chair? *That's it, fucker. I'm under a chair. Better check all of them. There's 150.*

I held my breath again, listened. *One chair, two chairs, three chairs, keep it up . . .*

I clenched my teeth. Was he really looking under chairs? Or was he drawing the gun, aiming it at the coffin?

The movement resumed. More deliberate this time, back down the aisle until the footsteps reached the stage. *One step, two steps, three steps, four, which puts him right next to your head. Hold your breath and flatten, flatten out . . .*

He passed the coffin. Kept walking, then stopped. More silence. Several seconds of it, like prayer.

Click, click, click, click. Then a faint buzzing sound. He'd found the houselights.

Fuck. The word so loud in my mind, I thought for a second I'd said it.

Footsteps. Towards the . . . *Bong.* A piano key. Low note. My back stiffened. *Don't make a sound.* Then one higher, then higher. All the way up the major scale. *E,G,B,D,F . . . Every girl's body dies finally.*

The piano lid slammed shut, and I heard his boots moving closer to the stage, heard them crunching against the dirt again, moving towards the diorama, then stopping, turning.

Best I could tell, he was by the foot of the coffin now, and I heard him moving, *crunch, crunch, crunch.* Closer to my face, then turning, *crunch, crunch crunch.*

No . . .

Crunch, crunch . . .

He was circling me.

"I know where you are, Samantha. Do you think I'm stupid?"

I shut my eyes tight, bit my lip, jammed my fingernails into the palms of my hands until I could feel the moist sting of my own blood.

"You're really going to make me do this, aren't you?" Peter said. He was standing right next to my neck, and his voice was impossibly calm.

He opened the lid, and stared at me, his eyes reflecting the pale flesh of my forehead.

I swallowed hard, didn't move.

"Get out of the coffin."

Slowly, I got out. My legs felt wobbly, as if I might collapse, but I managed to stand up straight. I kept my eyes on his face. I refused to look at the gun. I knew he wanted me to look at it, but I wouldn't. That was within my control. "What do you want from me?"

He smiled broadly, mirrored eyes drilling into my skin. "What do I want from you," he said. "What do *I* want from *you*?" He started to laugh. "You called the police on me. Why would you do a thing like that, Samantha? What did I ever do to you?"

I stared at him. "It's not . . . it's not what you did to *me*. It's what you *did*. It's what you *are*." I shut my eyes and waited for the gunshot. But none came.

Slowly, I opened my eyes and let them drift to his right hand. He was still grasping it, but it wasn't a gun. It was a collapsible umbrella.

I could go for the door. I could push him over again and run back up the aisle. I started to move, but he grabbed my wrist. His grip was strong. "How did you find out?"

"None of your business."

"Oh, it's definitely my business." His gloved fingers tightened around my wrist. "It's been my business ever since I saw you go into the Sixth Precinct, and ever since I got a call from that detective. It's been my business ever since . . . we . . . met."

"It was in the paper," I said. "Don't you ever read the *Post*?"

His hand loosened slightly. "You're crazy."

"I'm crazy? *I'm crazy?*"

"Like I really believe it was in the *New York Post* that I'm Canadian."

I stared at him for what must have been a full minute before I found my voice again. "What?"

"Let me tell you what I think this is about. You've got a thing for Yale, and you're jealous as hell that he and I got together. You act rude to me, but that doesn't work, so you do some digging. Maybe talk to some of my friends, I don't know. And then you run to the police and you tell them I'm an illegal alien so they can deport me, and Yale and I will never see each other again, and won't you be hap—"

"You're an illegal alien?"

"I mean, so *what*? I forgot to renew my work visa once. I'm going to take care of it."

He let go of my wrist. I started to back up, but my ankle turned, and I fell to the dirty stage floor.

"You okay?" *Did he really just ask me that?*

I stood up, brushed myself off. Looking at Peter, I suddenly lost my urge to leave. Instead, I was overcome by a starving curiosity, a desperate need to call his bluff and prove I'd been right about him all along. "Where did you get that tattoo on the back of your neck?"

"This place on St. Marks. Why?"

"It's a pentagram."

"So?"

"That's the sign of the devil."

"No, it's not."

My cheeks were starting to burn. "Yes, it is."

"It's Wiccan," he said. "I was into Wicca for about five minutes three years ago."

Peter's face was pink, his eyes wide and perplexed behind the mirrored lenses. "Wicca is an earth-based, goddess religion. It has nothing to do with the devil."

I clenched my teeth. "Tredwell put that pentagram there and you know it."

"Tredwell? From Ruby's?"

"What the hell other Tredwells are there?"

A metallic ringing pulsed out from beyond the lip of the stage, and we both turned to it. "That's my cell phone," I said. Peter followed the sound and answered it. "It's detective somebody." Eyes narrowed, he handed it to me.

Krull.

It wasn't Krull. It was Art Boyle. "Hi, Miss Leiffer. Johnny asked me to call you. Wanted me to tell you we got a make on the fingerprints from Yale St. Germaine's apartment."

"That was fast."

"Yeah. We had 'em on file because the guy had a previous conviction for shoplifting some . . . uh . . . paraphernalia . . . from the House of Pain down on Christopher Street."

I stared at Peter, my jaw tightening. "What was the name?"

"Tredwell Hague," he said. "You know him?"

After I hung up with Boyle, Peter and I sat cross-legged on the edge of the stage. Odd to be sitting there with him, unafraid, but everything about these past few days had been odd.

It didn't take us long to put it all together. Ever since Peter had taken the job at Ruby's, Tredwell had been trying to ask him out. Peter had repeatedly turned him down. "He's too young, I'm not into purple hair and have you noticed he's kind of stupid?" Peter said. "Besides, he kept trying to get me to go to these dungeon places, and I don't do S and M."

When he saw Yale and learned about his relationship with Peter, Tredwell had, quite literally, seen red. He'd followed me out of Ruby's, pulled me into Cheap Trix and fed me every horror story imaginable to get me to warn off my best friend. I remembered how long he'd taken in the bathroom there. Obviously straining his brain to come up with a frightening enough plot.

Before he'd received the call from Boyle, Peter had told several people—Tredwell included—about his date with Yale at Temple Bar. That was all Tredwell could take. Since I'd clearly failed to turn my friend against the love of his life, the spurned waiter had decided to take matters into his own hands.

Yale's address was listed. Obviously he was the only Yale St. Germaine in the phone book.

When Tredwell thought Yale was out with Peter ("I was actually at my cousin's place, hiding from the police"), he'd gone to the apartment and taken out twelve months worth of sexual frustration on Yale's belongings. The fact that he'd left not only his fingerprints but also his bow tie behind was, for Tredwell, typical.

"Total nut job," Peter said. "I can't even believe he told you we were dating."

"First you were convincing him to do drugs. When that didn't impress me, he said you'd coerced him into S and M—"

"Yeah, right. What a prick."

"And then you'd forced him to worship the devil."

"You believed all that?"

I had to admit it. Out loud, it sounded ridiculous. But I'd never questioned Tredwell, never thought for a second he might be lying. "I wanted to believe it," I thought and said at the same time. "Because . . . if it were true, it would've answered a lot of questions for me. I saw something . . . a crime. And if you were the one who did it, you'd be in jail by now. Everyone would be safe."

Peter had picked up a small handful of dirt from the stage and was slowly letting it sift through his fingers. "Sounds like you've been through a lot," he said, without a hint of sarcasm in his voice. I was actually starting to like this guy.

"It's those mirrored lenses, you know," I said. "The criminal has the same ones as you, and that's what got me going in the first place."

Peter removed a small plastic case from his jeans pocket and plucked the contacts out of his eyes. "I just thought you were trying to piss me off when you said they weren't one of a kind, but it turns out you were right," he said as he did it. "This actress came into Ruby's last night and she had them. Thought she was the cat's ass because she had an audition for some dumb soap opera . . ."

I shook my head at how small New York could be.

"I figured, a wannabe soap star who eats at Ruby's is not exactly on the fashion forefront. I was wearing these only to avoid the cops." Peter snapped the box shut and looked at me. His eyes were a dark, denimy blue and as stunning as the rest of him.

"Peter," I said, "the Sixth Precinct detective squad is not going to arrest you for being an illegal immigrant."

"They're not?"

"No. INS would be the ones to worry about, and nobody knows, anyway."

"Man, is that a relief . . . Now all I have to do is apologize to Yale for standing him up and kill Tredwell—not literally. What was this crime you witnessed anyway?"

I started to reply, but stopped when I heard a loud noise outside the theater door. It took only a few seconds to identify it as the sharp, leathery sound of a whip cracking. Peter and I stared at each other as the door slowly creaked open.

When it slammed shut, there was Hermyn at the back of the theater, chest thrown out to accommodate that acrobatic voice, fists pressed to her hips like a superhero.

"Oh, it's you, Samantha," she said. "I thought we were being robbed."

*   *   *

I had to admit, ever since Hermyn had announced her engagement, I'd been dying to know what her fiancé, Sal, looked like. "Think Sid Vicious with a water pick," Shell had speculated during her rant at the will-call window. And that image had stuck—I'd envisioned a pale, greasy-haired dentist built like a stick of gum, maybe with a few track marks. So when I finally saw him in the flesh that night outside the theater, sitting in the front seat of his Chevy Cavalier, I couldn't help but stare. He was emphatically *un*edgy—a sweet-faced man, not much bigger than me, with a neat, curly cap of brown hair and square, plastic-framed glasses. "So you're Sal," I said as Hermyn opened the back door for me and Peter and eased into the front seat beside her intended.

"Hello, there," he said without turning around. His head barely cleared the rest atop the driver's seat. "We're here to pick up Butterfly's belated Valentine's present."

"Don't call me that in front of other people, Sal."

"What with proposing and all, I completely forgot to give it to her—"

"You didn't have to give me anything."

"So I left it in Bu—Hermyn's cubbyhole last night because I wanted to surprise her at work today. Then she tells me you guys have the whole week off—"

"Did you see anybody else at the box office last night?" I asked.

"No," said Sal. "Was I supposed to?"

Hermyn pulled the red envelope out of her jacket pocket, and started to open it.

I figured I should probably go back for the doll's head, take it with me to show the police, but I couldn't stand to even think of it, let alone touch it. I'd tell the police about it later, send them to the box office without me, so they could seal the eyeless head in a clean, plastic evidence bag and take it far away. *Did that doll belong to Ariel? Did the blood on the ad?*

"We heard quite a racket there in the theater," Sal said. His voice was deep, especially for his size, and reminded me of a warm, heavy blanket. I imagined his patients had little need for anesthesia. "I guess everything carries in there. Makes for good acoustics. Hermyn does a great whip, doesn't she? Most talented woman I've ever met."

"Sweetheart, you're embarrassing me."

"I speak the truth, my love. Open your present."

"Tell me a joke first."

"Okay. What did one math book say to the other?"

"I give up."

"I have a lot of problems."

Hermyn cackled. "You are so funny."

"I hear most of them from my patient, Emmett. He's in the second grade."

"It's all in the delivery, Sal. Isn't his delivery wonderful, Samantha?"

"Excellent."

"Ohhhh, you darling man," Hermyn said as she gazed at the contents of the envelope.

"Well, show us, why don't you?" said Peter.

Hermyn kissed Sal deeply before passing a necklace into Peter's hands. He held it out so we could both look at it—a thin, sparkling chain with a delicate butterfly pendant—barely bigger than the gold applique on Hermyn's front tooth. A small diamond stood at the tip of each antenna and emerald dust had been sprinkled on its wings.

I found myself marveling at how Sal had walked into a store, noticed this sweet, fragile thing, and had immediately thought of Hermyn. No wonder she loved him. He was probably the only person in the world who looked at her boxy frame, her stern features, her spiky hair—and saw a butterfly.

"You all right?" Hermyn said to me. "You seem upset."

"I'm fine. Just . . . tired."

"So where are you two lovebirds headed?" Sal asked.

"I've *so* got to get back to work," Peter said. "They think I just went home because I forgot my wallet."

We drove to Ruby's in relative silence. When we got there, I saw two police cars parked outside and, through the frosty window, burgundy hair surrounded by blue uniforms. "Seems early for a bar brawl," Sal remarked.

As Peter left the car, I said, "Don't forget to renew that visa."

He turned and winked at me, then sprinted into the restaurant.

"He is so handsome, Samantha," said Hermyn. "Is he a model?"

"I think," I said, "he's just a normal waiter."

When I asked them to take me to Yale's apartment, I realized it was the only safe place I knew.

11

I'll Wait Here, Butterfly

"Incredible," Hermyn kept saying as she circled the great, multicolored pile of broken glass, china, pottery and shredded police tape sprawled at the center of Yale's living room floor.

Yale and I just looked at each other. When Hermyn had walked through the door and gasped at the jagged mess—which stood a couple of feet high and reminded me of one of the Watts Towers, collapsed—Yale had explained, teeth clenched, "It's art." Obviously, he hadn't expected her to take him seriously.

Hermyn knelt down, and grazed her fingertips over the headless body of Yale's porcelain dog. "Lost love and . . . ohh, yes, regret. Sal would go crazy for this."

Sal was waiting in the car. Hermyn had insisted on walking me upstairs, and when I'd mentioned several recent auto thefts that had occurred on Eighth Street after dark, Sal had said, "I'll wait here and watch the car, Butterfly!" I'd felt so sorry for Hermyn's fiancé, sitting out in the cold with the car turned off (he said he didn't want to waste gas) that I'd given him my huge, bulky coat, which he'd gratefully accepted.

When I turned around, I'd seen him in the front seat with the coat thrown over him like a blanket, wriggling underneath the folds of black wool, pulling the collar and hood over his small head. He reminded me of some sort of burrowing, baby animal.

Yale's apartment was barely recognizable. The couch was pushed up against the wall across from his two street-facing windows. But everything else in the room had been carefully swept into the center, including the police tape, which Yale had decimated as well, presumably to make one giant disposal pile. It made sense to me. Why bother with wastebaskets when your entire living room has been turned into one?

Tredwell's waiter bow tie had been placed at the top of the heap like an angel on a Christmas tree. I pointed at it and remarked, "Nice touch."

"I thought so," said Yale. He was wearing sweatpants that were rolled up at the bottom, an oversized *Cats* sweatshirt and thick ski socks. His face was flushed from stress and cleaning.

"Who is the artist?" asked Hermyn, who was still on her knees, stroking a remnant of a tragedy mask that bore a light gray dust from fingerprinting.

"Oh, Hermyn," Yale said, "this isn't art. These are my possessions—or what's left of them, thanks to a jealous little prick named Tredwell."

"Oh, good. Because honestly? It's kind of over the top."

"At least he's gonna pay for everything." Yale looked at me. "That's the one thing Peter really *is* forcing him to do."

Yale's buzzer gave off a long, painful bleat. I could tell someone was leaning on it.

"Jesus Christ." Deliberately, Yale walked to his door. "Who the fuck is it?" he shouted into the intercom.

A man's voice: "*I'm bleeding!*"

I looked at Hermyn, saw the color drain from her face in slow motion.

After five years in New York, I still had a California driver's license. But since Yale's Wisconsin license had expired two years ago and Hermyn had never learned to drive, it was understood that I would take the wheel of the Cavalier and drive us the few short blocks to St. Vincent's Hospital.

Sal had been shot. Exactly where, we didn't know, because blood was all over him and none of us wanted to hurt him more by exploring.

Driving was good because it gave me a place to sit and something to do with my hands, which were trembling so hard I could barely grasp the ignition key.

I had never seen so much blood in my life. Thick as paint and still warm and slick, it covered the front seat and both driver's side doors of the Cavalier. A few stray shards of glass clung to the left window, coated with the same bright, sick red. The rest had been shattered by the bullet. I felt ice-cold wind on my face and the tiny, prickly pieces through my pants and sweater, but it didn't hurt. And I wasn't cold. All I could hear or feel or think of was Hermyn's moaning, "Oh my God, oh my God," over and over again from the backseat while Sal, in the state he was in, tried to comfort her. "It's okay, Butterfly, I'm just . . . just a little dizzy is all . . ."

At one point, Sal said, "Did they steal my car?" and I realized how delirious he actually was.

Yale kept silent. His jaw was slack and I thought he might faint.

I wondered how Sal had been able to make it to the door and press the buzzer. His blood was all over the steering wheel. How horribly intimate it is to feel another person's blood, slippery and warm, on the palms of your hands.

The car screeched into a U-turn on Eighth Street. I said, "You never really do forget how to drive."

"Is that so?" Yale said. I glanced at him. Two tears trickled down his cheeks, but he seemed unaware of them.

"Did they steal my car? 'Cause I have insurance so it's okay. Lotsa car thefts on Eighth Street. Shouldn't

park cars there, but that's okay. It's okay, Butterfly . . ."

"We're almost there," I said, and ran a red light to
make a left on Seventh Avenue and narrowly avoided
smashing into a taxi.

"Hey, Butterfly, what do guns say when they don't
know the answer?"

"Oh, God, Sal."

"I don't know, but I'll take a shot! Get it? Boy, am I
queasy . . ."

By the time I braked in front of St. Vincent's, Sal
had passed out. Hermyn rushed in to get the paramedics as Yale and I hopped out of the car and opened
the back door. "Oh, please don't die," I whispered to
his still, frail body.

Yale just stared at him, his face gray beyond emotion.

In the waiting room at St. Vincent's, the air was hot
and a little moist. "I feel like I'm inside someone's
mouth," Yale said. "It can't possibly be sanitary in
here."

I probably would have smiled, if the situation had
been different. But I couldn't even work up a response.
It was hard enough to breathe.

"I mean a human's mouth, you know. Not a dog's
mouth. Dogs' mouths are supposed to be extremely
sanitary. You could probably eat out of a dog's mouth

and be safer than you would be at most delis. Of course, the dog probably wouldn't be too pleased . . ."

Yale kept talking and I just sat there, staring straight ahead at the blackness that pressed against the windows of the hospital waiting room. I wondered if they were bulletproof.

At least Sal wasn't dead. The bullet had entered the shoulder, breaking his collarbone but missing his vital organs. Hermyn was with him in the emergency room, even though visitors weren't technically allowed in there. There was a sign that said as much, but Hermyn didn't care. "Let me through, motherfuckers!" she'd yelled in her clear, piercing voice, like an opera singer playing *Shaft*. The ER staff had looked at her, admiring and afraid at the same time, and absorbed her into their group.

Yale and I had gone into the waiting room and received sporadic updates from the doctor who was working on Sal.

Sal had been hit in the left shoulder, which connected to his left arm, which connected to his left hand, where Hermyn would eventually place a wedding ring after the rabbi called her Amy and asked if she would take this man. That was her real name, Amy. She'd given it to the admitting nurse. "I'm his fiancée, Amy Rosensweig," she'd said, shedding the name by which we'd always known her as if it were a costume she'd been wearing for too long.

"Now, cats' mouths on the other hand. *Filthy* . . ."

A woman two seats over was holding a little boy who was probably her son. They both had the same huge, shiny black eyes, and the little boy was shaking. He was absolutely tiny.

The woman was talking very softly to the boy. I could hear her say *mi hijo,* a phrase I remembered from high school Spanish. My child.

"Strike that. A cow's mouth would be filled with cud, which is far more wholesome and probably smells better than anything in this so-called health care facility. Are you listening to me?" Yale hadn't stopped talking, not even to inhale. I'd never expected him to react this way in a crisis situation, which proves you can't truly know anyone, even your best friend.

"Mouths, right?" I said.

"Right."

Yale, the woman, the boy and I were the only people in the waiting room, which had to be rare. I looked at the big clock on the wall and saw it was just about eleven.

"Hey," I said. "Didn't Peter get off at ten? Why don't you call him? You can use my cell phone."

"Already spoke to him, after Tredwell finished *crying* at me. I mean, can you believe the absolute nerve of him—he destroys my valuables and I'm nice enough to drop the charges and then he expects me to feel *sorry* for him because Peter didn't want to play spanky-spanks or drip candle wax on his skinny ass—"

"Mi hijo, mi hijo. Te amo. No llores."

"I think you should go over to Peter's tonight."

"Well, my God if I wasn't sitting here I'd never *believe* you just said that. Too bad I don't have a *tape recorder* to document you of all people telling me to go over to Peter's, the *hostile, misogynist asshole* as you put it—"

"I like him. I made a mistake. You need a rest, and I don't think you should go back to your apartment."

"Why, Sam? I don't have a car. There have been four car thefts on Eighth in the past three weeks, two of them involving guns."

"Then why didn't they take Sal's car? He got out of the fucking car and rang your buzzer after he got shot, with the keys still in the ignition."

"They probably thought the cops would show up with all that hollering, and who could blame them? Good lord, that woman can *project*."

I just looked at him.

Yale took his time, breathing between words as if someone were extracting them from his mouth. "Sal was hidden beneath your coat."

"You figured it out."

"I was hoping you hadn't."

It was the last thing he said for a long time.

"Give me a cigarette."

"But you don't smoke."

"I don't care."

Yale raised his cupped hand against the wind, lit two

cigarettes in his mouth and handed me one. The cigarettes glowed warm orange in the purplish night, and, for a second, I felt like the heroine in a noir movie. Only this was real, and the lighting was a lot worse.

It was nearing midnight, and we were just outside the emergency room door. It felt good to be there, or at least less suffocating. "Aren't you freezing?" Yale said.

My coat was somewhere in the ER, covered in Sal's blood and destined for an evidence bag. But I wasn't freezing. The cold was there, of course, cutting through my thick sweater, biting my face and bare hands. But it didn't touch me, not really. Maybe the woman at the river had felt this way in her short-sleeved red dress. Surrounded by cold, but somehow beyond it.

I brought the cigarette to my mouth, took a deep drag and held it in. The smoke felt like hot, toxic liquid in my throat, but I didn't cough. I exhaled slowly, took another drag.

"My God, you're smoking," Yale said.

"Will wonders never cease."

"Sam, please don't start smoking. Between that and the way you eat, you're going to—"

"Die early?" For some reason, I found that incredibly funny. Laughter bubbled in my throat and spilled maniacally out of my mouth, and the grave way that Yale stared at me only made me laugh harder. "Oh, come on. Where's your sense of humor?"

I sat down on the sidewalk and leaned up against the emergency room window. The ash at the end of my cigarette extended at least an inch, so I tapped it and took another deep drag. "If you tell me it's unsanitary to sit on the sidewalk," I said, "I'm going to hit you."

Yale sat down next to me.

I liked the feel of the warm cigarette butt between my cold, gloveless fingers. I decided I could get used to smoking, if I were to have the luxury of getting used to anything. The butt was down to the filter, though, so I took another quick puff and reluctantly stubbed it out.

I stared out at Seventh Avenue, which looked strange and haunted without any people on it. A car drove by, its stereo blaring, and the thumping bass hung in the air for a few moments after it disappeared. I recognized the song. The Beastie Boys. "Sure Shot."

I pulled the cell phone out of my pocket and handed it to Yale. "I want you to call Peter—now."

"I . . . I don't have his number."

"Bullshit." I reached into the side pocket of his sweats. "You talked to him just before Hermyn and I showed up."

"Get your hand off my groin."

At the bottom of his pocket, I could feel a sharply folded piece of paper.

"Jesus, cut it out."

There was enough streetlight for me to read the printing on it: *Peter,* it said, along with a phone number.

"I know you so well."

Yale waited a few moments before responding. "I don't want to leave you alone."

"That's really sweet, but come on. What are you going to do? Jump in front of bullets?"

"Maybe."

"Look. It would make *me* feel better to know you're safe. I'm willing to pay you money to go to Peter's right now. Don't make me beg you."

"What are you going to do?"

"I don't know. Spend the night in the waiting room maybe."

Yale looked at me.

"I've spent the night in worse places."

"You're confusing yourself with me again."

I smiled.

"I'll call Peter under one condition—you have to call Detective Krull."

"Oh, come on. There should be police arriving any minute to question Sal now that he's stabilized. I'll talk to them."

"I want you to talk to Detective Krull."

"Why?"

"Because . . . he'll take care of you."

I was too tired to stand up, let alone argue with him.

He pulled his own cell phone out of the other pocket, punched in Peter's number with a huge, dramatic sigh.

I watched Yale ask, "Did I wake you?" watched him

say, "I need a place to stay tonight. I'll explain later."
Watched him listen as Peter gave him his address, no
questions asked.

After he hit "End," I said, "Was that so hard?"

"Now it's your turn."

"Sorry, I don't have his number."

"That's not fair. Where's that card he gave you?"

"At my apartment. And I'll bet you fifty bucks he's
not listed."

Next to me, I felt my friend's body stiffen. "Don't
make any sudden movements."

"Huh?"

"I want you to casually turn your head and look uptown. Across Twelfth and then half a block more."

As slowly and subtly as I could manage, I turned.

"Please tell me you've never seen him before.
Please tell me it must just be some guy cruising me."

But I couldn't reply, couldn't move, couldn't
breathe. Across Twelfth and half a block uptown stood
a tall figure in a long trench coat, a thick scarf tied
around the lower half of his face. It was too dark to see
the eyes, but I knew what they looked like, and I knew
where they were aimed.

In daylight, they would have burned us both.

"Get up, Sam. We have to go back inside. Please get
up. He's coming closer," said Yale. "He's walking towards us." My body wouldn't budge. I was the girl in
the Pinto all over again.

"Move," Yale breathed.

Easier said than done, I wanted to say. But that wasn't easily done either. I could not open my mouth.

"He's crossing the street. What is wrong with you?"

I don't know I don't know I don't . . .

"Fuck, Sam. Fuck, fuck, fuck." He was now less than twenty feet away. Yale put both his arms around me, and was on the verge of lifting me off the ground when suddenly, the man stopped walking. Yale tugged at me, but I was deadweight, staring, as he removed something from the pocket of his trench coat and held it out at us, jiggling it a little, like a treat: the naked, headless body of a doll.

"Whoa," said Yale.

Then came the siren. A police car sped around the corner and pulled up to the curb in front of us. I'd never been so happy to see cops in my life. *Saved by a kamikaze pigeon.* As if a spell had been lifted, I jumped to my feet.

I looked uptown. The sidewalk and street were empty. I would have sworn he'd been a hallucination if Yale hadn't seen him too.

Two uniformed officers—an orange-haired woman about my age and a young guy with a dewy, English rose complexion—got out of the car.

"Thank God you're here," Yale said.

"You know anything about the shooting?" she asked. As she took a notepad out of her pocket, I watched the back door open.

Yale was saying, "The man who shot Sal was just over there a minute ago, but now he's gone. I mean, we're positive he's the man who shot Sal, because he was watching us and he just did the *sickest* thing."

"Did either of you see him shoot Mr. Merstein?"

"No. Nobody did. Not even Sal. But this man . . . He was the same man Sam saw at the Hudson River on Valentine's Day."

Both cops stared at him. The redhead said, "Okay. That didn't make much sense."

"Who's Sam?" asked Rosy Cheeks.

"She's Sam," said the man who'd been in the back-seat. He slammed the door shut and turned around to face us. "Hello, Sam."

"Detective Krull," said Yale, as if he were at a cock-tail party. "She was just about to call you."

I said, "What are you, psychic?"

"No. Just a decent listener. When the report of the shooting came in, I recognized Yale's address. And the description of your coat . . . You must be freezing."

I had a nearly uncontrollable urge to fall into his arms, but I didn't.

The cops searched the block, but found no sign of the man in the black coat. By the time we went back into the waiting room, it was well past midnight. The woman and the boy had left, there was a new nurse at the admissions desk and the place seemed quieter and hotter than ever.

The heat was something of a relief now. It was so thick and stultifying that it actually felt protective.

The uniforms, Red and Rosy Cheeks, questioned Yale and me, and we told them everything—from the "eyes" phone call to my visit to the theater to Sal's shooting to seeing the man on the street—as Krull took notes. He didn't ask us anything directly. He just sat there, writing on his notepad, shaking his head every so often. Finally, he paged more uniforms and sent them to the Space to pick up the severed plastic head.

The new admissions nurse—who looked more like a surfer girl than a health care professional—took Rosy Cheeks and Red into the ICU to talk to Sal while Krull remained with us.

Before she left, the deeply tanned RN told us it was past visiting hours and that Hermyn was planning on spending the night. "Why not come back tomorrow, when he's, like, fresh?" she asked, as if Sal were a loaf of bread.

"Well, *she's* certainly from California," I said, after the nurse had left.

But Yale and Krull didn't reply. I was about to remark about how so many people in this city seemed to be from somewhere else, even if that somewhere else happened to be New Jersey.

If no one responded to that, maybe I'd cap it off with some cliché of an observation like, *How many so-called New Yorkers are truly from New York City anyway?* just to fill the silence. But Krull spoke first. "I'm through yelling at you, but I really wish you'd called me before you went to the theater."

Yale said, "Can Sam spend the night at your place, Detective?"

"Better go now, Yale, Peter's waiting."

"Yes, you can spend the night at my place. I don't have much furniture, but I do have a couch."

I looked at Krull and realized that when he'd said *I'm through yelling at you*, I'd actually felt disappointed. "Does the couch pull out?"

"No, but it's comfortable. And I've got cable."

"Sold."

Yale gave me a light kiss on the cheek, waved to Krull, then left. Through the big windows, I watched him hailing a cab.

"John," I said, "I know I should've called and told you about the e-mail before I went to the theater. I should've called you as soon as I found the magazine ad with the blood on it, and when I got the phone call from that freak, I should've called you again."

"Then why didn't you?"

"This is going to sound weird, but it's almost as if calling you and telling you would make the whole situation too . . . real. When I told you about the couple I'd seen at the river, the story solidified in my mind. And then it became true. The little girl was found in the ice chest, the messages I was receiving started getting worse, then Sal . . . I didn't want that to happen again. So I didn't call you because—"

Krull's eyes went soft. "I'm not bad luck."

"I know that. I do . . ."

"I believe everything you've said. I want to protect you, which is something I happen to be good at. And I have a gun. Put it all together, I'm the best damn rabbit's foot you're ever going to get."

I smiled.

"I want you to think of me that way. As your good luck charm. I want you to tell me everything that scares you, okay?"

I didn't say anything, but I did reach into my bag and take out the e-mail I'd received at the Space. "Maybe you could track down the return address?"

Krull looked at it. "Maybe I could."

Krull's apartment was in Stuyvesant Town, a large, East Side complex where I'd heard lots of cops lived. I'd never been there before, but Yale had, about four years earlier. With a cop, in fact. Yale had been so drunk he could barely see straight, and when he entered the cop's apartment, he'd been amazed. Hardcover, vintage books lined all four of the living room walls, from floor to ceiling. *A literary cop,* Yale had thought, falling head over heels in lust—until he realized that none of the books bore legible titles. When he reached out to touch the spine of one of them, he learned the sad truth: bookshelf wallpaper.

I told Krull that story as we careered toward his Stuyvesant Town apartment in the backseat of the police car with Red and Rosy Cheeks in the front. "I wonder if I've ever met that guy," Krull said, laughing.

Rosy Cheeks said, "I don't know any gay cops."

"How do you know?" I asked.

"Because I've never had a cop hit on me. Gay guys always hit on me."

Red, who was behind the wheel, turned and stared at him. "Why?"

"I dunno. They think I'm hot?"

She shrugged. "Maybe they think you're gay."

"No fucking way."

"Most gay men aren't interested in straight guys. They've got some kind of radar."

"Shut up, Fiona."

"I'm serious. My cousin told me that, and he's gay, so he ought to know."

"I said *shut the hell up!*"

Krull rolled his eyes. I couldn't think of anything to say that would diffuse this idiotic argument, so I watched the kid stewing in the passenger seat, his ears turning purplish. I didn't like the fact he had a gun on him. He seemed too emotional to be carrying something lethal. Besides, I'd had enough to do with guns this evening to last me a lifetime.

A lifetime. To me, the expression had always meant forever, and I supposed it still did. I supposed each person's lifetime was her own, personal forever. But for Ariel, forever had lasted three years. When Yale was touching the cop's wallpaper, she hadn't even been born.

Mi hijo, mi hijo. Te amo. No llores.

"Have you guys found out her real name?" I said.

"Who?" asked Rosy Cheeks, his voice still tight from anger.

"Ariel . . . The girl in the ice chest."

"Her name was Sarah," Krull said. "Sarah Grace Flannigan. Her parents reported her missing a week ago."

Fiona said, "She was with her dad last, at that playground on Tenth and Hudson? She was on the swing set, and he turned his back on her for half a second to get his video camera out of the bag. Turned around with the camera on and got a shot of an empty swing. She'd disappeared into thin air, poor little girl."

Not Ariel but Sarah. Sarah Grace, waving to her dad from a swing on a fenced-in city playground. Sarah Grace Flannigan in her purple jeans and her Disney T-shirt and probably a purple sweater and a purple coat. They'd taken the sweater and the coat before they squeezed her body into a shiny, pale blue picnic cooler. Because corpses don't need to keep warm.

"Do you mind if I crack the window back here?"

"Sure." Fiona released the auto lock. "How were the parents, Detective?"

"Pretty devastated," Krull said.

Mi hijo, mi hijo . . .

"Did they give you any leads?" asked Rosy Cheeks.

"Not really. The only unusual thing was that Sarah had found herself a new imaginary playmate in the past month or so. Which wasn't even that unusual because the kid was an only child, with an active imagination. She had a new imaginary playmate every week."

I think you're turning into quite the young novelist, eh, Daniel?

I said, "Was the playmate a man with sunglasses?"

"Her playmate was Cinderella," said Krull.

No one said anything else for the rest of the ride. I watched rows of low, darkened walk-ups flash by like dream fragments and breathed the cold air that streamed through the crack in the window, thinking about how sad it was to finally know Ariel's real name.

12

You Shook Me All Night Long

Krull's building occupied one of the nicer spots in the complex—across the street from the East River, with just one building to the left and nothing to the right but the tree-lined sidewalk. His apartment was on the twelfth floor, and the lobby was brightly lit and under-decorated with white linoleum floors, rows of shiny metal mailboxes and nothing else—not even a fake plant—to break the tidy monotony. As we entered the narrow, old-fashioned elevator, Krull muttered, "Jake's going to be pissed off."

"Jake?"

"You'll meet him. He waits up for me—hates it when I'm late."

I knew it. "Is Jake your . . . roommate?"

"You could say that. I'm going to warn you now,

he's *huge*. It's going to be hard, but try not to stare at him. He's very sensitive."

I winced.

We got up to the twelfth floor, and I followed Krull to the end of the long hallway. He opened the door slowly, whispered, "Jake," before he turned on the light. I sincerely hoped the big guy wasn't the jealous type. Of course, from my own experience, the word *sensitive* usually indicated that. Yale had gone out with more than one *sensitive* man who couldn't look at En or Roland or even me without spitting. I sighed heavily, remembering how the night before, I'd taken off all my clothes and propositioned a guy who, as it now seemed to be turning out, was a chubby chaser with a jealous boyfriend.

"Jake . . ." Krull whispered again. "Oh, there you are, sweetheart."

There was a light switch right next to the door, and when I flicked it on, I saw Krull on his knees, scratching the ears of the largest gray and black tabby I'd ever seen.

They both looked up at me. Krull smiled broadly. The cat narrowed his big yellow eyes. "Sam, meet Jake," Krull said. I burst out laughing, and Krull's enormous, sensitive cat raced out of the room before I could apologize, belly swaying beneath him like a hammock.

*   *   *

When Krull told me he didn't have a lot of furniture, he hadn't been exaggerating. His living room was nearly as sparse as the building's lobby. There was nothing on the walls, nothing covering the parquet floor, nothing on top of the squat piece of office furniture he was using as a coffee table. The TV and VCR were perched uneasily atop black plastic crates against the wall, as was the stereo system. His CDs filled one cardboard box, his books another.

The couch did look comfortable, though, and the view out of the one, east-facing window was stunning. I walked up to it, stared out at the starless sky, the bright cars whizzing up FDR Drive with the East River below, yellow and red lights from the Queensboro Bridge and Roosevelt Island churning on its black surface.

It made me remember the Pacific Ocean at night and how, as a kid, I'd lay in bed listening to it in our Santa Monica apartment, realizing how close it was, how strong. I'd always think, if the ocean wanted to, it could swallow us whole, and it would scare me from sleeping.

I could hear Krull in the kitchen, pouring dry cat food into a bowl. "So did you just move here or what?"

"Not really."

"You just like the Spartan look?"

Krull came out of the kitchen. "It was sort of imposed on me."

"What do you mean?"

He sighed. "My last girlfriend asked me if she could redecorate the place. I said sure, why not? So she got rid of a bunch of my furniture and posters, stocked it full of nice stuff—antiques, oil paintings. You wouldn't recognize the apartment. Of course Jake was a little confused . . ."

"Did you get robbed?"

"Sort of," he said. "It hadn't been working out between us for a long time. About six months ago, I said maybe we should think about separating for a while. She said, 'Fine, no problem.' The next day, while I was at work, she moved out and took all the stuff. I'd paid for a lot of it too."

"And you haven't redecorated since."

"She left me that couch, the bed, my service revolver and Jake. I don't need much more than that. The only thing I really miss is my Iron Maiden poster. Had it since high school. Can I get you a beer or anything?"

I looked into his black eyes. "She didn't try to get custody of Jake?"

Krull smiled. "No. She hated Jake."

When I looked at my watch and saw it was well past two in the morning, I wanted to cover my wrist so Krull wouldn't notice the time. We had been sitting on his living room floor for more than an hour, nursing a couple of beers, listening to AC/DC, playing gin with a deck of cards he'd produced from a drawer in the so-called coffee table, and I'd felt relaxed for the first time since Valentine's Day.

Jake was sound asleep in my lap; he felt like some sort of fur-covered, vibrating boulder. I found him extremely therapeutic. If someone could market a synthetic version of Jake, they'd have quite a successful cottage industry. He beat the hell out of healing magnets.

Krull had been winning steadily for at least ten hands and I'd never particularly liked AC/DC, but still the whole situation was comforting. There was safety here—not only in Krull's warm, gigantic cat, but in his sparse bachelor's apartment, in his heavy metal record collection, in his deck of Bicycle playing cards, in his soft, dark eyes. Maybe he *was* a good-luck charm.

"Gin," Krull said as the lead singer shrieked "Honey! What'll you do for mo-ney?" out of the speakers and Jake dug a set of claws into my knee.

Krull collapsed onto his back and threw an arm over his face. I expected him to say something like, *You ready to turn in?* or *Big day tomorrow.* But he didn't. What he said was, "You suck at gin."

"I know," I said. "You want to play again?"

"Not really."

"Oh . . . Well, how about blackjack?"

"Look, I know you're scared. I'll stay here with you for as long as you like. I just don't feel like playing cards anymore."

I looked at him. "It's that obvious?"

"You wouldn't be human if you weren't scared."

What kind of a cop says things like that? Carefully, so as not to disturb Jake, I adjusted myself until I was lying next to him. My eyes were tired and sandy, but I kept them open and watched the white ceiling as I listened to the first lines of "You Shook Me All Night Long."

"What exactly are American thighs anyway?"

Krull's words slurred together dreamily. "In high school, three of my buddies and I formed an AC/DC tribute band called Hell's Bells. I played lead guitar."

I pictured the detective fifteen years younger and in skin-tight jeans, his wavy brown hair delinquent length, strutting across a stage, then leaning into a guitar solo as groupies pelted him with their bras. "Were you good?"

"I sucked worse than you suck at gin. We thought it would be a good way to meet girls and make money doing something we loved. But the problem was most girls hated AC/DC and we weren't good enough to make any money, so we basically just played in my garage and irritated everybody within earshot. Of course, it did piss off my father, which was the most important thing, anyway."

"Was your father a cop?"

"Hardly. He was—is—a research scientist at Columbia Presbyterian. He hates that I'm a cop. I think he'd be prouder of me if I were still in the AC/DC trib-ute band."

"What about your mom?"

"She died when I was twelve. Cancer. Which is sort of ironic because my father does cancer research."

"That must have been hard for you."

"It was . . . strange. Like somebody punching you in the face for no reason. You're just kind of standing there, going, 'What the hell?' "

"Like she disappeared into thin air." *Turned around with the camera on and got a shot of an empty swing.*

Krull looked at me.

"Wasn't it like that?" *She'd disappeared into thin air, poor little girl.*

"We were all in her hospital room, my dad, my little brother and me," he said. "She was intubated, and I re-member how the machine made her chest go up and down, like waves. It was so dependable, I figured it could keep her alive forever. Then my brother said he had to go to the bathroom, and my dad went with him. And all of a sudden I got this weird feeling . . . like I should be looking up at her instead of down. When they came back, I pointed to her body and I said, 'She's not in there anymore.' My dad looked at the monitors and told me I was right."

I rolled over on my side so I was facing him. Jake grunted and plodded over to the couch.

"She didn't disappear," he said. "I saw her go."

"John, can I ask you something?"

"Sure."

"Why did you become a cop?"

"Because I wanted to help people."

"Can you help me?"

He smiled his sad, warm smile. "I thought you'd never ask."

Beneath my skin, some powerful, nameless emotion flexed itself and expanded until I felt like crying. Tears even began to well up in my eyes, but before they could spill out I leaned forward, just a few inches, and kissed him.

Krull's body was big and dense and solid, and when he was on top of me I felt protected from the world. That hadn't happened to me before. I'd always felt vulnerable during sex, like I was being dangled at the edge of a steep cliff by the hands of someone I didn't trust.

I wanted to tell him how good it felt, the weight of him. But I never liked to talk during sex and he wasn't saying anything either, which relieved me because I'd laughed more than once at guys who had tried to provide commentary when we were fucking.

In fact, neither one of us had said a word since the kiss. We'd just fallen into each other on the living room floor as the last song on the AC/DC CD—"Rock and Roll Ain't Noise Pollution"—came to an end. Jake may have walked by, I wasn't sure. But otherwise there was nothing in the room. Nothing but the sounds of breathing and movement and clothes coming off.

I ran my hands down the length of his smooth back, and let them rest at the love handles, thinking how reassuringly human and sexy it was that he had love handles—not like Nate, whose waist felt like a professionally wrapped gift, all tight and impersonal.

That was the last real thought I had, because as he moved up inside me, my head went as empty as the walls of his apartment.

At some point, I opened my eyes and watched his face. It looked so good up close—not bloated or babyish or wide angle, like faces up close usually did. Beautiful.

An electric sensation shot up my spinal column and I cried out, I actually screamed, before the motion sped up and he groaned and shuddered and finally collapsed on top of me.

I thought, *That's the second time he's made me scream.*

"I hope no one called the cops," he said, and we both started to laugh.

We made love once more in his bed. I fell asleep feeling like someone who'd eaten a gourmet meal after subsisting on drive-through for years.

When I woke up the next morning with Jake sniffing my face and dull sunlight trickling through the one bedroom window, it took me several seconds to remember where I was, until I saw Krull's dark hair on the pillow next to mine. His clock radio went off as if on cue. Then he mumbled something that sounded like "branch" and hit the snooze button.

It was six-thirty. I knew I had to get up, put my clothes on, call in sick at Sunny Side, but I didn't want to move. I felt vaguely depressed that Krull's arms hadn't been around me when I'd awakened. We'd fallen asleep curled into each other's bodies. Exactly when had he rolled over and turned his back?

I watched Jake climb onto Krull's pillow, then pat him dully but persistently on the back of the head. "Stupid cat." The detective definitely wasn't a morning person.

He stretched, rolled over onto his back and, to my surprise, smiled. He grabbed my hand and placed it flat across his forehead. "You've sapped me for the day," he said. "I'm no good."

I didn't reply, just leaned over and kissed him on the mouth.

"Well, maybe I'm good for one thing." He pushed Jake to the floor and pulled me on top of him.

Seconds later, the clock radio went off again. I felt him freeze beneath me and I groaned. "Hit the button."

But Krull didn't move.

I would've reached over and turned the radio off myself, if the news announcer hadn't been reporting the discovery of another child's body. This time it was an eight-year-old girl who had been found in a foot-locker left alongside a row of garbage cans just a few blocks from my apartment. Like Sarah Grace Flannigan, she had been strangled. No mention was made of her eyes.

"Why didn't you tell me?" I asked, as Krull pulled on his worn khakis.

"You were keyed up. I didn't think it would do you any good to hear we'd found another kid."

"Another *strangled* kid. With . . . something done to the eyes."

"Yes." He buttoned up a white shirt, selected a burgundy tie with wide, mustard-colored stripes. "I was planning on telling you eventually."

"Sure you were."

"I figured, after we'd had a beer, relaxed a little . . . But, um . . . you know, other things took precedence. I didn't think you were going to seduce me."

I felt an awful burn in my chest—a hard question, needing to be asked.

"What?" said Krull.

"He killed the girl in the footlocker because of me, didn't he? If he hadn't seen me at the river—"

"No," Krull said. "He killed Graham two years ago, and then for some reason he started again with Sarah Flannigan. The same thing that made him kill Sarah— *that* was what made him kill the footlocker girl. *Not you.*" His words were quick and defensive. And they had the sound of having been said—or thought— before.

Krull unlocked his bedstand drawer, pulled out a

gun and a shoulder holster and put them on. After he'd covered it all up with a polyester maroon sport coat, he turned around and faced me. "You know how to use a gun?" he said.

"Of course not."

"I'm going to show you later. Don't leave. There's coffee in the kitchen and food. I'll be back really soon. I just have to pick up a car and check a few things out." From the blazer he'd worn the previous night, Krull removed the e-mail I'd given him and jammed it into a briefcase.

"Can't I do anything? Can't I come with you?"

"Just try and relax. Spend some time with Jake. Watch TV."

"But not the news, right?"

"The press always gets things wrong. That's why I let Art deal with them. He's got a better sense of humor about it than I do."

He paused for a moment and smiled at me. "You know, you look really good in my bed." His eyes glittered and I wanted to say: *Please don't go. Just stay here and I'll stay here and neither one of us will ever leave and Jake will be happy and I'll be happy and I'll never steal your furniture I promise.*

But I didn't. I just winked at him. "Someday I'm going to help you pick out some new clothes," I said.

Jake's bowl was empty, so I found his dry food in one of the kitchen cupboards and filled it up. As soon

as the cat heard the faint creak of the cupboard door, he
came clambering into the room, his paws thudding on
the wood floors. Jake's step was unusually heavy, even
for an animal of his size. If Elmira had been Krull's
downstairs neighbor, she would have already sued
both him and the cat.

Jake buried his head in his bowl, tearing at his dry
food enthusiastically like a dog, without looking up.
"You do like your breakfast, don't you, big guy?" I
freshened up his water bowl and placed it next to him.
"Don't forget to breathe, okay?"

I watched him polish off the contents of his food
bowl, then lap at his water noisily. He was a weird cat.
There was nothing even remotely feline about him.

I wandered back into Krull's bedroom. Being alone
in here wasn't so bad. I had an urge to open up his
closet, bury my face in all of his awful suits.

I was wearing the top sheet, which I'd wrapped
around my naked body like a toga. I figured I should
put my clothes back on and make the bed—at least it
would be something to do. I didn't feel like listening to
the TV or the radio, didn't want any contact with the
world outside. Contact with the bed, on the other hand,
I could handle.

Just after I unfastened the toga and let it drop to the
floor, the phone rang. I smiled. Krull had probably just
arrived at work, and his timing was impeccable. "Hi."

A voice floated back—a thin whisper, barely audible. "Samantha."

"John? Why are you whispering?"

"It isn't John." A small, bitter laugh, with no tone behind it, just air.

I gritted my teeth and said nothing.

"Schoolteacher Samantha . . . They're best when they're little."

"Who the fuck is this?" Of course I knew who it was. By now I knew.

"More little corpses. Then little you." The whisper was toneless, genderless, but strong, like an icy wind.

"Leave me alone."

"Have you ever touched a corpse's skin? It's cold and stiff. Perfect."

"I said—"

"Soon you'll feel like that. Touch your face."

I let the receiver drop back into the cradle, put my clothes on fast, then pulled Krull's blanket around me. Suddenly, my whole body felt deeply, painfully cold.

When Krull showed up about half an hour later, I hadn't moved from the floor. I heard his voice in the kitchen. "Where are you, the bedroom?" But I couldn't answer.

The minute he walked in, and asked, "What's wrong?" I jumped up and threw my arms around him.

"What happened?"

I took a deep breath and told him about the phone call.

"Right after I left?" he asked.

"About ten minutes. I thought it was you, so I picked it up."

"Did anyone call after that?"

"No . . . No one. I've been . . . sitting on the floor."

He picked up the phone.

"Who are you calling?"

"I'm going to dial star sixty-nine. He was probably calling from a blocked cell or a pay phone nearby, since he seemed to know you were alone. But who knows? It's worth a shot."

I watched him tap in the digits, watched him listen as the recorded voice listed the origin of the last received call. Slowly, his face went white.

"What is it?" I asked.

His voice flat beyond emotion, Krull recited the seven digits. It was my phone number.

We drove to my apartment in the unmarked police car that Krull had picked up at the station. It was beige, a few years old, American. It reminded me of Sal's Cavalier, which reminded me of blood.

I was wearing the same outfit I'd had on the day before, plus Krull's leather jacket to replace my ruined coat. It was the same one he'd been wearing when I'd first seen him at Sunny Side, and it felt good—protective, like strong arms around me. I wanted him to insist I keep it.

Art Boyle and a couple of squad cars were going to meet us outside the building. Then they'd either capture Mirror Eyes, or, at the very least, recover whatever evidence he'd left. The thought of his mouth on my receiver still made me cringe, but otherwise I was weirdly energized. *I'm working with the cops*, I kept thinking. "So am I an operative or an informant?" I asked Krull.

He didn't reply.

Krull hadn't wanted me to come with him, but I'd insisted. If he was angry about it, I didn't care. I didn't want to be alone again in his empty bedroom, worrying about what was happening to him outside.

The detective stared straight ahead with his teeth clenched, his jaw squared. I examined his profile. He hadn't shaved that morning, and faint black stubble highlighted the strong bones in his face. His eyelashes *were* beautiful, I realized. Soft and lush and sweet looking—not like the hard stubble, not like the prominent bump at the center of his nose. "How'd you break it?"

"Break what?"

"Your nose."

He looked at me. "I did something I shouldn't have. Something that was not safe, that I had no business doing. If I had stayed where I should've stayed, it never would've happened." I knew he was trying to sound stern and punishing, but he wasn't doing a very good job of it.

"Oooh, what did you do? Get into a brawl with some skel?"

He let out a short, involuntary laugh. *"Skel?"*

"Yeah, you know. A skel. A perp. A jailhouse Johnny."

"Where do you get these expressions?"

"Jailhouse Johnny come at you with a shiv?"

"Not quite, Mickey Spillane."

"Some rat fink squealing punk wouldn't give up the goods, so you had to leave the negotiating to Mr. Fist and his five little friends?"

"You have really been watching some crappy cop shows."

I could tell he wasn't angry anymore, so I put my hand on his thigh and squeezed it. "It ain't easy being the Man, huh?"

He put his hand on top of mine. "You bet it ain't easy, dollface," he said. "But that's not how my nose got broken."

I looked at him. "Then what did you do that wasn't safe?"

"I jumped off our roof when I was seven years old. I was pretending to be Superman."

I smiled. "Ah."

"Broke my leg too, but that healed better."

We were about half a block away from my building; Krull pulled over to the curb. Through the rearview mirror, I watched a dark blue Impala slide in behind us, watched Art Boyle squeeze out of it and walk up to the driver's side window. "Freakin' car only gets AM radio, so I'm stuck listening to that freakin' all-news station that gets everything wrong."

"Since when do you say *freakin'*?" Krull asked.

"I'm a gentleman." He smiled at me. "There's five uniforms up in your apartment, Miss Leiffer, and they say nobody's there."

"Well, that's a relief." It wasn't, really.

"I bet we find lots of trace," Boyle replied, as if he'd been reading my mind. "You'd be amazed at what people leave behind, without even knowing it. Probably be able to get a full DNA sample from your phone."

I got out of the car. As we walked toward my building, I turned to Krull. "Hard to think of him as having DNA."

"Yeah, too human."

Inside my apartment, I saw three of the uniforms standing near the door, and I realized one of them was Rosy Cheeks, the gay-paranoid cop from the previous night. "You might want to keep away from my CD collection," I told him. "There's a lot of Liza in there."

"Huh?"

Near the coffee table, Krull and Boyle were speaking to two more officers—a Latin guy with an eagle tattoo on his arm and Rosy Cheeks' redheaded partner, Fiona. "Miss Leiffer," she said, "do you like your refrigerator? I notice it's a Kenmore, and I'm thinking of getting one."

Well, that was out of left field. "I don't keep a lot of

things in it other than coffee and leftover Chinese food."

"Mind if I take a peeksie?"

"This is a crime scene, not Macy's," Boyle said. "Go shopping on your own hours."

A crime scene. "To tell the truth," I said, "it feels kind of nice to talk about . . . kitchen appliances. It feels normal."

Fiona looked at Boyle.

"Knock yourself out," he said.

Krull put a hand on my shoulder. "Take your time. Look around, and see if anything seems out of place or different," he said. "If it does, just point it out, we'll collect it."

I paced the area, looking at the phone stand, the bookshelves, the positioning of the couch, TV, stereo. Everything was where I'd left it, including the cordless receiver at the center of the dinette table, next to Krull's business card. "That explains where he got your number," I said, pointing to the card.

Krull nodded. "Good detective."

I spotted the blinking light on my answering machine. "I didn't have any messages before."

"Let's give it a listen," Boyle said as Fiona moved towards the kitchen.

When he hit the button, I noticed the rubber glove on his hand, and it struck me as funny, this sterilized object in an apartment with dust bunnies under the couch.

The electronic voice said, "You have two messages."

"Probably from my mother. She's concerned I might
be a drug addict."

"Why?" Krull said.

I shrugged my shoulders. "She's a self-help author."

"Is your mother Sydney Stark-Leiffer?" said Boyle.
"I saw her on *Oprah*."

"New message. Three a.m.," said the machine.

Next came a female voice, but it didn't belong to
Sydney. It was small and trembling and, if I'd ever
heard it before, I couldn't place it. "Hello . . . Samantha." A sharp intake of breath. "You don't know me,
but you've . . . seen me. Your number was here, with
your name. He wrote it. He only writes down numbers
of people he . . . I need you to know I didn't kill them.
He did. I was afraid. I wanted to run away, but I
couldn't. Um, it's early in the morning. Meet me by the
river at . . . noon? At Shank's. I want to help you.
Please."

"Shank's Dredging and Construction," I said. *The
woman in the red dress*. Krull and I stared at each
other.

The call had come in five hours after Sal had been
shot, three hours after Yale and I had seen the man outside St. Vincent's. "It was a new message—not saved.
The only way he could have heard it is if he was in
here when she called."

"He probably didn't," Krull said. "We know he

called you at seven. That's four hours he would have had to—"

"New message. Six-thirty a.m.," the machine interrupted. Again, the caller was female, but older this time, and angry: "Young lady. I am calling from downstairs and this is *outrageous*. I know you are in there, and I know you are awake because I hear your boots clomping on those hardwood floors." *Elmira.* "If you do not take them off this moment, I am COMING UP THERE AND I MEAN IT!" I felt my jaw drop open.

Rosy Cheeks and the tattooed cop were pulling the couch across the room. And as it moved, the body that had been shoved underneath revealed itself like a sick, slow striptease: skinny legs first, then hips, chest, head. *Elmira.*

Krull said, "Turn around, Samantha."

My eyes went to the feet, to the acid green mules.

"Shit, man," said one of them. Rosy Cheeks, I think.

"Do not look!" Krull shouted.

I heard my own hollow gasp, saw blue-white skin, a torn green nightgown with a gaping dark bloodstain, a knife—*my kitchen knife*—submerged to the thick, pine hilt at the center of the stain. I saw eyes, wrenched open, pupils so huge and black that the whites were obscured. *No . . . not pupils. Hollow, empty sockets.*

"Shit, man, shit. My first corpse and it looks . . . looks . . . Help me . . ."

"Act like a man, for chris—"

"Sam, close your eyes!"

But I couldn't respond, couldn't move. Blackness crept into my field of vision, and I felt my knees start to buckle, saw the dusty wood floor rushing up to my face.

I was vaguely aware of a woman's voice in my kitchen. "Found something!" it said, half shout, half scream. As I lost consciousness, I realized it was Fiona. She must have opened my refrigerator.

13

Area Unsafe

"She's dead."

"Naw, look at her."

"I am lookin' at her and she ain't moving."

"She's just out, is all."

The first voice was male, the second female, and I didn't recognize either. I thought they were probably talking about Elmira, and I wanted to say, *Are you crazy? Didn't you see what was done to her?* But all that came out of my mouth was a groan.

"See, I tol' ya," said the man's voice. Slowly, I opened my eyes and let them adjust to bright lights. I felt big, gentle hands on my face, figured out they were attached to John Krull. "You okay?" he said.

"Sure, she's okay," said the voice of the man who stood over Krull's shoulder. He was thin and weathered with large dog eyes. A small, pale woman stood next to him. "We thought you was dead, honey," she said, and I recognized them as my next-door neighbors, the Schultzes—or the Schwartzes, I still wasn't sure—to whom I'd barely said anything more than *hi* during four years of living here. "Uh . . . Hi."

I realized we were in the lobby of my building. Someone must have carried me down—presumably Krull. I was on the floor, my head and shoulders propped up on his knees.

My eyes went to the vaguely familiar people who stood staring behind the Schultz/Schwartzes—people whose names I'd never heard; people I sometimes nodded at, maybe exchanged forgettable remarks with, but only about the weather, only if we happened to be sharing the elevator and only if the weather was in any way remarkable. Looking up at them now, I felt overexposed and kind of silly. "What happened?" I asked Krull.

"You passed out. I took you out of there."

"That I could've guessed."

He turned to my neighbors. "She's fine, everybody. Move along."

As the small group dispersed, I recalled the open mouth, the vacant, bloody sockets. I looked up into Krull's warm black eyes and shuddered. "Elmira . . ."

"I know."

"He just . . . scooped them out."

"Ssssh. Don't think about it."

I struggled into a sitting position and stared at him. "A woman's eyeballs were in my refrigerator! You can't not think about that."

"I know. But for now, you've got to try and focus on other things."

"Where were they, the butter tray? The fucking *crisper*? Jesus . . ."

"Let me take you down the street, buy you a cup of tea."

"A cup of tea," I repeated stupidly. I wanted to say more, but my thoughts were moving so quickly . . .

Graham, Sarah, the girl in the footlocker. Elmira, barely bigger than a child herself . . .

More little corpses. Then little you.

I was on my feet, pushing the glass lobby door open and running outside, past the cluster of police cars, past the small group of gawking pedestrians, past the scaffolding on a neighboring building and then directly under a ladder, the first time I'd ever done something so blatantly unlucky. Keinahora. *Fuck that. You can't get rid of the evil eye once it's here, and it's here. It's in the refrigerator.*

I kept running to the edge of my block, out into the avenue and in front of cars, with their horns blaring and their tires screeching as I stood at the center of one of New York City's clogged and dangerous arteries, thinking, *Go ahead and kill me. Run me over and kill me, and then I'll be the last little corpse.*

Somebody yelled, "Get the fuck outta the fuckin' street, ya fuckin' psycho!"

I heard Krull's voice calling my name and then I felt his arms around me, pulling me back onto the sidewalk and holding me there as I struggled, body trembling, breath cutting through my lungs like that thick-handled knife.

Krull pressed me to his chest. "It's okay. It's okay," he said. I could feel his chin moving on top of my head, the curve of his warm neck, his heart beating as hard as mine through his heavy coat.

"He's going to kill one of my kids."

"He won't. I promise."

I pulled away, looked up at his face. "What if I had called the police Friday night as soon as I got back to the box office? You'd have caught him. Sal wouldn't have gotten shot. Elmira would still be alive, and so would that little girl—"

"You think they would've sent out even *one* squad car because you said you saw two people dropping an ice chest in the river—one of them a disappearing guy with mirrored eyes?"

"If I'd insisted enough."

He shook his head. "Anyone you spoke to would have tried to humor you like I did."

"It's my fault."

"No. It's mine."

"Give me a break."

"Do you know why I came to your classroom with Genovese and his dog puppet?"

"Because you were interested in community service."

He looked into my eyes long enough to make me feel uncomfortable. "Two years ago, our unit caught that other case—the boy in the Tenth Street Dumpster," he said finally. "He was such a small kid for six. His name was Graham, which is my younger brother's name. My brother used to be small for his age too, and I was big, so I was always sticking up for him at school. I'd scare off some bully, and Graham would say, 'You saved my life, Johnny,' because he's always been kind of melodramatic like that . . ."

A guy on a cell phone passed us. "Whatever, we don't do magazine events!" he shouted into the tiny piece of machinery, gesturing so emphatically that he knocked Krull in the back. I pulled him closer.

"My brother became a scientist like our dad."

I watched him swallow to smooth out his voice, and I could almost hear the words as they entered his mind: *What can you become in six years?*

"I told Graham's family we were going to find the murderer. Staked my life on it. Amanda said it was stupid to say that, and she was right—"

"You tried."

"I went to your classroom with Genovese because I wanted to look into the faces of some of the kids I'd let down."

I moved closer, bringing my hands up to his face, running them lightly against the beard stubble, across the nose he'd broken playing Superman.

His eyes glistened slightly, from the cold or from emotion, or from a combination of the two. "We did discover one thing about Graham. He'd been sneaking onto Internet chatrooms, using his older sister's account. It could be where he met the killer."

"He was young to be doing that."

"He was advanced. Spent all his time on the computer and putting together these intricate model airplanes. He wanted to be an engineer. At six. His parents said he'd tested as a genius."

I swallowed hard, thinking of Sarah Grace Flannigan—half Graham's age and too young to have tested as anything. *What can you become?*

"I called Graham's folks when I went back to the station this morning, to double-check the screen name. His sister had gotten a new address after he was killed. But when I logged on with her old password, I saw that it was still open, still receiving mail."

I stared at him.

"ER425160. The numbers are jersey numbers—hers and her two best friends'—from junior varsity basketball. ER stands for the team name, the Edison Royals."

"John," I said. "Can we please just nail this fucker?"

I was relieved to hear that Krull had called in absent for me, placed Sunny Side under surveillance and given Terry my temporary NYPD cell phone number so he could call me in case of emergency. It was one less thing to worry about on a dauntingly long list.

Near the top of that list—just under my butchered neighbor—was the wire. I was about to be fitted with one—a real, FBI-style listening device, which I would wear to meet the woman who had called me. *Meet me by the river at noon,* she'd said. *I want to help you.*

Well, sweetheart, you are going to help me. You're also going to help some NYPD detectives catch your freaky boyfriend, whether you want to or not.

In less than two hours, I would meet a blond murder accomplice at an abandoned construction site, wearing a wire and a bulletproof vest. It was so over-the-top B movie, I had to say it out loud.

"You going to start talking about skels again?" asked Krull.

"Skels," Boyle snorted. I was sitting in the back of a disguised police van ("Gordy's Plumbing" was painted on the side) with Krull and Boyle, plus one other detective unit of three, finishing up the coffee and bagels that the friendliest of the new detectives, Munro, had provided. Munro was around Boyle's age, but more or less his physical opposite—thin and sinewy with sharp, serious features, his silver hair tied back in a ponytail.

"Some of the DAs use that expression—skels," Munro said. "Makes 'em feel like tough guys."

"I've never heard it," said Krull. "They probably say

it around you because you look like Clint Eastwood and served in Vietnam."

"You really think I look like Eastwood?"

"Lotta people tell me I look like Nick Nolte," said Boyle.

One of the other detectives chuckled. A short, laconic guy named Pierce. "Yeah, and I look like Cher."

"Fuck you, Pierce, you fuckin' Scorpio."

"What happened to *freakin'*?" said Krull.

"Are you going to fit me with the wire?" I asked him. From what I knew of wires—which came entirely from late-night cop show reruns—the transmitter fit into one's crotch or cleavage, and the wire part ran across the back and down the arm. I couldn't imagine any of these guys putting one on me.

"Not much fitting is needed," Munro said. He opened the glove compartment, produced a tiny, expensive-looking cell phone and handed it to me.

"If her boyfriend shows up and tries to kill me, I'm just supposed to *call* you guys?"

All of them laughed, which made me angrier.

"That's the wire," Krull said. "It's got the transmitter inside. Just clip it onto your bag and you're set."

I frowned at the device. "How very James Bond."

"It works great," Boyle said. "We park this boat where we can see you, put the receiver through the roof vent, you're covered."

"Nobody finds out," Munro added. "Most people

still expect you to be wearing them on your body, so if she wants to frisk you, you're okay."

I pictured this terrified little woman frisking me. "You sure?"

"We've been using these almost exclusively for the past couple of years, and I've never seen anyone figure it out." Munro gave me a smile. "You're going to do great," he said.

"Yeah," I said. "I have to."

"Showtime," said Boyle.

I looked at my watch, and indeed it was. Eleven forty-five, or, as we'd say in the box office, fifteen minutes to curtain. I was going to talk to her, get her to give me as much information as possible about her boyfriend's whereabouts. The cops in the van would relay that information to another, on-call unit of detectives, which would hopefully have Mirror Eyes's ass in custody by the time Blondie and I were through with our chat. If by some chance he showed up at the site, there were six sharpshooters positioned around the area. I even had a code word to say. Freezing. If anything freaked me out, all I had to say was "I'm freezing." Or "It's freezing out here," and every heat-packing civil servant within wire range would come running. Presumably.

I glanced at Krull. How tired he looked, with those purplish half circles pressing against the bridge of his nose.

"Time to gain five pounds in two minutes," said Munro, and handed me a bulletproof vest.

I put it on over my shirt, then pulled on my sweater and that comforting leather jacket. "Does this make me look fat?" I asked Krull.

"It's completely unnoticeable."

"But what if she frisks me?"

"Tell her you bought it from a spy store," said Boyle. "You were concerned for your safety."

The vest was weighty and stiff—it reminded me of the lead aprons that dentists give you to wear during X-rays. "This thing is heavy. How come people are always running in them in the movies? I can barely stand up."

"You get used to the feeling," said Munro. "Sort of like wearing a backpack—only the weight is more evenly distributed. Ever go hiking?"

"Not if I can help it."

Krull said, "Before you go, can I talk to you, alone?"

I followed him out of the van, ignoring Pierce's wolf whistle, glad Krull had asked because I wanted to be alone with him, too. I didn't want to *talk* to him alone, though. I just wanted to *look* at him alone, once more for good luck. We headed up half a block, to a closed storefront behind a parked SUV, and I stared up at his face, pale in the flat sunlight.

"You're sure you want to do this?" he said.

"Absolutely."

"Because we can still head right in there ourselves and arrest her—"

"And give him a chance to get away? No fucking way."

Krull looked at me. "You really kick ass, you know that?"

I ran my eyes down the length of his body. "That is such a bad outfit."

"Who wants to get blood on an Armani? Show me a well-dressed detective, I'll show you a guy with the wrong set of priorities."

"So . . . when all this is over and you take me out to dinner, you're not going to dress like that?"

"I'll put on the hand-tailored suit my dad got me for Christmas, if it'll make you happy." Krull tilted my face up to his and gave me the softest kiss imaginable. "But I'd rather stay in."

As I turned and left him there, I kept it all in my mind: his bad clothes, his wide, strong back, his soft lips and, most important, the way he'd just looked at me, dry eyed and smiling, as if we'd both be safe forever.

"Out of curiosity," Munro had asked in the van, "did you ever go to that construction site before Valentine's Day?"

"No."

"What made you decide to stop there, then?"

"Sometimes I just do things like that."

As I made my way to the construction site, I tried again to figure out the answer to his question. Then I recalled how, twenty years earlier, I'd left my friends from Brownies to take a shortcut down that deserted street.

"Samantha, where you going?"

"I want to go home a different way."

"We're supposed to stay on the busy streets, remember?"

"And we're supposed to look in both directions before we cross."

"I don't care."

"Well, I do."

"You would, Tracy. You're a scaredy-cat. All you guys are big chickens."

"Am not!"

"Am not!"

"Am not!"

"Are so. And I should know 'cause I'm a brave girl."

"Says who?"

"Says my daddy."

"You don't have a daddy."

"Samantha thinks she has a daddy!"

"Samantha's crazy!"

I'm not crazy. Sometimes we just do things like that. We listen to the wrong voices in our heads, we take the wrong turns, walk down the wrong streets and meet men in Pintos. We borrow big, hooded coats from the

*wrong people to keep warm in a cold car, we go to the
wrong apartment to complain about noise, we turn our
backs on our children just for a minute, just to get a
camera out of a bag . . .*

"Testing, one two three," I said, not really to test the
wire but to interrupt my thoughts.

Up ahead by no more than a few car lengths loomed
the tops of the three piles of cement blocks, and I
hoped the men in the van had heard me. I crossed fingers on both hands, held my breath and counted to
eleven for good luck. *Okay, that's enough compulsive
behavior for one day.*

Before I slid under the fence, I told myself to calm
the fuck down and act like someone else, someone
without such an imagination, without so many nightmares. After all, nightmares are a luxury when you're
wide-awake and sliding under a fence, carrying a wire
that may or may not work. And crossing your fingers
is pointless when you're about to meet a woman who
dropped a dead little girl in the river.

On the other side of the fence, the first thing I noticed was the white, rusted trailer with the broken sign
in front: "RK AND RIDE." I'd assumed she'd be waiting in the trailer, but I saw nothing through the windows. "Hello?" I said.

No answer.

I spun around, eyes scanning the site. I didn't see

any sharpshooters. *You're not supposed to see sharp-shooters. That's the whole point.*

I looked at the piles of cement blocks, and realized I had no idea what lurked behind them. I had assumed that they marked the end of the construction site, but that wasn't necessarily true. There could be another entrance on the other side. If the trailer had two doors, the man and woman could have gone through that entrance and into the trailer, hidden by the stacks, and exiting—ice chest in tow—through the southern door, where I'd seen them. Or they could have left the ice chest in the trailer days earlier, then returned on Valentine's Day to dispose of it.

Either way, it could explain how they seemed to materialize out of nowhere.

I got my face up between the nearest two and peered into the tiny space. Around twenty additional feet of empty asphalt stretched out to meet a tall, wooden fence on the other side. I had to change positions a couple of times before I could see the far corner of the metal bordering fence. But sure enough, it had been folded back. Another entrance.

Beneath the vest, my shoulders started to relax. The place seemed so empty, and I didn't hear any footsteps. I couldn't imagine hearing any in the future either, and it gave me an odd sense of relief.

I backed up, inhaling the sweet, pasty smell of damp concrete, the residue of some quick rain I'd never noticed, pulling the leather jacket closer to my chest. *She's not going to show.*

"Hello?"

The voice sounded so much like my own that, at first, I thought maybe it was some sort of delayed echo.

But then she said, "Samantha?" and I knew she was in the trailer.

I stood in the doorway and saw her sitting on the floor, wearing a long green coat. *Dressed for the weather this time.*

She had clean, gold hair and a face I'd seen somewhere before. *Why is she sitting on the floor? Is she afraid if she stands she'll be seen through the windows?*

"You're here," she said. "I'm glad."

The trailer was nearly empty, with a thick coat of gray clinging to what little was in it—a broken office chair in the corner, a metal-edged counter that may have once been used as a desk, the shell of a filing cabinet, linoleum—so you couldn't tell anything's real color. Grime from the city air: car exhaust, stirred-up dust, remnants of dead, decomposing things. Amazing how it could conquer a whole place like this, with no one around to intervene.

I crouched down and put myself on the woman's level, the way you would with a shy child. "You look familiar. Have we met before?"

"People tell me that." Her eyes were very, very blue,

and her skin was pale and smooth. "Help me, Samantha."

"Nobody helped Sarah Flannigan." *No, you're not supposed to say that. Be nice and get her to talk.*

A tear began to leak down her cheek.

"I'm sorry," I said. "I didn't mean that."

"Yes, you did, but it's okay because you don't understand. Not yet." The woman stood up, and she was taller than I remembered. We stared at each other across the dark stretch of trailer, with the winter sun streaming in behind her like a dying spotlight. *You look so familiar.*

I remembered her in her sleeveless dress, remembered her shaking back. "You were scared. When I saw you, with the ice chest, your arms . . . you were crying then too."

She nodded.

"Why were you dressed like that?"

She wiped away the tear, watched me for several seconds without speaking, as if she were having difficulty discerning me from the rest of the dark, grimy trailer. "I wanted," she said, "to be as cold as Sarah."

What could I do, but let her take my hand, let her draw me out the northern door of the trailer and into the cold air on the hidden side? It was the same here—a little cleaner, without all those broken cement chunks. It seemed quieter, if that was possible.

What if the sharpshooters couldn't see me? I started

to suggest we leave, go somewhere, get a cup of coffee, but the woman put a finger to her lips.

I glanced over her shoulder for just a second, so as not to draw attention, looked fast and hard at the wooden fence and thought *see me, see me, see me.* Then back into her blue, blue eyes. *Are those colored contacts?*

"I wanted to die that day. Like her."

"I understand."

"I know you do," she said.

"Who is he? Why little kids?"

"They're the right size."

"For what?"

The woman moved closer to me, placed both hands on my shoulders. In the course of conversation, we'd switched places, and now the trailer was behind her like a backdrop from some cheap slasher film. Her delicate face was in the foreground; the face of the film's doomed heroine. *They are colored contacts.*

"Did you ever want to get rid of your stale, old, rotting body?" she said. "They make you so pretty for your funeral."

Suddenly, I remembered where I'd seen her before.

"You and I, we're standing here rotting. We die more and more every day. That's what he says."

She was the woman in the camel coat, who had exited Ruby's when I was on my way into the Sixth Precinct to tell Krull about Peter Steele. The woman who had asked me for a light, who had screamed at me when I'd ignored her. *Hey, Patchwork Bag, I'm talking to you!*

"The eyes rot first," she said.

"You've been following me."

She opened her mouth as if to say, "No, I haven't," or "You must have me confused with someone." No words came out, though. Just a scream. She turned and ran from me, disappearing back through the trailer. *What the . . .*

Behind me, I heard heavy footsteps, Boyle's voice shouting, "Stop!"

She must have seen the surveillance van, or maybe she figured out the cell phone was a wire.

"Stop or I'll shoot!"

He'll never catch up with her. He's too damn heavy. I started after the woman myself when I heard a fire-cracker exploding, and something that felt like an invisible car knocked me off my feet and onto the pavement.

When I could breathe again, I realized I'd been shot. Bullets bounce off vests in movies, on cop shows, but not in real life. The bullet socks the air out of your lungs and throws you to the ground. *If it's this bad with a vest, could you imagine it without one? No, you couldn't because you'd be dead, but you're not dead now. You just. Can't. Move . . .*

I figured one of the cops had accidentally shot me. *Friendly fire. What a joke.*

"Hold your fucking fire!" Krull's voice. *Fucking fire. Fucking friendly fire . . .*

Firecrackers. Why were they still shooting?

John, I wanted to say. But I couldn't talk. I managed to half open my eyes, turn my head slightly. And for one moment, just before Krull got in front of me, I saw that the shooter wasn't a cop.

Mirror Eyes, standing by the wooden fence, with his black scarf and his long black coat and in his black-gloved hand, a black gun. *That's why she screamed. That's why she ran . . .*

He stopped shooting, began to raise his arms.

Krull leaned over me, put a hand on my neck. "Play dead," he said into my ear. As he stood and turned away, I closed my eyes.

"Drop your gun!" Krull said.

A long, heavy silence followed, in which the tiniest noises echoed, as if someone had turned up the volume on this whole strange scene. A hard-soled shoe, scraping against concrete. A seagull's cry. An ambulance siren, miles away.

Another gunshot.

I opened my eyes, saw Krull open fire, saw spent shells spilling onto the pavement. The man clutched his arm, but kept the gun out in front of him, kept shooting at Krull.

Where are the fucking sharpshooters? It's freezing, freezing, freezing.

I hadn't moved at all since I'd been shot. Not because of what Krull had said, but because I hadn't been able to. I was paralyzed, the way you are in a dream. The way I'd been in the Pinto.

Stock-still on the cold ground with wet concrete pushing into the side of my face, I saw Krull fall. Saw him clutch his neck and topple backwards, dropping his gun. I saw the blood, Krull's blood, pouring over his fingers and all I could think was, *Shot in the neck, shot in the neck.*

Krull's black eyes went wide, then closed as he lay there, still holding his throat, blood still pulsing over his long, gentle fingers.

Shot in the neck. I didn't care about playing dead, didn't care about anything but the fact of his bleeding.

A thick, tingling heat flooded into my arms and legs. I could move now, but in a weird, pitching way, like my legs were full of Novocain. I felt as if someone was hugging me and realized it was the vest.

I threw my body forward, on top of Krull's, put my hand over his face, over the razor stubble, over the broken nose. I felt his soft lips move under my hand, air pushing through them, mouthing a word with a *t* at the end. Maybe it was *Don't.*

In the distance, I saw Munro, Pierce and about six other cops running, but they were too far away to do anything, and he was starting back under the fence. I heard a few shots—sharpshooters, probably.

Krull was down, and here he was, Mirror Eyes,

scurrying under the fence like a rat on a subway rail. My voice came back: "You sick fuck!"

He stopped and stared at me, aimed the gun. I stared back at that half face, at those lifeless eyes over the black scarf. What was behind that scarf? What kind of nose, what kind of mouth? What if there was nothing there at all—no features, just flat skin? And what a strange image that was, what a strange image to be the last image ever to enter my mind . . .

Click.

Again. *Click.* Out of bullets. I felt Krull's breath faltering, felt his eyelids flutter.

I leaned back a little, grabbed Krull's gun off the ground and pointed it up, between those eyes.

"Wait!" The word was surprisingly clear behind the black scarf. Was it fear that made his voice pitch up like that, like the voice of a child?

Under my hand, Krull's face went still, and silence spread all around me, rushed into my ears, clouded my vision until all I could see were mirrored eyes in front of the barrel.

"*You* wait," I said. I pulled the trigger.

14

Souvenir Bruise

I couldn't stop staring at the nurse's name: Debbie Reynolds, RN. It was printed in red letters across the white plastic name tag she wore on her sky blue pantsuit, giving her broad chest a sort of patriotic look. We were in a tiny, single-bedded room at St. Vincent's, and she was trying to get me to relax enough to speak—probably using the hospital personnel equivalent of verbal judo, though I didn't know for sure, didn't care. I hadn't been able to say a word since I'd fired the gun.

"You've been through so much," Debbie Reynolds kept saying. "Don't you want to take a sip of water?"

Why didn't she at least call herself Deb or Deborah? Maybe Debbie was her full name, and her parents were the kind of witty sadists who name their kids Justin when their last name is Case, or Cherry when their last name is Baum. Maybe she had a brother named Burt.

"How about some apple juice? Your blood sugar's pretty low, and that might perk you right up."

I let my head roll back till I could see the faded Monet print on the wall behind me. Upside-down *Water Lilies*.

It felt so dark in here, even with those headachy fluorescent bulbs over the bed. There was a big window, but the blinds were closed and I couldn't get myself to ask Debbie to open them. The room probably faced a brick wall anyway, knowing my luck. My rotten luck. Finally meet a nice guy, somebody shoots him in the neck.

My back still ached from the gunshot. According to the doctor who had examined me, I'd soon have "a hell of a souvenir bruise" between my shoulder blades.

"You know you almost got him," said Debbie. "You are one plucky little gal, shooting at bad guys."

I wished I could crawl underneath the bed. Lay on the floor and hide forever from Debbie Reynolds, RN.

"So," she said. "This fellow was wearing those Magic Mirrors, huh?"

Fellow?

Who could blame his girlfriend for running away, fast as she did, without looking back? Boyle had chased her several blocks, then returned wheezing and sweating and even redder than usual, saying, "Oh fuck no," again and again, when he saw what had happened to Krull, to me. And when he saw that the shooter had just . . . disappeared.

"My daughter borrowed some of those Magic Mirrors from one of her girlfriends," Debbie was saying. "Got herself a nasty case of pinkeye, just in time for the school play."

Debbie blinked at me a few times. "I bet you want to cry, don't you?"

I shook my head, because I couldn't cry. All I could do was replay the scene in my mind.

Mirror Eyes, staring at me as I squeezed the trigger.

The force of the shot, knocking my arm into its socket.

The gun dropping out of my hand, clattering to the ground.

Concrete, socking me in the back of the head.

Next to me, Krull's face, chalky and still, bright red seeping into his collar.

I'd lain there, hurting too much to move, until I heard the paramedics' sirens.

Krull was rushed to the hospital, but the man had run into an alley and disappeared, leaving some blood—Krull had tagged him in the arm—but nothing else. Cops later found an old, open manhole in the alley, a tarp thrown over the top, nothing inside but more blood. Obviously he'd hid there, like a rat, until it was safe to leave.

How could I have shot at him and missed?

According to the paramedics, I had a mild concussion from hitting my head on the ground. They'd asked me my name, and the current president's name, and even though I'd appeared to know the answers, I hadn't said a word. So they'd gurneyed me into the ambulance and driven me to St. Vincent's for observation.

"That detective is going to be fine," said Debbie.

"How the hell do you know?" The words flew out, along with tears. I was crying now, and Debbie was leaning in, putting both of her big arms around me, letting me cry on her clean blue uniform.

"He's still in surgery," I said. "He's been in surgery for a long time, and how can you say he's going to be fine when he was shot in the fucking neck?"

"He is going to be fine," said another female voice. "Because if he's not I'll be pissed. And you don't want to piss off a woman with postpartum hormones and a gun."

I looked up, saw Boyle standing in the doorway with a slim, sandy-haired woman wearing gray NYPD sweats and a badge around her neck. "Hi, Miss Leiffer, this is—" said Boyle, but I didn't need an introduction.

"You're the third partner."

She walked up to the bed and stuck out her hand. "Amanda Patton."

"Congratulations," I said, still crying a little. "Boy or girl?"

*　　*　　*

It was a boy. Patton and her husband had named him John—after her father, not Krull. But that didn't stop me from crying again as soon as I heard the baby's name.

"I'm sorry," I said, as Patton opened her handbag, and handed me a Kleenex.

"Do you have any idea how much I've cried since John was born? Between the lack of sleep and the post-partum and the breastfeeding, which is really hard—nobody ever tells you that—and then *this* . . . But Krull's going to be fine. He's strong and tough. It's not like he's a six-pound baby who's starving to death because his mother can't even get her fucking milk to let down."

Boyle cleared his throat.

Debbie had left the room. I was sitting up in bed in my pink hospital gown, with Patton in the chair and Boyle standing next to her. I looked at these two people, whom I barely knew, and felt such a deep longing that I couldn't even cry anymore. I missed my clothes. I missed that damn leather jacket.

"John will live," I said.

Neither of them asked which John I was talking about.

After a while, we all got thirsty, so Patton went looking for a vending machine.

"What was the deal with those sharpshooters?" I asked Boyle.

"They were positioned, just couldn't get a clear shot."

When I tried sitting up straighter, I felt a vicious yank between my shoulder blades. "Well, he did pretty good."

"The more targets you have, the easier it is to hit one," Boyle said, as Patton returned to the room with three cans of orange soda.

"I heard the fuckwad bled a little," she said.

"Are you guys running tests on the blood?"

"It's pretty corrupted," said Boyle, "And even if it wasn't, we probably wouldn't have anything to match it with."

I looked at him.

"He washes those bodies clean—including your neighbor, Mrs. Bean. Nothing under her nails. Not a stray fiber on her."

"Did he give her a makeover?" asked Patton.

He shook his head. "Probably not enough time."

"A makeover?"

"This guy makes . . . improvements on the corpses," Boyle said. "Maybe he feels guilty about taking their eyes—I don't know. Johnny was the one talking to the profilers, and I don't much believe that shit anyway."

"Right, just astrology," said Patton.

"Hey, the moon is full and Mercury's out of retrograde during the Aquarius/Pisces cusp. Last time that happened was when we found Graham, so you tell *me* what to believe."

"There are other factors and you know it." Patton started to say more, but then she looked at me and stopped.

I thought of Elmira, thought of the child found dead on my block, thought of the other gruesome discoveries yet to be made since I'd locked eyes with him on Valentine's Day. *More little corpses, then little you.*

"What kind of improvements did he make?" I asked.

"Weird ones," Patton said. "Sarah's nails were painted to match her purple pants, and somebody put her hair in pigtails. There were freckles drawn on Graham's face with an indelible pen."

"John never mentioned that."

"The last girl, in the footlocker?" said Boyle. "He dyed her hair yellow. Looks like he may have used some kind of paint, mixed with water. The funeral home's going to have a hell of a time getting it out."

Patton looked down at her hands. "I'm sure they'll have a closed casket."

"That reminds me," said Boyle. "I gotta call Forensics."

After he left, Patton gestured towards the closed blinds. "Mind if I open them?"

"Please."

She pulled the cord, revealing more darkness on the other side of the window. A brick wall.

"Figures," I said.

"At least you have some privacy. You wouldn't believe how many reporters are out there."

Patton returned to the chair, collapsed in it. She put her face in her hands, and for a minute I thought she might be crying. But when she lifted her head to talk, I saw that her eyes were dry, her voice smooth. "John Krull let me beat him at arm wrestling. My first day on the job, in front of the whole squad."

I looked at her.

"Here I am the first female detective in the precinct, and everybody's staring at me like I'm some kind of space alien with tits, so of course I find the strongest-looking one of them and challenge him to arm wrestle."

"Why?"

"I have no idea why I do these things. But before I know it, there's this huge crowd around us, and everybody's betting on Krull. He doesn't know me from a crack in the ceiling, and his own partners have put up fifty dollars apiece against me, but still he lets me win. Can you believe that?"

I smiled, because actually, I could.

Just then, Boyle returned, his face squinted up like he was trying to determine the origin of an unpleasant odor.

"So?" Patton asked.

"Miss Leiffer, do you remember the substance covering the eyes of the doll in the Schoolteacher Barbie ad?"

My jaw clenched up. "Whose blood was it?"

"Nobody's."

"Excuse me?"

"Acrylic paint." He turned to Patton. "Can you imagine? The guy jimmies kids' eyes out, but when he wants to scare Miss Leiffer, he gets squeamish and fakes it with paint?"

"There was . . . paint in the girl's hair," I said.

Boyle nodded. "What they're doing now is looking at different brands of acrylic paint after they've dried, trying to find the best match for the color found on the ad. The closest one's called Black Cherry, brand name Liquitine."

"Who's that used by, artists?" Patton asked.

"Sure, but it's also real popular with . . ." Boyle's voice trailed off.

Nurse Debbie Reynolds stood in the doorway, arms crossed over her chest like thick ropes. There was a doctor behind her—a tall middle-aged woman with glasses and a white coat and tired brown hair. "Detective Krull is out of surgery," the doctor said.

"Is he going to be okay?"

"That's anyone's guess right now. The bullet didn't hit anything but muscle, but he's lost quite a bit of blood and we had to intubate him." For a second, I thought she'd said *incubate*.

"He's in Intensive Care."

"Can we visit him?" I asked.

"You'll need to get the attending physician to discharge you first, and no more than one in the room at a time and . . ."

"And?" Patton said.

"And . . . it might be . . . a bit upsetting to look at him."

Boyle coughed. It was the only sound in the room.

Typically, only blood relatives were allowed in Intensive Care, but Krull's father was at a conference in Russia and difficult to reach, and his brother couldn't get a flight out from Seattle until the next day. So by default we achieved family status—his two partners and last night's lay.

The overhead lights were dim in Krull's Intensive Care room, and thick curtains blocked the floor-to-ceiling windows that overlooked the nurses' station. There were two armed guards on the other side of his door and, in the waiting room just outside the unit, a guy from the Police Benevolent Association, a woman from Internal Affairs and—before three orderlies escorted them out—a few of the more persistent tabloid reporters, all waiting for Detective John Krull to open his eyes or die.

You'd never know that here, though, in this quiet room, with its dull lights and softly blinking medical equipment, where only one conscious person was allowed at a time. Here, the only sound was that of Krull's ventilator.

At first I'd found it comforting, that deep, echoing gasp—like En's yoga breathing—and I'd liked the way it made Krull's chest rise and fall so reliably. But then a nurse had told me that the machine was doing his breathing for him, thus weakening his lungs, and the sooner they weaned him off it, the better his chances for survival.

I'd been standing next to Krull's bed for the past ten minutes—watching him the way you'd watch a baby sleep, with that same awkward reverence. His neck was heavily bandaged and his soft lips, taped clumsily to the long, plastic air tube, were chapped and grayish. But other than that, and the IVs that ran into each arm, Krull looked like he was sleeping.

I wondered how many people had died in this room. You could smell death here, in snaking, antiseptic fumes. "Please live," I said.

I placed my hand over his. It felt cool and dry, almost inanimate.

The two big orderlies remove the reporters from the waiting room, arms grasping their backs as if they were old, drunken friends.

Patton turns to me and whispers, "I didn't think Krull should be handling this Ariel thing, to tell the truth."

"Why?"

"He's too much of a fucking sweetheart."

It couldn't have happened more than fifteen minutes ago. Yet in my mind, the reporters, the orderlies—even Patton and myself—seemed as static as magazine pictures. The room, the machinery keeping Krull alive—

this was reality. And it wasn't easy for my mind to stay in it for long.

I dragged a chair up to Krull's bedside and sat down, put my head next to his on the pillow. When I turned, I saw nothing but white bandages edged in dried blood.

One of the reporters has a pointy, pale face. He reminds me of a ferret. "You the girlfriend?"

Patton says, "Ignore him," but I stare anyway.

He leans forward in his chair, smiles. His teeth are tiny. "What was John like?"

My throat tightens. "Where do you get off using the past tense, asshole?"

The Internal Affairs woman stops typing. Police Benevolent lowers his magazine and stares. Patton leaves the room.

The reporter says, "Well, isn't he on life support?"

Don't say anything, don't say a word.

"Isn't he?" repeats the smiling ferret, but now Patton is back with the orderlies.

"Hey, don't I know you?"

I lifted my head. Standing over me was the surfer nurse from the emergency room.

"Remember me, from last night? It's totally okay if you don't. They move me around all the time."

Last night. It had been less than twenty-four hours. "How is Sal?"

"Much better. Amy took him home this morning. She is such a sweet girl."

"She does a great whip impersonation."

"Awesome. Anyways, I'm going to have to ask you to leave. The doctor's coming in, and we're gonna try and wean him off the ventilator."

I got up from the chair. "You think he's ready?"

"Ready as he's gonna be."

I'd hoped for a more positive response than that, which the nurse seemed to sense.

She put a hand on my shoulder, and I glanced at her name tag. *Gretchen Trask.* Such a solid-sounding name for such a frothy-looking girl.

"Everything is going to be all right," she said.

When I returned to the waiting room, everyone had left except Boyle. Internal Affairs and Police Benevolent had presumably gone home for the day, while Patton was in the lobby, calling home. Somewhat guiltily, I mentioned I still had her phone, but Boyle said, "That one's NYPD property. She's got her own personal cell for calling her husband."

I leaned close to Boyle, as if the reporters were still here. "They're trying to wean him off life support."

Boyle held up a hand, crossed his fingers.

"Superstitious?"

"Can't hurt."

I heard Amanda Patton's voice asking someone where the waiting room was, and two seconds later, she walked in. "This place is such a friggin' maze."

"How's the baby?" Boyle asked.

"Sleeping. I miss him. I think I'm gonna go home."

I started to tell Patton she might want to wait a little while, because they were weaning Krull off the ventilator, but then I realized I had no idea how long it would take. Probably hours. I wasn't able to say or think much more than that, because Gretchen was standing behind her, shaking her frosty blond head, saying, "Sorry, guys. Not today."

15

Intaglio

Since the doctor had asked for the atmosphere in Krull's room to be as serene as possible, that meant no visitors at least until morning.

"I guess that's our cue," said Boyle, after Gretchen finished telling us as much and returned to the ICU.

"I'll take Samantha to the hotel," Patton said.

I frowned at her. "Hotel?"

"The NYPD has booked you a lovely, guarded room at the Days Inn on Twenty-third."

"Guarded."

"Two uniforms outside the room, just like Krull's," she said.

I watched her face. Her cheeks colored slightly.

"Do I really need that much protection?"

"Couldn't hurt, right?" Boyle said. The way he avoided my eyes made my shoulders tense up.

"You guys think he's going to come after me, don't you?"

"Hey, you can never be too safe," Patton gave me a forced smile. "Plus, you can order all the room service you want, on us."

I started out the waiting room door and followed them down the hall to the elevator, trying not to imagine my own eyes scooped out of my head and placed on the shelf of a hotel minibar.

Just as Boyle hit the "down" button, though, Dead Man's Fingers rushed up my back. I pressed my shoulder blades together, felt the pressure of the gunshot as if it had just happened.

The elevator door opened. Patton and Boyle started in.

"Just a minute."

Again. Another galloping chill, this time stronger, this time in italics. *Dead Man's Fingers*. Just like Valentine's Day. Two times in a row.

I took a step back, and once more it sliced into me. Three times. Yes, a bad premonition. Bad times three. But was it about me?

"What's wrong?" said Patton.

I pictured Krull, alone in that quiet room, ventilator pulsing in and out. *It was so dependable, I figured it could keep her alive forever.*

"I think I'm going to stay here," I said.

*   *   *

Gretchen gave me some pillows and blankets, and I set up a bed for myself on one of the couches in the ICU waiting room. She told me I could even order a pizza, so long as I paid for it in the lobby. "Sort of like a slumber party," she said. "Only . . . um . . . with just one person."

There were at least four uniforms patrolling the hallways around me. They'd been there all day, in shifts. I'd assumed they were there for Krull, but apparently I was also part of the deal.

After Gretchen left, I sat on my makeshift bed for a few minutes, listening to the silence. There was a small TV across the room, but I didn't feel like turning it on; I was too afraid of catching a news story about Krull, or Elmira, or the murdered children. Or me.

I looked at the newspapers and magazines on the small coffee table. All the magazines were about parenting or fitness and at least six months old.

Today's *Times*, *Post* and *Daily News* were there too—probably left by one of the reporters—with follow-up Ariel stories on all three front pages. When they'd come out this morning, the girl in the footlocker hadn't even been found. What would the headlines be tomorrow? The next day?

I picked up the *Post*, went straight for Liz Smith.

Liz's featured photo was a headshot of a young blond woman, lit from behind like a haloed Mary in a Christmas pageant, but dripping with lip gloss and shimmering eye shadow. Her shoulders were bare, and she smiled suggestively at the camera, so she appeared to be wearing nothing more than a long string of pearls, which hung past her prominent collarbones and out of the frame.

The picture was high drama, even for a headshot in a gossip column, and it took me several seconds to get past gawking and realize I actually knew its subject. Miranda, former supporting player in *No Tears for Addie*. Shell Clarion's stalkee.

Under the photo, the caption read, "Leading Lady for *Let Live*'s Lucas."

I read the column. Not only had **Miranda Boothe** been cast as Lucas's long-lost love Carrington, but rumor had it she and **Nate Gundersen** were involved off camera as well. "At her audition, I couldn't stop staring at her," the "scrumptious" Nate told Liz. "She was wearing these outrageous mirrored contact lenses."

"Well, fuck me stupid," I said to no one.

The strange thing was, I felt nothing. No emotion at all, other than surprise at how quickly some soap operas were cast, and how quickly some actors became "involved."

Amazing what a few days could do to one's outlook on life, if they included sex, murder . . .

I dialed Yale's cell. He sounded smooth and dreamy when he picked up; I knew he was still at Peter's.

"Hi," I said.

"Sam!"

"How's Peter?"

"Award worthy."

"Glad to hear it."

"More important, how are you? Are you still at Detective Krull's? Has he caught the killer?"

Where do I start? "How'd you like to have a slumber party at St. Vincent's?" I said. It seemed as good a place as any.

Half an hour later, Yale showed up in the ICU waiting room, wearing the same outfit he'd had on the previous night, carrying a large pepperoni pizza and saying, "Like I said before, screw nutrition."

I knew it had been only a day since we'd seen each other, but to me, he seemed like something out of a time capsule.

"What's wrong, Sam?" he said. The question was so well meaning and simple it made me want to laugh—or cry, I wasn't sure which. I put my arms around Yale's neck and hugged him tight, like he had just saved my life.

Then I sat him down on the couch, put the box of pizza on the coffee table and told him everything that had happened since he'd left the hospital the previous night.

After I was finished, he watched me without speaking for at least a full minute. Finally, he said, "I thought you were here because of Sal."

"No, he's fine. Hermyn took him home. Or should I say Amy?"

"My . . . God."

I gave him a smile, put a hand on his shoulder. "You leave me alone for just a short time and look at what happens."

"Is there anything I can do?"

"As a matter of fact, there is," I said. "You can get that morose look off your face, you can help me eat this pizza, you can tell me every single detail of your night with Peter and most important . . ." I took out the *Post*, opened it to Liz's column. "You can read this, and get ridiculously, irrationally outraged about it."

Like any best friend worth the title, Yale did as he was told.

Early in the morning, I woke up on the waiting room carpet with a rollicking cramp in my neck and Yale snoring into my ear.

Gingerly, I got up and headed down the hall to ICU. The cramp was just an inch or so above my left collarbone—the exact same place where Krull had been shot—but I tried not to think of it as an omen.

I picked up the wall phone outside the unit. A nurse answered, her voice flat and businesslike, more or less the opposite of Gretchen's coconut oil lilt, and sure enough when I asked for Gretchen, the new nurse told me her shift had ended an hour ago.

"What is John Krull's condition?"

"Critical."

"Oh . . ."

"Of course, this is critical care, so *everybody's* critical. After we finish transfusing him, we're gonna attempt weaning again."

Krull was still not allowed visitors, but the nurse promised she'd let me know about any change in his condition.

"By the way," she said, "did you know he has a heart murmur?"

"It . . . uh . . . never came up in conversation."

"Well, he does. It's very slight."

I hung up the phone, thinking about all the other things that hadn't come up in conversation. So many facts left to know about Krull—his birthdate and his favorite food, his political affiliation and his blood type and the strangest place he'd ever made love.

Back in the waiting room, I found Yale awake, folding blankets and stacking them on the couch. "How'd you like me to take your class this morning?" he said. "I've got a few new show tunes I'd like to try out on the kids."

"Sure. I'll okay it with Terry." My mouth was dry. And between the lingering pain from the gunshot bruise and the brand-new pinch in my neck, my whole body felt pummelled. "John Krull has a heart murmur."

"Really? So does Peter."

"How do you know that?"

"He told me. I think we were talking about the forms you have to fill out at the dentist's, and it just . . . Hey, what's the matter?"

"Well, let's see. The first guy I've been able to care about since Nate is hooked up to life support. My downstairs neighbor was slaughtered in my apartment with my knife. Oh yeah, and did I mention there's a fucking serial killer out there who's either going to murder more kids or me—or most likely both? And I can't go to my apartment or my job or even a goddamn deli and I haven't had a fucking shower in two days and . . ."

"Ssssh. It's okay." Yale put his arms around me. He smelled like clean laundry.

"My life sucks. And . . . and there's probably not much more of it left."

"Please don't say that."

The faint, blond stubble on his chin picked up the light as he spoke. It reminded me of the glitter my class had used to make valentines. "Can you please sing to me?"

We sat down on the couch, and quietly, Yale started to sing "There's a Place for Us," from *West Side Story*, which, although he had no way of knowing, made me cry as a kid. I used to put the soundtrack on our record player, pretend it was my dad singing to me.

Yale's voice reminded me of dark, polished wood, but I was too tired to tell him that. So I just sat and listened, feeling the soft vibration of it, until I fell asleep in his arms like a baby.

*   *   *

The next time I awakened, it was around 11 a.m. Yale was long gone, teaching my class (having okayed it with Terry himself, according to the note he'd left.)

Amanda Patton was sitting on the couch across from mine, reading the Halloween issue of *Child* magazine. "Good morning," she said.

She put the magazine down and handed me a bag with a café chain logo on it. "Brought you coffee and a doughnut, but the coffee's probably cold by now."

It was lukewarm, but the doughnut was chocolate covered, and I loved her for that.

"So," she said. "We're getting closer to Mr. Freakshow."

I stopped eating.

"Remember when Art was talking about the paint on the magazine ad? He said it was called Liquitine, and I asked if it was used by artists?"

"Yeah."

"Well it is, but more commonly, it's used by hobbyists."

"Hobbyists?"

"I don't know if Krull told you, but the first victim, Graham—"

"Made intricate model airplanes."

"Exactly."

"So you're thinking he's a model builder?"

She nodded. "They usually find some activity that puts them closer to their victims. Lots of kids like to build models."

"But Sarah Flannigan was only three. I seriously doubt she—"

I was interrupted by a ringing and noticed, for the first time, the wall phone across the room.

I picked it up. "Um . . . Waiting room?"

"Hi, honey." The ICU nurse, her voice flat and unemotional as ever.

"Yes?"

"We have consciousness."

"Consciousness of what?"

She laughed a little, and then I knew. *Krull* had consciousness. Krull was awake.

Smiling so hard it hurt, I rushed across the room and threw my arms around Patton. "Thank God," we both kept saying, over and over again. "Oh, thank God."

"I can sneak one of you guys in," warned the nurse through the wall phone outside the ICU. "But it has to be brief as all get-out or his doctors will kill me."

Patton insisted it should be me: "You were the one who spent the night in the waiting room."

I walked her to the elevator. "Give your baby a big kiss for me," I said.

Patton winked. "Right back at ya."

"He's not my baby. I've only known him four days," I said. But the elevator doors had already closed.

The nurse buzzed me into the ICU, and I started to panic. What if I'd built this relationship up in my mind to be much more than it was? What if he was just a nice guy, a sweetheart like Patton said, and he'd been protecting me because that was his job? What if he'd told me about his dead mother and his furniture-stealing ex-girlfriend and his AC/DC tribute band to get my mind off of Mirror Eyes? What if he'd fucked me for the same reason?

Before I entered Krull's room, I nodded at the two guards and took a deep, steadying breath. "You Sam?" said the one on the right, a young guy with a black buzz cut and a marine's body.

"Uh . . . Yeah."

"Want to hear something funny? My name's Sam too."

Yep, that was hilarious all right.

"That's not the funny part. When detective Krull regained consciousness, the first thing he said was, 'Sam.' The nurse thought he was asking for me. You should've seen the look on his face when *I* showed up in his room!"

"He said, 'Sam'?"

"You'd better get in there fast before he decides to go unconscious again."

I opened the door to find Krull propped up on fluffed pillows, the plastic tube removed from his mouth. Somebody had given him a shave, which made him look younger and a little vulnerable, especially in that thin, pale hospital gown. "Sam." His voice was croaky from the tube.

There was so much I wanted to say, to do. Run across the room and jump on top of him, for one thing, but I figured that would probably upset the IV. "How are you feeling?"

"I'm so glad you're okay."

"You're glad *I'm* okay?"

"The last I saw, you were . . . shooting my gun at that . . . God, you're beautiful."

"That has to be the morphine talking." I moved closer, took his hand in mine. It was warmer now, and so soft. "Your pupils are huge."

"Thank you." He gave me a half smile.

"I didn't get him, by the way."

"It was a good try—" He grimaced. "Please don't ever get shot in the neck, because it hurts."

"You probably shouldn't be talking so much."

"Do I look that bad?"

"Pretty crappy."

"These drugs . . . My head feels like it's full of cotton candy."

I could hear voices outside the room, the handle on the door turning. *Do they want me out of here already?*

I wished there was something I could say to him, some meaningful words or a piece of good news to cut through the drugs and make him strong again. But there was no time for words, and I didn't have any good news.

So I kissed him on the mouth. It was like breaking

the surface of deep water after a long time under. "That was from Amanda Patton," I said.

"Her husband's going to kill me."

"Sorry, honey." I looked up and saw the ICU nurse, heavyset and thin lipped, as serious as her voice.

"That was fast."

"I'll let you back in soon, when he's a little stronger. In the meantime, you've got two visitors in the waiting room."

It wasn't until I'd left his room that I began to wonder who those visitors might be.

As I headed toward the waiting room, an image flashed into my mind: Mirror Eyes and his girlfriend, sitting side by side on the waiting room couch, next to the stacked-up blankets and pillows from the previous night, staring at the door.

I almost bypassed the waiting room altogether and headed for the lobby to dial 911. In fact, I would have done it if two cops hadn't been standing in front of the elevator, if the waiting room door hadn't swung open, and if Yale hadn't flown out of it and nearly knocked me over. "Fabulous news about Detective Krull. Now get in here immediately."

He grabbed my arm, pulled me into the room, which was empty save Veronica Bliss, who sat on the couch, looking at me like she expected to get socked in the face.

"What are you doing here?" I said.

"I don't know. Ask your friend."

"Sam, have you ever dated anyone named Intargio?"

"Intaglio," Veronica said. "Evan Intaglio."

"No."

"I didn't think so," said Yale.

I looked at Veronica. Her cheeks burned the same pink as the embroidered strawberries on her navy Shetland sweater. "Are you sure?"

"Who is Evan Intaglio?" I said.

"Someone . . . who . . . was looking for you."

Yale nodded at me and narrowed his eyes and I began to understand. "You've been talking to—"

"I thought you knew him. He said he was your ex-boyfriend, and you have so many ex-boyfriends—"

"How did he—"

"He called school on Monday and said, 'Is Samantha Leiffer there?' I guess he'd called that theater where you work, and they gave him our number."

"Probably Hermyn," Yale said. "She's not used to talking on the phone."

"It was early, and nobody was there but Anthony and me. So I took the call."

"Veronica, how could—"

"Evan said he'd met you in Chicago."

"I've never been to Chicago!"

"How am I supposed to know that?"

The hairs pricked up on the back of my neck. I gritted my teeth to stop the sensation.

"He sounded so . . . sweet . . . And he said he missed you."

I remembered the way Veronica had looked at me on Monday, with that glint of perplexing envy. How could anybody be jealous of a hangover, I'd thought. But it wasn't the hangover. It was him. Evan Intaglio. Mirror Eyes. "All he wanted was your home phone number."

"You gave him my home phone number?"

"And then we started talking, and we found out we had a lot in common."

Like what, Veronica? Wanting to see me dead?

"We talked about God, and doing good works and, frankly, I couldn't see what he saw in you. You didn't seem to share any of his interests."

I stared at her. The fact that she could still find a way to make snide comments when she'd just admitted to putting a serial killer on my trail was so astronomically bitchy I almost admired her for it.

"It gets worse," Yale said, and my mind went straight to the magazine ad in my desk.

"Did you let him into the school, Veronica?" I was trying to stay calm, but my voice cracked, like a teenaged boy's. "On . . . Tuesday morning?"

She picked at a cuticle. "I didn't," she said. "But Anthony may have."

"What do you mean, he may have?"

Her voice was barely audible. "Evan . . . got in somehow."

"Tell her how you know that," said Yale, making no effort to stay calm.

"He . . ."

"He left a dozen red roses on Veronica's desk."

I stared at him, let the scene play through my mind. A man shows up at Sunny Side before school hours, well dressed, with a dozen roses. He's wearing sunglasses. Anthony sees him at the gate. A nice-looking guy in sunglasses with roses for Veronica. Poor Veronica, who never gets roses. The man tells him his name. Evan Intaglio. Anthony's last name is Ciriglio. Intaglio/Ciriglio. They could be cousins . . .

"I never met him in person," said Veronica.

"No," Yale said. "But you chatted online with him that night."

"Did you give him my e-mail address at the Space?"

"I think so," she said quietly. "But he said he wasn't interested in you anymore. He said he'd seen you at a bar recently, near your apartment, drinking like a fish."

"Jesus."

"I thought you were just out sick yesterday. I had no idea we were under surveillance. Terry never told me. He never tells me anything. I found out from Yale."

Veronica took off her glasses. Without them she looked doughy and slightly cross-eyed, like an overgrown baby. "Poor detective Krull."

Please don't let her cry. I can't take her crying right now. "Did . . . Evan . . . happen to say anything about model airplanes?"

"Um, no . . ."

"What about acrylic paint?"

"Paint?"

"Nothing about any hobbies he might have?"

"Just charities. Toys for . . . Tots." She winced as she said it, as if she were just at this moment figuring it all out. She looked into my eyes, and before I turned away, I saw it there. The awful comprehension. The murdered children.

"I'll talk to the police," she said. "Anyone you want me to talk to, I will."

"Thank you," I said, but still, I couldn't make myself look at her face.

After we phoned Art Boyle and told him about Evan Intaglio, Yale and I bypassed the guards, stuffed Veronica into a cab and sent her off to the Sixth Precinct.

It seemed like years since I'd been out of this hospital, and I was surprised at how normal everything looked. The reporters were gone. Krull's doctor had given a press conference and presumably, they were all back at their newspapers, writing their stories. It was cold, and overcast, and people slammed past us in their thick coats, just like any afternoon on any day in late winter.

For the first time since Friday, I didn't feel watched, and I wondered if Evan Intaglio had taken off his black scarf and his Magic Mirrors and left the city. If he were

smart, he would've done that, maybe killed his girlfriend first for good measure.

I wondered how long it would take before her body
turned up in a Dumpster or a footlocker or a cooler in
the river, with her nails polished purple and paint in
her hair. *They make you so pretty for your funeral.*

"I hate that motherfucker," I said to Yale as we
walked back toward the building.

"Try not to be so hard on her. She didn't know."

"Not Veronica," I said. "Evan Intaglio."

Yale stopped at the revolving door. "What kind of a
name is that, anyway? There's something made-up
about it."

"Oh really, Yale St. Germaine?"

"Well," he said. "It is unusual . . . Hey, I've got an
idea."

"You're not going to suggest we look him up in the
phone book."

"No, of course not. But we could call Peter, get him
to talk to his contact lens salesman, and see if an Evan
Intaglio ever bought Magic Mirrors from him. He
might have a credit card or something, and we could
give it to the police."

I shook my head. "Krull said they've already collected receipts from every optical store that's sold
Magic Mirrors to anybody in the tristate area. Which is
a hell of a lot of people—probably more now that
they've made Liz Smith's column."

I remembered first seeing Miranda with them, on

Monday night at the box office. She'd said Magic Mirrors would be "totally hot in about a week," but it turned out she'd been off by a few days. *The makeup artist on Addie? She's got 'em too, and so does my friend William who works at* Allure. *I even saw this clerk at that toy and hobby store on Twenty-eighth who was wearing them. Scared my poor niece half to death* . . .

"Where are you going?" said Yale, but I didn't reply, just let him follow me as I rushed back towards the street and hailed a cab. I let him get in beside me as I asked the driver to take me to Twenty-eighth Street.

As the cab lurched along, I took out my cell phone, called the Sixth Precinct and asked for Boyle. When the desk sergeant couldn't find him, I asked for every detective whose name I knew. Not one was available—not even Pierce—so I told her it was urgent that someone, anyone, meet me at the toy and hobby store on Twenty-eighth.

"Miss Leiffer, where are you right now?"

"I'm in a cab."

"Headed?"

"I just told you!"

"What's the address of the store?"

"I don't know."

"What's the name?"

"I don't know," I said. Then the connection failed.

"Perhaps we should have clarified our plan before leaving," Yale said.

"Screw you."

"All right. Never mind. But I've got two questions."

The cab turned east on Twenty-eighth. "Slow down please," I said to the driver. "We'll know it when we see it."

"Question one: 'What if the club kid Miranda saw working at this nameless toy store is not our Evan Intaglio?' Question two: 'What if he is?'"

"If he is, and the cops still haven't found us, I'll call 911. If he isn't, at least we can feel like we've done something."

"Sam, you've been shot in the back. I'd say you've done quite a bit already."

The driver turned around and stared at me, but I kept my eyes out the window. "I just . . ." I said, "hate that he's put himself in my mind."

"Stop." At first, I thought Yale was talking to me, but then the driver obeyed. As Yale fished money out of his wallet, I looked out his window, saw a small storefront on a crumbling brownstone with a sign that read, "Cinderella's Toy and Hobby." And not a police car in sight.

"That was her playmate's name," I said.

"Who?"

"Sarah Flannigan. Ariel. She had an invisible playmate named Cinderella."

We were standing on the brink of the store's three front steps. I tried calling the precinct again, but couldn't get a connection; the phone's battery was low.

Yale patted his pockets. "I left mine at Peter's."

"Oh, well."

"Maybe we should wait for the police anyway."

"They might never show." I made myself walk up the steps. "What could happen anyway? It's business hours. There are plenty of people outside."

One, two, three . . . I held my breath, crossed my fingers, pushed open the door. *Go!*

The first thing I noticed was an electric train buzzing around a miniature, snowy mountain town atop a large table in the center of the store.

It looked like it had been set up for Christmas. There were tiny, multicolored lights in the miniature flocked evergreens, tiny people waving, frozen, out of cabin doorways, as the little train chugged by.

Glass counters encircled the train set area, filled with colorful antique toys. Shelves full of brightly labeled paints and hobby kits lined the walls, with completed projects interspersed—candles, mini–stained-glass windows, Christmas ornaments, jewelry, dolls.

A chorus line of vintage Barbies popped cleverly out of a pink silk hatbox against a wall. One was dressed like a stewardess, another was in a nurse's uniform, still another wore a bikini. Not a Schoolteacher Barbie in the bunch.

There were plush stuffed animals in antique chairs,

model airplanes and spaceships hanging from the ceiling. It was cheerier in here than I would've imagined—inviting really, despite a complete lack of human life. "Nice place," said Yale. I wasn't sure he'd followed me in until then.

There was a counter with an old-fashioned cash register and a silver bell, which I rang for assistance.

After several rings, a guy about my age lumbered into the room. He had spiky blond hair and a goatee, and he easily weighed 250 pounds. No way was he Evan. "Can I help you?"

I cleared my throat. "Does anyone work here—a man, who has Magic Mirrors contact lenses?"

His big face colored slightly. "No."

"You sure?"

"Well . . . My girlfriend bought me a pair, and I wore 'em to work one time. Thought I looked cool until I made a little girl cry."

Yale gave me a nudge. "False alarm."

"Excuse me?"

Make sure. "You don't happen to know an Evan Intaglio, do you?"

"No, but I know his brother, Earl Flangeneck."

We stared at him.

He chuckled.

"What's so funny?" I asked.

"Oh . . . Sorry. You're seriously looking for somebody by that name?"

"Yeah."

"Because Intaglio is a doll maker's term. I've never heard of it as a last name."

"I told you it was fake," Yale said.

"What . . . does it mean?"

"Intaglio means concave in Italian, I think. It's an effect done on antique dolls' eyes. They scoop out the area, paint the iris in the concave space. Makes it look like the eyes are following you around the . . . Are you okay?"

The electric train whistled, turned a corner. *Chugachugachugachuga . . .*

"Do you want to sit down or something? You look kind of—"

Scoop out the area.

"Sam?"

Finally, I found my voice again. "Have you ever heard of . . . Liquitine paint?"

"Who hasn't? I mean, in this business."

"What's it used for?"

"Everything, pretty much. Model building, paint by numbers, doll restoration . . ."

"Doll restoration." *Chugachugachugachuga . . .*

"You can mix it with water to color dolls' hair, use it to restore facial features or makeup. It's pretty versatile." *Chugachuga woooooo.*

I said, "They're the right size."

"Who is the right size?" said the clerk.

"Kids. Dolls."

Yale said, "He's a doll freak?"

Have you ever touched a corpse's skin? It's cold and stiff. Perfect. "The makeovers. He's restoring them. The eyes . . ."

"Intaglio."

"Right."

"What is up with you guys?"

I looked at the clerk's name tag: *RANDY.* "Thanks Randy, you've been a big help. See you later."

Just outside the store, my cell phone rang. The battery was so low, I could barely hear the voice on the other end. After shouting "hello" a few times, I realized it was Sam, Krull's guard from the hospital. "Where . . . you?" he said.

"I'm—"

"You've got . . . here. The . . . detective . . . see you."

"What?"

". . . nurse couldn't find you . . . blood pressure . . . He's really worried . . ."

"Oh, shit."

"Just get back here. Please." He hung up.

When I told Yale, he said, "You go to the hospital, I'll go to the precinct house. We'll confab later."

A free cab pulled up and he let me take it. Like a gift from God, the driver had an old cell phone similar to mine, and a charger plugged into the cigarette lighter.

I held out the near-dead phone. "Please," I said, and he quickly removed his cell, plugged mine in. Perfect fit. *Thank you.*

"Where to?"

"St. Vincent's." The driver sped off, leaving my stomach in his wake.

I read his ID tag; his first name appeared to be Enog. Gone spelled backwards.

After about a minute's thought, I borrowed Enog's phone, called the hospital and asked for the ICU.

"He's stabilized," said the nurse. "We gave him some more sedatives."

"Can you do me a favor and just tell him . . . tell him I'm having lunch . . . in the cafeteria."

"Will do."

When I handed his phone back, Enog winked at me, as if I'd passed him a note in class, then kept driving. He jolted forward and stopped suddenly so many times, it became almost rhythmic. I found myself reminded of the train whistle at Cinderella's. *They scoop out the area, paint the iris in the concave space.*

Finally, we arrived at the hospital. Queasily, I took my cell phone and got out of the cab, paid Enog his money and listened to him rev off. *Chugchuga-chuga . . .*

Just I was about to enter the lobby, the phone rang. I pushed "Send" and said, "I'm on my way up to his room."

"Ms. Leiffer?" The voice was clear. I recognized it immediately.

"Daniel?"

"Yes . . . hi."

I started to ask how he'd gotten this number, then remembered Krull had given it to the school. Terry must have posted it on the bulletin board.

"I miss you," said Daniel.

"Me too, honey. But I'll be back soon. You know, you really shouldn't be calling this number. It's for emergencies—"

"Ms. Leiffer, what's your favorite color?"

"Daniel."

"Please." His voice trembled when he said it.

My breath caught in my throat.

"Please answer the question!"

"Green, honey. It's green. Are you okay?"

Daniel started to cry.

"Where are you?"

"The monster's going to make my hair that color!" he sobbed.

And a new voice took over. A cold whisper. "Gotcha."

I could hear Daniel crying in the background. "Don't you dare hurt him," I said.

"More *little* corpses. I told you. Don't you know what *klein* means in German?"

I wanted to hang up, call 911, call the Sixth Precinct, take the elevator to ICU and alert all those guards. *But he's got Daniel. Daniel's with him, and he's called me. He got this number, he's got Daniel. Calm down. Calm down and get him to talk. Calm down and . . .* "What do you want from me?"

"Interesting question."

"Anything."

"You're small. *Kleine* Samantha."

You fucking, fucking sick fuck. "Yes."

"Not as small as Daniel. But you're a girl and I like the girls better." I could barely hear him. Why the whisper? Why the need for mystery now?

I made myself say it. "Do you want to make a trade?"

"Yes." The *s* sibilant, like the hiss of a snake. I couldn't hear crying anymore.

"Where is Daniel?"

"He's here. Say, 'Hello,' Daniel."

Daniel's voice, a wet squeak. "Help."

"Come here, alone, we'll make the trade. Your body for his. Tell anyone, tell a soul, I slit his little throat and leave his eyes to rot."

"Where do I—"

"Go to the northeast corner of Tenth and Sixth."

The line went dead.

I tore down the sidewalk, slamming into the shoulders and legs of strangers, Krull's leather jacket slapping at my sides. "Fuckin' watch it!" someone said.

"Ouch! Hey!"

"What's the rush, baby?"

Well, since you asked . . .

On the northeast corner of Tenth Street and Sixth Avenue was a parking garage. I scanned the entrance for Daniel, for Mirror Eyes, but all I saw was an empty glass booth where the attendent was supposed to be. I pulled Krull's coat closer to me, felt a small, hard object against my chest. Making sure no one was watching, I checked the inside pocket. Miniature Swiss Army knife.

First, I tucked the tiny knife into the cuff of my sweater sleeve. Then I started towards the booth.

"Hello?" I said, but when I peered inside, I found no one hiding there. "Is anybody here?"

Like an answer, a black sedan pulled out of the garage and screeched to a halt beside me.

Behind the wheel was Randy, the toy and hobby store clerk.

16

The Last Laugh

We drove in silence, Randy and I, the garage shrinking in the rearview as the sedan headed west.

He'd taken my patchwork bag and Krull's coat, reached into my jeans pockets to make sure they were empty. "Give me the cell phone," he'd said, just before shutting the back door. Not a word since.

I tried looking at him a few times, but he kept his eyes off mine, kept his eyes on the road like any good executioner. *Nothing personal, you understand. Just doing my job.*

He stopped at a traffic light, just before a crosswalk. I watched an older woman push a stroller in front of the car, and for a moment, everything seemed to move in slow motion—the woman, the stroller, Randy's fat hands on the steering wheel. I watched the woman, pressed my gaze on her like my eyes could emit light and heat, thinking *Look at me. Look at me and call the police.* But she didn't turn, just kept walking, and when the light switched to green I saw Randy's eyes fixed on me in the rearview.

"He has a new fish," I said.

"Who?"

"Daniel." Without looking down, I checked my sweater cuff, touched the edge of the tiny Swiss Army knife.

The car lurched along. The street we were on was tree lined and peaceful, with brownstones and florists and specialty food shops. Then we crossed another avenue, and the buildings abruptly went boxy industrial and empty looking. The meat-packing district.

On the side of one windowless building was a faded mural of a pig in a chef's hat. "Polowski's Pork," it read. I looked at Randy, then the pig on the mural. Stupid, grinning animal, happy to cook his dead friends.

The sedan turned up another avenue, then right on a side street, left through a wide alley and right onto another street full of walk-ups and old warehouses. Where were we going? Where was Daniel?

We stopped in front of one of the walk-ups—its old exterior black from grime, who knew what color it had been originally?—and a powerful chill shot up my back. Dead Man's Fingers. "Little late."

"What?" said Randy.

"Nothing."

He double-parked, got out of the car, opened my door like a chauffeur. *We've arrived at your destiny, ma'am.*

This was the plan I had: Get Daniel to run away. Then scream. Then take the knife out of my cuff, stick it in the fucker's eye. *It's good to know how to scream.* It was good to have a knife too. Too bad it wasn't bigger.

There were a few steps in front of the walk-up, leading down to a basement apartment. Randy nudged me toward the door, unlocked it. "Wait a minute," he said.

He ran his oily hands down the arms of my sweater, slipping his fingers into the cuffs. Out came the knife. "Nice try."

Before Randy pushed me into the apartment, I stared him in the eyes—looking for some human emotion, something within him that might take that NYPD cell phone and call for help. "Why would you do this for *him*?" I said.

But Randy didn't answer. He was wearing colored contacts—deep purple, like a bruise. Strange I hadn't noticed them earlier.

Alone in the basement apartment, what reached me first was the smell—a flat, clean, unnatural odor I quickly identified as paint. It was dark here, with no lights on and the shades drawn, but it wasn't pitch-black like a black box theater. I could see shadows. Nothing moved.

Randy had shut the door behind me and stayed outside. Probably following orders, but still, I got the feeling he was afraid to go in. *What is in here?*

I felt something near my back—put my hand behind
me and touched cloth, soft and inanimate, stretched
against a frame. *Chair, no, longer. Couch. Okay.*

"Hello?" My voice came out thin, a whisper.
"Daniel?"

Clink. My foot knocked into it, and I felt something
wet hit my sock. I looked down at a squat cylinder.
Paint can. Paint on my sock.

My eyes were beginning to adjust. I looked down
and saw five paint cans lined up against the back of the
couch. To the right a wall of exposed brick and some
kind of hallway.

I turned around, rested my hands against the back of
the couch, the only thing I could trust. I could make
out a more complex shape against the opposite wall. A
shelf unit lined with small silhouettes, all of them perfectly still. All of them human.

*Don't scream, not yet. Where is the light? Need
light. Calm, calm . . .* "I'm ready to make the trade!"
My voice was louder this time, and like a reward, the
lights went on.

The forms on the shelves were dolls: some porcelain, some plastic. I recognized many of them as collectibles. The same collectibles I'd seen on the
shopping channel, with working limbs and plush
clothes and names like Clarissa and Scarlett and

Sebastian. Just like on TV, only with one difference: Someone had removed all their eyes.

The couch was a spotless white, its back cushions removed to make way for a large cardboard box. From where I stood, I could see its closed top.

"Hello?"

No answer still. I moved closer to the box and touched it. "Daniel?"

Holding my breath, I pulled back the cardboard folds and looked inside.

Dead white skin, bloody lips.

"Shit."

I jumped back, threw my hands over my mouth.

Stay quiet. Breathe in, breathe out. Now. Take a step. Look again.

In the box was a face, yes. But not Daniel's. Not human. A chalk-white doll's face, lips painted red, resting atop many other painted doll's faces. Looking closer, I saw the box was packed with bald, porcelain heads, their lips gleaming and lurid, their cheeks rouged, bright blue and purple and green paint smeared generously over their eyes, which were all open, all intact.

When I closed the lid again, I noticed three words, printed on the bottom left corner in neat, capital letters: *THE BAD ONES.*

The lights flashed off, then on again.

All right asshole, you want mind games, I'll give you mind games. "Show your face," I said. "Or I break all the *good* ones!"

I moved around the couch, headed straight for the shelving unit. But before I could get there, I slipped on something wet, fell to my hands and knees on the cold cement floor.

I got up fast, saw blood on my hands, blood on the floor. And then I saw a man's body, lengthwise against the front of the couch with the paint cans looming over him, throat slit so deeply he'd nearly been decapitated.

His eyes were opened wide, as if he still couldn't believe what had happened, couldn't believe he'd seen his own death coming at him so strong, so soon. And he was still wearing his mirrored contacts.

> "Cinderella / dressed in yella /
> Went upstairs to kiss her fella /
> How many kisses did she take?"

I whirled around, and saw the girlfriend. The frightened blonde with the perfect face.

"One, two, three, four . . ."

She wore her short-sleeved red dress, and dragged Daniel by the arm like a rag doll. Over his mouth stretched a thick piece of gaffer's tape. In her other hand, she grasped the black handle of a butcher's knife.

It hit me all at once: *The phone calls, always a whisper. Her voice, not his. Her notes, her paint, her makeovers. She's the doll freak. She's the murderer.*

"It's okay, Daniel," I said.

"Don't lie." She grinned. Her lips were painted a bright bloodred.

I glanced at the dead man on the floor, then back at her. "Why did you kill him?"

She started around the couch. I moved in front of the head, trying to block it from Daniel.

"He was big and ugly," she said.

I looked at Daniel. Tears ran down his cheeks.

"Plus, he brought me nothing but bad ones."

"Bad ones?"

"The ones with the obvious flaws you can never fix, no matter how much paint you use. The oversized ones. The nasty ones that hit and bite and run away."

"You're not talking about dolls. You mean children."

She rolled her eyes. *"Projects."*

"But . . . you were crying at the river. I saw—"

"You saw me from the back." She said it as if she were talking to a slow student. "I was *laughing*. At him, for being such a pansy. He was the one who always cried."

She took a few more steps forward. "Randy will be much better. He's not an ugly pansy like Phil."

My eyes went back to the body. "Evan."

"Evan. Do you want to know who Evan is?" She let go of Daniel's hand for a moment, strode over to the shelf unit and picked up a male doll, with shining yellow hair and red velvet overalls. "This is Evan," she said, kissing each of its eyeholes. "My favorite of the boys."

"Run, Daniel!" I yelled, but he just stood there, staring at me. *I know how you feel. Once upon a time, there was a princess who couldn't move.*

"My goodness," she said. "You are stupid." She stepped closer to me, touched the blade of the butcher knife to the side of my face. "Pretty, though."

I thought of John Krull. Did he still think I was in the hospital cafeteria?

"The best projects," the red mouth said, "are pretty to begin with." With the index finger on her other hand, she tapped my lower lip—softly, as if she were testing its resilience. "Close your eyes, *Kleine* Samantha."

What else could I do, but obey? What could I do, but wait as she dragged the cool blade down the side of my face, 'til I felt the point at the hollow of my throat? *Please don't watch this, Daniel. Please look away.*

The sharp point lingered there for several seconds and suddenly, I had her figured out: I knew she wouldn't slit my throat. I was too pretty for that, too small for the big blade. If she did that, I'd be wrecked, like Phil, beyond restoration. *No. What she's going to do is drop the knife and strangle me—just like the children. She's going to wait like a spider until I'm paralyzed with fear, and then she's going to do it.*

When I felt the knife come away from my throat, I knew I was right. I knew that was exactly what she'd done with Graham, with Sarah, with all the others. They'd died feeling the same way I'd felt in the Pinto.

Frozen. *Once upon a time there was a princess who got angry.*

At the exact same moment, my eyes flew open and my knee shot up, connecting with her stomach. "You . . ." she wheezed, and the knife came at me, still clutched in her hand, point grazing my chest through the thick wool of my sweater. I felt a sting, knew I was bleeding, but not deep—at least, not deep enough to matter.

I balled my hand into a fist and socked her in the face. I'd never punched anyone before, and it was surprisingly painful, like hitting a brick wall.

She fell back, clutching her face but still holding the knife. Shaking the pain out of my hand, I turned to Daniel. Daniel, now sitting on the floor in his dapper little overcoat. I looked into his face, at the gaffer's tape over the mouth, the tears still streaming down his cheeks, and thought of his mom, Erika. What she must be thinking . . .

"Run, run, run!" I screamed, louder and higher than I'd screamed, four days earlier, when I'd first seen John Krull. "Run!"

"Shut the fuck up!" shouted the woman, and I couldn't help but wonder, *Where is Randy during all this?* Maybe he wasn't standing guard. Maybe he'd betrayed her and left, maybe he had called the police. Or maybe the walls were soundproofed.

I lifted Daniel to his feet, and pushed him. Finally, he moved. He backed up, away from Phil's body, around the side of the couch. *Atta boy. Now go faster.*

She was coming at me now, knife raised, red lips stretched into a grin, like the pig on the mural.

She flew forward, and I grabbed the hand with the knife in it. But she was ready this time. She didn't let go. I pushed the knife hand back with all my might, but still it moved closer and closer to my throat.

I could feel the huge cardboard box pressed against the small of my back, and I knew we'd reached the couch.

Out of the corner of my eye, I could see the little boy—still motionless, still watching. *Oh, God, Daniel, would you please just run away!*

The knife moved closer until the point touched the soft tight skin above my trachea. My grip on her wrist was weakening, my arm tiring of holding her off. I looked at her face, the bright blue contacts, the lipstick smeared across her chin, the cheek purplish where my fist had made contact and thought, *This is it.*

Suddenly, she screamed and dropped the knife, and it took me a few seconds to compute what had happened. Daniel—tiny Daniel, frozen with fear—had ripped the tape off his mouth and bit her in the leg.

He raced out of the room, and she headed after him, all anger, all reflex, unaware she'd dropped her knife.

I snatched it off the floor as she caught up with Daniel, grabbed him by the hair and jerked him back towards her.

"Let him go!" I yelled, and when she spun around to face me, Daniel took off again.

"Bitch." She grabbed for my neck with both hands, ready to kill, but there was no time. No time for her now.

In one motion, I plunged the blade straight into her chest. It was like pushing through thick ice, then a release, like hitting running water below. That's how I tried to imagine it. Just ice. Just water.

Her arms went lax, and I waited for her to drop, thinking of absolutely nothing.

It wasn't until she fell to the floor and I noticed her gold hair fanning out behind her and the blood spreading out from the hilt of the knife in a widening circle, that I remembered she was a person.

I watched her face. Behind the contacts, her eyes seemed fixed, motionless. Then she smiled, blood leaking out of her mouth, staining her white teeth and mingling with the smeared lipstick as her breathing stopped. From deep in her chest, I heard the rattle as life finally left her body. But she kept watching me, still smiling, as if she'd had the last laugh.

The room that Daniel had run into wasn't a room at all. It was a large closet that smelled of cedar. Nothing was hanging in it, but there were several stacks of magazines on the floor. *Doll Fancy*, *American Doll*, *Doll Collector*, *Doll Aficionado* . . . Must have been where she'd gotten the ad for Schoolteacher Barbie. Daniel was curled up between two of the stacks with his head down, his knees pressed into his chest. It made him look smaller than usual, almost like a baby.

My sweater had been covered in the woman's blood, but I'd taken it off, used it to wipe the blood off my hands, so Daniel could see me without getting more frightened.

I lifted a bunch of magazines out of the way, got on the floor and put my arms around him. How tiny he was beneath that grown-up overcoat.

After a long time, I said, "You are a very brave boy."

Tentatively, Daniel sat up. He reached into one of his overcoat pockets, handed me a photograph he'd been carrying.

It was of the blond woman—the doll restorer— sitting on a bench in a small city park. A light snow dusted everything around her, and she was smiling her perfect smile, holding a little red-haired girl in her lap. It would have been an ideal Christmas card photo, were it not for the serious set of the little girl's lips, or the strange, imploring way in which her eyes watched the camera. The blond woman wore the same camel-hair coat she'd had on three days earlier, when she'd accosted me outside the Sixth Precinct house. The girl wore an unzipped purple parka and underneath, a Little Mermaid T-shirt.

Epilogue

The Rudder

After I killed the doll restorer, Daniel didn't say a word—not even when the police arrived at the apartment, on a tip from a pedestrian who'd heard screams.

"You okay, little fella?" said one of the officers, and still, he said nothing. Not until he noticed three more cops, opening another door at the end of the long hallway—a door I hadn't noticed earlier.

Then he started to scream and, hard as we tried, we couldn't get him to stop. When Erika Klein finally showed up, he fell into her arms, sobbing and coughing.

The room was the doll restorer's project gallery, where she kept all her finer, more exotic paints, her vats of plaster and homemade hair dye, her knives, her scalpels, and the jagged eye scoopers she'd fashioned from soup ladles and welded saw blades. There were more dolls there, of course—good ones and bad, works in progress.

And one human project. A little girl, later estimated to have died nearly six months earlier, her body too decomposed for proper identification. Daniel had been tied to a chair, facing this project for a long time, as Phil yelled at the blond lady in the other room.

Three weeks later, the Kleins left New York. They never said where they were moving but, Erika assured me, it was "someplace warm."

On the last day of school, I got a manila envelope in the mail, with a postmark from New Mexico. There was no note inside—just a brown crayon drawing of a long-eared, four-legged animal, a child's handwriting underneath. MY DOG FRED, it said. LOVE DANIEL.

The doll restorer's name was Cynthia Jane Gray, and she was the sole owner and proprietor of Cinderella's Toy and Hobby. It's how she met the children or, as she might have put it, how she found her projects.

Four weeks before her disappearance, Jocelyn Reed, the girl in the footlocker, had bought one of Cinderella's vintage Barbies and joined the store's Barbie Collector's Club, which met Wednesday afternoons. After walking alone to her third meeting, she never returned. An anxious-sounding Cynthia had phoned Jocelyn's parents, telling them their daughter had never shown up—was she all right? And no one had doubted her concern—not the Reeds, not the police who'd questioned "kind, caring" Cynthia Gray.

I learned that Jocelyn had been murdered a week before Sarah had. Seeing me at the river had not made Cynthia kill more kids, but it had rattled her. Rattled her enough to stalk me, to murder Elmira, to kidnap Daniel, to drop her carefully crafted mask of sanity by making my death an all-consuming goal.

As for the others, Graham was from New Jersey, but had corresponded with Cynthia when he tried to order model airplane kits from her Web site.

Sarah Flannigan had lived just one block away from Cinderella's Toy and Hobby. More than once, her parents had panicked when Sarah suddenly disappeared, then breathed sighs of relief when they found her talking to that beautiful blond woman who owned the neighborhood toy store.

That's what Cynthia was—a beautiful blond woman. It often placed her beyond suspicion. When she'd shown up at Sunny Side, claiming to be Daniel Klein's visiting cousin, Daniel had forgotten all he'd learned from Buster the Safety Dog and walked willingly away with her. Terry hadn't thought twice about it. Not until Daniel's mother arrived twenty minutes later.

Before she bought the store, Cynthia had two interests: dolls and her job. She worked in a funeral home, embalming bodies, painting faces.

A week after she was laid off, the funeral home owner discovered a body missing—that of a five-year-old girl. Her family threatened to sue, and they settled out of court. While the body was never found, the owner had creeping, unvoiced suspicions. ("Pretty," Miss Gray used to croon as she painted lips and cheeks. "So pretty, pretty, pretty . . .")

With more free time, Cynthia devoted it to dolls. She scoured eBay for collectibles, went to conventions. "She could drive a hard bargain," said a fellow hobbyist. "What she liked best was porcelain girls."

Cynthia was from Pennsylvania, a rich only child who rarely went to school. Her parents, a former housekeeper said, sent Cindy to her room when she talked too much or got, as they put it, "too lively." It was a room filled with beautiful antique dolls.

Cynthia's parents died when she was seventeen. They were discovered in bed together, their wrists slit, holding hands. Double suicide, everyone assumed. Cynthia's mother—who'd never liked makeup of any sort—had been wearing a deep garnet shade of lipstick. Odder still were the freckles drawn on her father's cheeks with eyebrow pencil.

I learned all this by reading the tabloids, which had a field day with Cynthia Jane Gray. "Cinder-hell-a," she was dubbed by the *Post*. Not many living people knew her well—except possibly Randy, who was talking through lawyers, proclaiming his total ignorance as to the horrific crimes his boss had committed.

As for Mirror Eyes, his real name was Phillip Allen Brewster, and he was thirty-two years old. He was a schizophrenic who'd spent most of his life in mental institutions and probably couldn't believe his luck when a woman who looked like Cynthia Gray showed interest in him. They had met three summers earlier, when, recently released, he'd applied for a job at her store. Soon after he got the job, he stopped taking his medication and sent his sister a letter. *I'm doing good works,* he wrote. *I'm helping an angel who makes little ones beautiful and sends them to God.*

You could say I learned a lot from these people: Trust your intuition, but not too much. Don't think you have everything figured out, because you don't. Things are never truly as they appear. But the main thing I learned was this: I am capable of killing another human being.

Who wants to talk about that with anyone, let alone reporters? (Though, I must say, I did generate some excellent headlines. "Schoolboy Saved by the Belle!" was my favorite.)

A week after I killed Cynthia, my mother flew out to New York with Vito the hairdresser in tow, and served as my spokesperson while actually cooking me dinner several nights. Sydney and Vito were staying at the Plaza, but frequently, she'd share my pullout bed, so that when I woke up, sweating and weeping in the middle of the night, she'd be there.

Sydney referred to Krull as "that policeman" until

he was released from the hospital and she met him face-to-face. Then she decided I "certainly could never do any better than that, so please, Samantha, don't ruin this with any of your intimacy issues."

Well, it's six months later, and to Sydney's shock and my own, I haven't ruined anything. I've moved all my Rent 2 Own furniture into Krull's formerly sparse apartment. I've met his father and brother. We've chipped in on a summer share on Fire Island, babysat for Patton's son, said the *L* word to each other more than once. I never thought I'd believe it, but my mother was right. Love *is* the rudder.

Otherwise, not much has changed. I still work at the Space and Sunny Side, where I spend most of my days alternately amused and annoyed.

This afternoon, we're going to Hermyn and Sal's wedding. It's at a converted mansion in Tarrytown, and we're driving there with Yale and Peter. En and Shell—who recently outed themselves as a couple after two years of secret-but-consistent "buddy sex"—will be there too. And Argent is going to sing.

Krull will wear the hand-tailored suit his father gave him for Christmas and since I'm in the bridal party, I'll be wearing a hideous lime-green taffeta gown chosen by Hermyn's mother.

But now, dawn is breaking and I'm taking a walk. I'm just about there, now—the construction site on the Hudson River where this whole thing started. The place formerly known as Shank's.

I've been walking here every morning at sunrise for the past week, and it's made me feel good—the warm air, the glinting water. It makes me think, *No more ghosts.*

The site has been leveled. There's nothing here now but concrete, and soon that will be gone too. The area will be planted with grass, and there will be a plaque—a tribute to Sarah, Graham, Jocelyn and all the other children taken away. I was one of the people who lobbied for it. There had been too many morbid tourists here, posing for pictures in front of the "Shank's" sign. Too many "Ariel Raves," with teenagers doing drugs and dancing around the trailer.

I walk down to the river, inhale the smell. It's so warm now and the air is thick and wet, summer breathing its last gasps.

Funny how different this place is.

Somehow, with the bin and the trailer and the stacks of concrete blocks, it seemed emptier. Now that it really is empty, it feels like any other part of the city.

When I was a kid, my superstitious grandmother used to say the same few words every night before dinner, which was as close to prayer as we ever got. I'm thinking of those words now as I look out at the churning, brown-green water where Sarah's body was dropped: *That nothing bad should ever happen here.*

I put my back to the river, gaze up at my crowded, messy, beautiful city. In the distance, I hear the insistent cry of a police siren. "That nothing bad should ever happen here again."

I say it three more times, for good luck, then gaze up at the dawn sky. It's a strange, chemical purple, pink rays seeping into it like blood from a deep wound.

Read on for an excerpt from Alison Gaylin's
next novel, the sequel to

Hide Your Eyes

coming in January 2006

"Haven't I seen you somewhere before?" said the voice behind me. The voice was deep, with some sort of European accent—French? Belgian? Swiss? A tasteful trace of accent, like a carefully chosen accessory. Like a black leather three-button jacket, bought brand-new at Barney's because it looked "so vintage," but costing more than I make in a year. He was probably wearing the coat too, despite it being ninety degrees outside.

"I don't think so," I said without turning to look at either him or his inevitable coat.

I was sitting in a Starbucks at Tenth and Sixth at 6:30 in the morning on the first day of school, making name tags for my class, wondering how we'd all get along. I loved imagining faces to go with the names, trying to pick out the shy ones, the precocious ones, the troublemakers. After writing each name in red felt-tipped pen on a rectangle of yellow construction paper, I'd close my eyes, repeat the name in my head and make a serious attempt to visualize the student. Deep down, I suppose I enjoyed believing I was psychic. Like my superstitions, it gave me a sense of control.

Yes, I still had my superstitions. I'd had them so

long they were like birthmarks and I barely noticed
them anymore. But my mother did. She wanted them
removed.

A year and a half earlier, I'd stabbed a serial killer to
death with a butcher knife after nearly getting murdered myself. And then, just as the residual nightmares
were starting to fade, September 11 happened. My
mother couldn't understand how I could go through all
that and still think it made a difference whether or not
I walked under a ladder. Sydney said I suffered from a
disorder with a clinical term: magical thinking. But I
didn't care. My mother lived three thousand miles
away and could not physically stop me from stepping
over cracks in the sidewalk. And besides, magical
thinking didn't sound like a disorder. It sounded like a
compliment.

Visualizing this new group of kids from the sound of
their names was proving harder than usual, though. There
was a Charlotte, an Ida, two Harrys, an Abraham . . .
When I closed my eyes, all I could see were friends of
my grandmother.

"But I'm sure I know you. Look at me, please."

Man, this Eurotrash was persistent. Maybe it wasn't
a come-on. Truth was, I'd heard that question many
times since moving to New York from men and
women, gay and straight, and only a few of them had
said it because they wanted a date. Though puzzled at
first, I'd soon discovered that small, dark-haired,

vaguely Semitic girls like me were about as common as pretzel vendors here.

Plus, I looked a lot like my famous mother and had been in the press myself after the serial killer incident. So there were quite a few people I'd never met who thought they'd seen me before.

I turned, looked at the stranger with the overpriced accent. And instantly, I felt guilty for being so rude. He was young but dressed thirty years older, in gray polyester slacks and a short-sleeved yellow Oxford with a white T-shirt underneath. His black hair was short, but not fashionably so, and he had large dark eyes and an olive complexion. Maybe he was from Puerto Rico, maybe Morocco, maybe Lebanon or Saudi Arabia. He was the type of person who got pulled aside and questioned by airport security guards, who got glared at on subways and hassled for no reason. I'm sure he'd heard the question too, but with such a different inflection, such darker intent. *Haven't I seen you somewhere before?*

"I'm sorry," I said. "You probably just have me confused with someone. It happens all the time."

He smiled. "We will go out together. You are pretty."

Oh, give me a fucking break. "Pretty taken."

But the guy didn't move, just kept staring.

"Uh . . . Bye." I looked at the door and, as if I'd willed it, Krull walked through, along with another Sixth Precinct detective, Pierce, who'd helped out on surveillance during my serial killer case. Krull's partners didn't like Pierce much—Amanda Patton thought he had Short Man's syndrome and Art Boyle was prejudiced against Scorpios. Nonetheless, Pierce and Krull had become friends, working out at a nearby gym together most mornings before work. Sometimes he ate dinner at our place, and I didn't mind him.

The main problem with Pierce was, he overreacted to everything—even himself. He was short and small-boned, but he overreacted by working out so much that his neck swelled huge and his body became this collection of uncomfortable-looking bulges. And a few months ago, when his hair had started to thin, he'd overreacted by shaving his head until it gleamed. I've never seen a man more resemble a fire hydrant than Pierce, and it made me feel sorry for him. He tried so hard.

This morning, I'd told Krull that I planned to come to Starbucks before class, but still I was surprised they'd actually shown up. *He remembered.* A sense of relief rushed through me, and then I wondered what I was so relieved about.

From his shirt pocket, the stranger produced a piece of paper and put it in front of me. "I want you to have this," he said.

It had been carefully folded into a tiny, tight triangle.

"It is my name and my phone number for you to make frequent use of." This was said loud enough to embarrass me.

The two detectives moved toward my table. I wanted Krull to kiss me, deep and passionately enough to show each and every Starbucks patron just how pretty fucking taken I was, but that was not like him, not lately. I found myself envying the shoulder holster he wore under his drab, blue suit coat, just because he was comfortable to have it that close.

I wanted Krull at least to say, "This guy giving you trouble?" But he didn't. Pierce did.

The stranger raised both hands in a corny gesture of surrender and made a fast retreat for the door. *Guess he knows law enforcement when he sees it.*

"Looks like a terrorist to me," said Pierce.

Krull rolled his eyes, sat down at the table. "Only thing he was interested in terrorizing was my girlfriend."

I smiled at him. *My girlfriend.*

"What's that?" Krull pointed to the tiny paper triangle sitting next to my stack of name tags.

"His phone number." I flicked it across the table. "Prefolded and ready for distribution. Way to make a woman feel special."

Pierce said, "So, what do I hear about your mother moving to New York?"

It took me several seconds to digest the question. "What?!"

"I thought I heard it on the radio. I could be wrong, but I don't think so. Dr. Sydney Stark-Leiffer, right? *The Art of Caring?*"

"Number one, she's not a doctor. Two, I'm sure my mother would tell me if she were—"

"She's not a doctor?"

"You must've heard wrong. You—"

"Look at that," said Krull.

For a long moment, I stared at Pierce, amazed to absolute silence that someone I'd shared a bed with for a year and a half could hear this news—this life-altering, potentially catastrophic news involving my *mother*—and interrupt it with a directive as irritatingly dismissive as "Look at that." What was he looking at anyway, a dessert? An unusual hairstyle? Pierce didn't seem to get it, though. "What?" he said.

I turned to Krull. He had opened the paper triangle. *So that's what's so important. Some guy's phone number.*

He handed it over.

There was indeed a phone number on the small slip of paper, but no name to go with it. Just a sentence, printed in neat, capital letters with a red, felt-tipped pen similar to my own: YOU ARE IN DANGER.

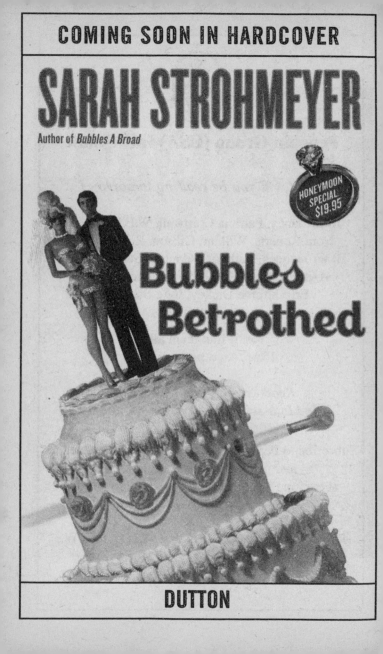

Coming Soon in Paperback

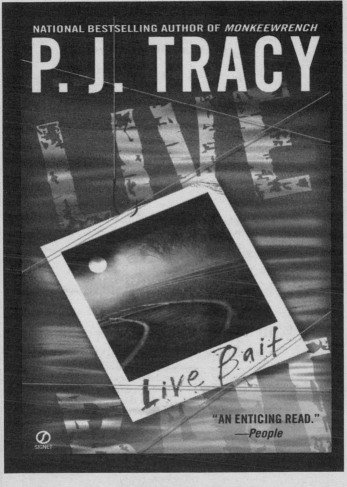

NATIONAL BESTSELLING AUTHOR OF *MONKEEWRENCH*

P. J. TRACY

Live Bait

"AN ENTICING READ."
—*People*

SIGNET

Penguin Group (USA)
is proud to present
GREAT READS—GUARANTEED!

**We are so confident that you will love
this book that we are offering a
100% money-back guarantee!**

If you are not 100% satisfied with
this publication, Penguin Group (USA)
will refund your money!
Simply return the book before
May 1, 2005 for a full refund.

**With a guarantee like this one,
you have nothing to lose!**